Easter at the Villa Victoria

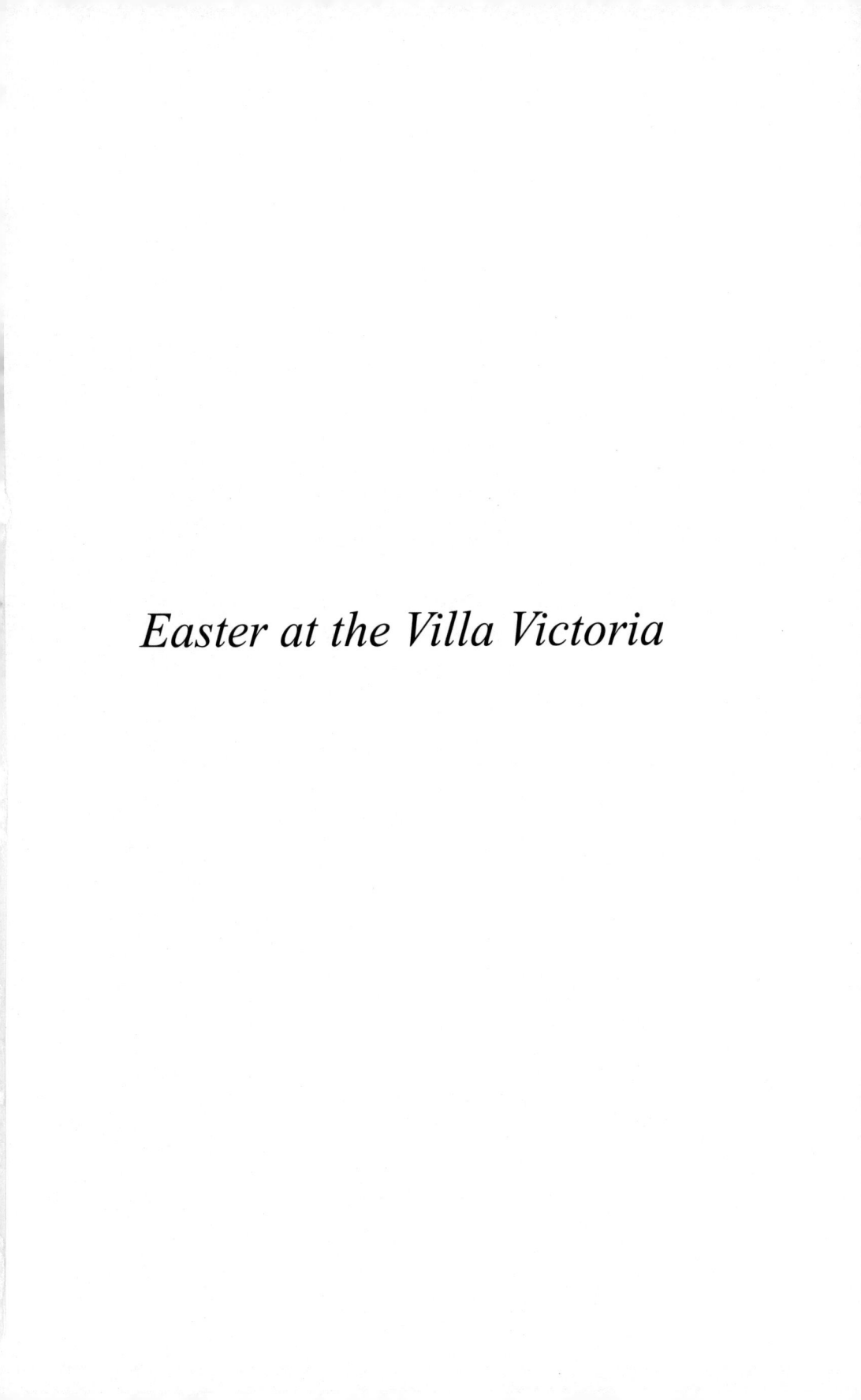

By the same author:

Soldier of the Raj
Admiral of the Blue
Bloodline
Lifeline
The Night Hunter's Prey

Easter at the Villa Victoria

IAIN GORDON

Copyright © 2016 Iain Gordon

The moral right of the author has been asserted.

Apart from any fair dealing for the purposes of research or private study, or criticism or review, as permitted under the Copyright, Designs and Patents Act 1988, this publication may only be reproduced, stored or transmitted, in any form or by any means, with the prior permission in writing of the publishers, or in the case of reprographic reproduction in accordance with the terms of licences issued by the Copyright Licensing Agency. Enquiries concerning reproduction outside those terms should be sent to the publishers.

All characters in this book are imaginary and any resemblance to any person either living or dead is purely coincidental.

The photographs used in this book are downloaded from Wikipedia Commons and are either in the Public Domain or licensed under the Creative Commons Attribution 3.0 Unported Licence and are attributed to the individual originators as shown.

Matador
9 Priory Business Park,
Wistow Road, Kibworth Beauchamp,
Leicestershire. LE8 0RX
Tel: (+44) 116 279 2299
Fax: (+44) 116 279 2277
Email: books@troubador.co.uk
Web: www.troubador.co.uk/matador

ISBN 978 1785899 997

British Library Cataloguing in Publication Data.
A catalogue record for this book is available from the British Library.

Printed and bound by CPI Group (UK) Ltd, Croydon, CR0 4YY

Matador is an imprint of Troubador Publishing Ltd

In fond remembrance of
'The Old Riviera'
1850-1950

The Descendants of Captain James Stewart and Victoria Morton

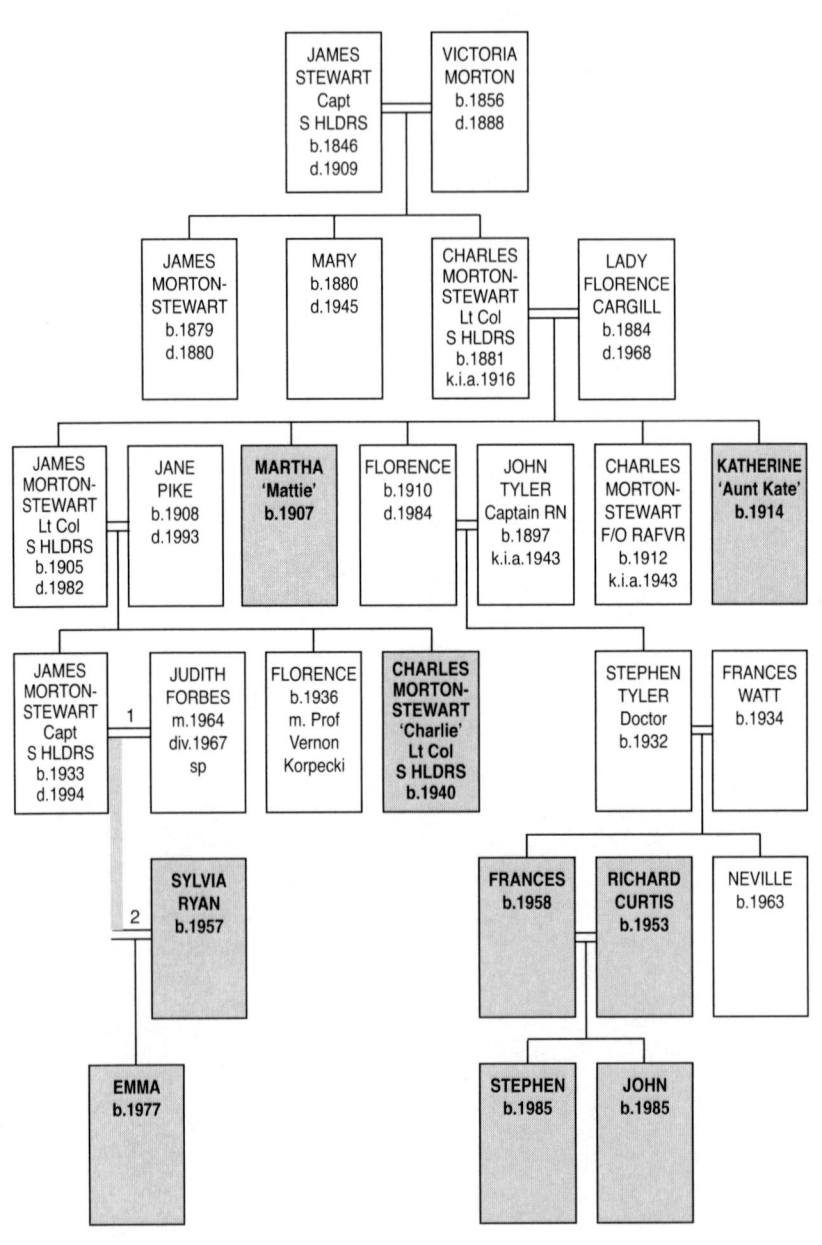

Dramatis Personae

FAMILY

Miss Katherine Morton-Stewart, 81, 'Aunt Kate', the more starchy of the two old sisters, 'The Aunts', who have lived in the Villa most of their lives.

Miss Martha Morton-Stewart, 88, 'Mattie', the more relaxed sister.

Lieutenant-Colonel (Retired) Charles Morton-Stewart, 55, 'Charlie', recently retired army officer, nephew of the Aunts and present owner of the villa.

Mrs. Frances Curtis, 37, daughter of Charlie's cousin, Dr. Stephen Tyler.

Richard Curtis, 42, Husband of Frances, MD of London Advertising Agency.

Masters Stephen and John Curtis, 10, twin sons of Frances and Richard.

Mrs. Sylvia Morton-Stewart, 38, widow of Charlie's 'Black Sheep' brother James.

Miss Emma Morton-Stewart, 19, daughter of Sylvia.

STAFF AT THE VILLA

Miss Bridie Hogan, 62, Irish housekeeper from West Cork who has been with the family for 40 years.

Dhanibahadur Limbu, 72, 'Dhani', ex-Gurkha rifleman, gardener, chauffeur and general factotum at the villa.

Manjulika Limbu, 65, 'Manju', Dahni's wife, a superb cook, trained and worked in 5-star establishments in Hong Kong.

Henri, late teens, the garden boy.

Monsieur Verrechia, late 60s, retired waiter at the Martinez who helps out at the villa for important dinner parties.

FRIENDS & ACQUAINTANCES

Steve Fitzgerald, late 20s, Emma's boyfriend. American diplomat, works in US Paris Embassy, of Boston-Irish stock.

Lady Wroughton, early 80s, 'Frills', widow of senior British officer, lifelong friend of the Aunts, lives on Cap d'Antibes.

Dr. Marcel Chouard, early 40s, the Aunts' doctor, an Anglophile and Epicure.

Madame Elise Chouard, late 30s, Marcel's glamorous and flirtatious wife.

Rupert Saint John Powell, (pronounced Sinjun Pole) mid 40s, Christeby's Art Expert from London, a social climbing name dropper.

Herbert Pontefract, mid-40s, Christeby's manager in Nice and an expert on English furniture.

Mrs. Maud Pontefract, mid-40s, Herbert's wife.

Tour Grimaldi, Antibes

Photo: PATRICK ROUZET

Prologue

Henri, the garden boy, preferring the frivolous levity of French patisserie to the wholesome solidity of good Irish baking, was neither overjoyed by the extra slice of fruit cake which Madame Hogan, the housekeeper, slid maternally onto his plate, nor caring of the cordiality which the gesture bespoke.

'Non, non, non.' he said rudely with a dismissive sweep of a deeply tanned and unwashed hand.

Bridie Hogan, aware that the boy's interests extended no further than his noisy motorcycle and the new waitress at the pizzeria on the corner, and that he spoke no English anyway, resumed the discussion of her employers with Manjulika Limbu, the Nepalese cook whose husband, Dhanibahadur, was gardener, chauffeur and handyman at the villa.

'I don't know what's for the best, chust, what's for the best.' Bridie always repeated things twice – the two pronouncements linked by the word 'chust'. It was a habit which was of particular value to foreigners who had difficulty in understanding her West Cork brogue which remained unalloyed though she had not seen Ireland since the age of seventeen – forty-five years ago. 'It would kill them to be put to a home,' she continued, 'chust, it would kill them to be put to a home.'

'Oh yes,' Manjulika affirmed, 'it would kill them. Isn't there anyone in the family who could come down here to live with them and take over some of the responsibility?'

'Colonel Charlie could come himself. He's retired now and he has no ties, chust, he has no ties.'

Henri, the garden boy, rose from the table scraping his chair noisily on the quarry-tiled floor of the kitchen. He left the room without a word, scratching himself.

Prologue

'That boy!' said Bridie in an exasperated tone, scrubbing pointedly at the butter he had smeared on the table, 'I don't know how much longer I can put up with him. He's a proper little tinker, chust, a proper little tinker.'

Presently she had an inspiration: 'He should get them all together,' she said, 'Colonel Charlie should get the whole family down here together to discuss how they can help and what's to be done, chust, what's to be done.'

She crossed the room and closed the window savagely to shut out the sound of Henri who was crooning in the whining, nasal fashion of a Kentucky hillbilly as he watered the rose bed beneath the window.

* * *

By the time BA345 from Nice had touched down at Heathrow, Lieutenant Colonel (Retired) Charles Morton-Stewart had reached much the same conclusion as Bridie. He had been pondering the matter since his pre-flight drink in the Pullman Bar in Nice Côte d'Azur Aeroport where, his thoughts undisturbed by the depressing presence of the masses, who were excluded by the exorbitant bar prices, he had started to address the problem which he knew would not go away. Now, with a two hour wait until his connecting flight to Inverness, he headed for the bar in the domestic departure area of Terminal 1 to develop his thoughts and to cauterise, with a large glass of whisky, the unpleasant taste of the in-flight meal.

He must assemble the family, he had decided, and involve them in the decision as to what to do about his two ancient aunts and the house in Antibes.

By the time his flight landed at Inverness Dalcross, he had drafted a letter which he would drop off on his way home with the worthy Mrs. Urquhart on the Muirtown Estate, who worked for the Clydesdale Bank in Inverness and obliged him with the odd bit of typing as and when he required it:

> *Mrs. Urquhart – I wonder if you could very kindly type these letters for me. It is the same basic letter to all recipients with*

Easter at the Villa Victoria

individual postscripts as indicated. I have to come to Inverness on Thursday so could collect them from you on my way home (about 6.45 pm) if you can manage it by then? If I don't hear from you before Thursday, I will assume they will be ready. Hope your daughter has now fully recovered from the measles.

*Many thanks,
Yours sincerely,
Charles Morton-Stewart   4/12/95*

Letters to:

1. Mrs. Sylvia Morton-Stewart
   The Flat, 4a Cannock Mews,
   Kensington, LONDON W8

2. Dr. Stephen Tyler, MD, MRCP,
   Vereholt House, Little Snodbury,
   near CHULMLEIGH, Devon

3. Mrs. Richard Curtis,
   137 Twickenham Way,
   RICHMOND, Surrey

4. Neville Tyler, Esq.,
   c/o Dr. Stephen Tyler,
   (address as at 2 and mark 'Please Forward'

5. Mrs. Vernon Korpecki,
   32 West Side Residence
   University of Santa Cruz,
   California, USA

Prologue

(Friday's date please)

(Dear . . . I will top and tail)

I have recently returned from spending six weeks in Antibes and fear there are some major decisions which must be made in the course of the next few months regarding both the house and the future plans for the Aunts.

As you know, Mattie is now 89 and Aunt Kate 82. Mentally, Mattie is still as sharp as a button but she has become increasingly frail over the past year and is very deaf. Poor Aunt Kate suffers terribly from her arthritis and is now entirely confined to her wheelchair.

Having lived at the villa continuously for nearly eighty years now, apart from their internment during the war, it would be a terrible wrench for them to leave. Yet common sense suggests that the time may now have come when we should at least consider the alternatives. It cannot be too long before Aunt Kate requires round-the-clock nursing care. Already she has to be lifted in and out of bed by Bridie and Mrs. Limbu neither of whom is themselves in the first flush of youth nor trained for this sort of work

Overlaid on this is the financial situation: the Aunts have, I suspect, been living above their income for some years (which is not helped by the current strength of the Franc) and their capital must necessarily have been eroded. I do not think they would understand that economies could be made (Champagne is still served at 11.30 every morning!) and it would be unreasonable to expect them to change their ways radically at this time of their lives. There does not appear to be a financial crisis but I believe it is another aspect which we must look at.

Easter at the Villa Victoria

You are aware, of course, of the understanding between Father and myself that, when I inherited the house from him, the Aunts would be allowed to finish their days there, or stay on as long as they wished. This, naturally, is sacrosanct – their wishes must be paramount whatever we decide. However, I got the impression when I was with them these past few weeks that Mattie, in particular, was getting worried about the future and that they were both finding the daily business of running the house increasingly onerous.

The house has been in the family for 116 years and I consider myself merely as its present custodian. Any major decisions on its future must, I believe, be corporate family decisions and this is why I am writing to you.

Would it be possible, do you think, for as many of us as possible to spend a few weeks out there with the Aunts, perhaps over Easter, so we may jointly review the situation and decide what, if anything, must be done? Do come for a month if you can.

Now that I am a free agent, I can fit in with the plans of others so, if this idea is feasible for you, would you please propose some alternative dates so I can try and get something arranged.

PS for Mrs. Sylvia Morton-Stewart (1) 'Is Emma working now? She must come too, of course, if she is free.'

PS For Dr. Stephen Tyler (2) 'I am sending a copy of this letter for Neville. I don't know where he is at the moment so perhaps you could forward it.'

PS For Mrs. Vernon Korpecki (5) 'I realise it will probably be impossible for you and Vernon to come (unless you are

Prologue

planning a trip to Europe around that time anyway). If you cannot come, I would, nevertheless, appreciate any views or comments you may care to make – you were always closer to Mattie than any of us and I know you will share my concern for them both.'

* * *

'What on earth does he mean?' Frances Tyler said to her husband with obvious irritation, 'Why shouldn't the Aunts be expected to make economies? Everyone else has to.'

'They are very old and set in their ways, Frances.' Richard replied. 'At that age it must be very difficult to change the habits of a lifetime.'

'Nonsense. The hard fact of the matter is that they are leading a 1920s lifestyle in the 1990s and, if they can no longer afford it, it's up to us to do something about it. There must be plenty of nice nursing homes in Cannes which would cost a great deal less than keeping them on in that house.'

'You are talking about your aunts, Frances, not a couple of old dogs.'

'Old dogs; old people; there are hard decisions which have to be made about both when they can no longer look after themselves properly.'

'So you want to go to this meeting that Charlie suggests?'

'Of course. There will have to be *somebody* there who is capable of facing up to reality.'

'It will have to be during the twins' Easter holidays then. You'll have to talk to the school and see if you can wangle an extra week or so either end.'

'I expect they'll be delighted to be shot of the little brutes for as long as possible.'

'Will you do that then? And write to Charlie and propose some dates?'

'Yes. I just hope he hasn't invited that whore Sylvia.'

* * *

Easter at the Villa Victoria

'I wonder if Charlie knows about hoists.' Dr. Stephen Tyler said to his wife. 'If getting Aunt Kate in and out of bed has become a problem, a hoist might be the answer. They are quite simple and comparatively inexpensive.'

'Why don't you get hold of some literature and send it to him when you reply to his letter?'

'Yes, I will. It's a pity we can't go down there and give him some support but I'm afraid it's out of the question to let young Rowbotham loose on the customers just yet.' Dr Tyler was due to retire in seven months time and was in the process of inducting the young man who would be taking over his single-practitioner rural practice. Straight from the A&E department of a busy general hospital in Plymouth, young Rowbotham had much to learn about the refinements of general practice in deepest Devon.

'Absolutely,' his wife agreed, 'and I'm really not fit enough yet to leave home for that length of time anyway.'

'Quite. I'll make our apologies and send Charlie some bumph on hoists.'

* * *

In their neat modern condominium on the university campus, Charlie's sister Florence read the letter out to her husband Vernon who had the Chair in Ancient History.

'Poor old Charlie,' Vernon said, 'a very difficult decision for him to have to make but there's no way we can get to Europe next year.'

'No, of course not. I'll write and explain and tell him he has our proxy in all things. Charlie is so fair and sensible; I have no doubt whatever that he will ensure that the right decisions are made and that the Aunts' welfare and happiness are safeguarded. The house is less important.'

'Of course.'

'I wonder if he's inviting *Sylvia*.' Florence said with a mischievous twinkle in her eye as she reached for her pen and notepaper.

* * *

Prologue

In her small flat off Kensington High Street, Sylvia Morton-Stewart called out to her daughter: 'Emma, we've been invited to a family conference at the villa in Antibes.'

'What? Us? Emma replied incredulously, 'the pariahs of the family?' she took the letter from her mother and read it. 'Will we go?'

I think perhaps we should. If it was just me, I wouldn't go, of course; but it is *your* family and they are *your* great-aunts so I think you should be there to have your say. I'll come to give you moral support.'

'But they're so stuck up and hostile towards us.'

'Not your uncle Charles. He has always been very decent and civil to us.'

'He hasn't exactly sought us out though, has he? We haven't seen him since Daddy's funeral.'

'No, but at least he came to it, which is more than any of the others did.'

Emma was 19 and worked part-time in a gallery in Ebury Street.

'Will you be able to get time off?' her mother asked, aware that she seemed to come and go more or less as she pleased.

'No problem.' Emma replied, 'If you really think we should go, you can tell him that we can fit in with whatever dates he arranges with the others.'

* * *

Charlie received no reply from Neville Tyler who was believed to be backpacking in Thailand at the time.

Easter at the Villa Victoria

1. *Frances and Richard*

'How do you *know* she's a tart for heaven's sake?' said Frances irritably. 'Because nice girls don't hitch-hike alone along the RN7 in mini skirts, six inch heels and fish-net stockings.' Richard replied.

The twins, sniggering and whispering to each other, strained round and peered through the luggage in the back of the Volvo estate car to get a better look at the girl on the kerb, who had already attracted the attention of a lone male motorist who had stopped abruptly, in the middle of the heavy traffic, nearly causing an accident and provoking a crescendo of Gallic road rage.

'Why is he stopping for her?' asked Stephen, the first-born twin.

'Shut up.' said his mother.

Richard pulled the Volvo off the RN7 in the outskirts of Antibes and began the long climb up the hill at the top of which stood the Villa Victoria. The house stood in its own grounds of about three acres surrounded by walls augmented, where necessary, with ten foot-high security fencing, woven from tight, green hurdling through which it was impossible to see. The whole was topped off, as appropriate, with spikes, barbed wire or broken glass. There were two main gateways into the grounds, one of which had been sealed off and barricaded in the mid-1980s when crime on the Côte d'Azur began to reach epidemic proportions. The main gates, whose original wrought iron magnificence had been somewhat diminished by the addition of bolted-on steel panels, to guard the house from prying eyes and the ingress of very thin intruders, were controlled by an entry-phone system and a closed-circuit television camera. Entry by pedestrians through the wicket gate required a four-digit code, divulged only to trusted regular tradesmen, to be punched into a small keypad.

During the hours of darkness, these deterrents were reinforced by heavy steel bars which Dhanibahadur Limbu, the gardener, chauffeur and

Frances and Richard

handyman, would lock in place across both gates. But all these measures were insignificant compared to the ultimate deterrent to uninvited visitors which was Dhanibahadur himself. Five feet six inches and 72 years of age, he was underestimated at one's peril.

Dhani, as he was called by the family, was Nepalese and had served 24 years in the Gurkhas – one of the fittest and most ferocious infantry outfits in the world. His watery brown eyes were always moving over the boundaries for any sign of disturbance and his hearing was as keen as an animal's. He occupied a small flat in the basement with his equally diminutive wife, Manjulika, who was the cook and who shared the household duties with Bridie, the Irish housekeeper. In pride of place in the Limbus' sitting room hung Dhani's kukri, the curiously curved knife of the Gurkhas which, swung with terrifying efficiency in the strong hands of these gallant little soldiers, had wrought terror among the enemies of the British Empire for the past two centuries. A Gurkha soldier's manhood was measured by his ability to sever a goat's head with a single blow of his kukri. Dhani's was kept razor sharp and, as well as being used for a variety of utilitarian jobs in the house and garden, accompanied him upon his patrols of the grounds. These were not undertaken with any regularity but as and when, during the course of the day or night, he felt the desire to check the integrity of his boundaries.

On such occasions, he would slide silently from terrace to terrace, from bush to bush, always smiling, his kukri swinging comfortably in his hand with the familiarity of a lifetime's use. He would pick the odd deadhead here, tighten the occasional fastening on one of the hurdles there, but what he was really looking for was some sign of an intruder.

There had been one such incident three years ago when two German beach bums had parked their motorcycle by the sealed-off entrance and, risking serious personal injury from the eight-inch iron spikes on top, had scaled the gate. They made it as far as the edge of the lower lawn where their way was suddenly barred by a small brown man with a wicked looking knife in his hand (Dhani had had trouble with Germans before). There was something in his poise and smiling face which told them they should not proceed but, when they turned and ran for the gate over which they had entered, he was suddenly in front of them again, crouched and gesturing with his hand that they should sit down on the ground. They sat and waited until the police arrived fourteen chilling minutes later during which time the smile never left Dhani's face.

The two German intruders had long, shoulder length hair, one in a pigtail, when they entered the grounds of the Villa and had difficulty in explaining to their friends, who visited them in the Antibes police cells the following day, how they now both had neat bobs. Dhani kept the pigtail in a polythene bag and on occasions when the television failed to please him, would take it out and stroke it, smiling and chuckling to himself in delighted recollection of that night.

Dhani was at the gate of the villa, without his kukri, as Richard announced himself on the entry-phone and waited for the electric motor to swing the gates open.

'Hello Dhani. How are you?'

'Very well Mr. Richard.' replied the smiling Dhani standing to one side as the Volvo pulled in, his eyes scanning the road outside in the hope of spotting a potential intruder about to sneak in through the open gates behind the car.

Richard stopped at the side of the house where cars were parked – the Aunts did not like vehicles at the front – and had started to unload their cases from the back when Charlie appeared at the side door and walked over to greet them. The men shook hands and Charlie embraced his cousin formally and playfully knocked the twins' heads together.

'Good journey?'

'Perfectly bloody,' said Frances, 'the traffic on the autoroute gets worse and worse; it's suicidal at this time of year.'

Charlie had arrived in Antibes two days earlier so he could be there to welcome the family. Sylvia and Emma were due the following day, on the lunchtime flight from London, and they would then be complete.

Frances and Richard

As Dhani carried their cases upstairs, four at a time, one in each hand and one under each arm, Frances rushed ahead, threw open the windows of their bedroom and sighed with wonder at the view which never failed to delight her. The front elevation of the house faced south-east so all the principal bedrooms, which were on the south-east and south-west sides, enjoyed much the same spectacular view.

The eye was immediately drawn to the Old Town of Antibes – compact, ancient and challenged only by the old hill towns of Eze and Cagnes for the title of 'Most Picturesque Town on the Côte d'Azur'. Its Roman-tiled roofs, in every russet shade, and pitched at a multitude of different angles and projections, crowned little houses of natural stone or white stucco, dotted with windows of different shapes, sizes and levels, some overlooking the narrow, shaded streets and others with a view across the massive 16th-century fortifications of the Old Town to the sea, port and countryside beyond. Dominating the Old Town were the tall, twin towers of the cathedral and Château Grimaldi, irresistible to every visiting artist and photographer and the symbols by which the town had become known. Separating the Old Town from the yacht port to its east was a section of the Old Town wall in which a great arch opened out from the maze of narrow, steep streets in the Old Town to the wide, modern roads of the port area. The inner port was packed with yachts and pleasure craft of every size and type with a small jetty reserved for commercial fishing boats. The inner port led to a larger, and more recently constructed, outer port area, protected from the sea by a long, stone breakwater with a wide road running along its full length and a lighthouse at its end which marked the southern tip of the harbour entrance. This breakwater, known locally as 'Millionaires' Row', was where the very large yachts moored, their sterns to the jetty and their bows held out at right angles by fixed chain moorings on the seabed. These craft, the playthings of middle-eastern royalty and multi-national companies, had permanent crews on board throughout the year and often lay for months on end, awaiting the whim of their mega-rich owners.

On the north side of the harbour mouth the ground rose steeply to Fort

Carre whose grim bastions had guarded the town of Antibes through three centuries of changing fortune and intermittently violent proceedings. Now unoccupied and structurally too unsafe to allow entry by tourists, the deserted fort lent a sinister aura to the coast with its great gun embrasures gaping and the Tricolour flying from its uppermost bastion. Beyond the fort the full sweep of the Bai des Anges opened up to the east with the city of Nice shimmering in the distance with its dramatic backcloth of snow-capped Alps.

'Wonderful, isn't it?' said Frances to her husband who had joined her at the window.

'Yes,' replied Richard, 'every time it takes your breath away.'

Turning slightly to their right, they could see Cap d'Antibes rising above the elegant houses and cool boulevards of the New Town. At the highest point of the Cap stood a little church, the Sanctuaire de la Garoupe, beside a tall lighthouse, the brightest light on the coast, whose flashing loom swept the walls of the bedrooms at night with its regular, reassuring rhythm.

In the middle ground were the houses and apartment blocks of the town's northern suburbs with cars, looking like Dinky Toys, passing along its tree-lined avenues and traffic lights like coloured pinheads in an elaborate model.

At the foot of the villa's gardens was the weathered, pantile roof of the Mas de la Farigoule, now a small hotel but once the 'home farm' of the Villa Victoria with land stretching down almost to the coastal railway. Since the war, with ever increasing demands for residential building land on this beautiful hill, the cultivated terraces of the Mas had given way to neat houses and gardens, well-planned apartment blocks and a network of tidy roads.

Beyond the coast, Frances could see the sweep of the deep blue Mediterranean from Cap Ferrat, beyond Nice, to Cap d'Antibes. Dotted with little white triangles of sail and with the odd cargo ship plying the trade routes on the horizon, she always thought it was like the archetypal seaside scene portrayed in early railway travel posters and so loved by British people. It lacked only the screaming gulls and saucy postcards but, unlike British resorts which seldom seemed to deliver the clear blue skies shown in the posters, this magical place was always warm and bathed in sunshine.

In late afternoon, as it now was, with the sun well down in its arc to the west, the buildings and battlements of the Old Town were illuminated from a low angle. This was when the view was at its theatrical best, the Old Town appearing in knife-sharp focus in the ultra-clear air of late afternoon, the whole vista of the coast, with its long shadows and vivid colours being more like an extravagant stage set – far too perfect to be real. No wonder, she always thought, that the greatest artists have always been drawn to this coast.

Inside the walls and fences of its boundaries, the gardens of the villa were a haven of peace and beauty. Terraced lawns descended the sharply sloping land with grass as green, and as like a proper English lawn, as it was possible to achieve in the dry climate of the South of France. Paved walkways rambled between herbaceous borders alive with colour in every season. The arching fronds of immaculately-coifed palm trees gave welcome shade to the house and along the broad paved terrace beneath the verandah which ran the entire length of the south-west front. An ancient bougainvillea stretched itself in the fierce sun on the boundary wall, banks of waxy cyclamens flanked the stone steps which curved down to the southern boundary where a double row of old, gnarled olive trees blocked from view the more intrusive of the modern buildings below, and provided privacy from the guests at the Mas.

The climate laid few constrictions on nature's ambitions in this beautiful, sheltered garden. The seasons had little relevance; even in the coldest month of January, with its occasional morning frosts, the beds played host to multi-coloured polyanthus, wallflowers, cyclamen, yuccas and arum lilies. Now, Jasmine and exotic fuchsias bloomed around the boundaries, orange and lemon trees hung heavy with fruit and swaying mimosas wafted through the house the heady scent which, for many, is the scent of the South of France.

Easter at the Villa Victoria

On the east side of the villa was the old coach house with garaging for cars and a staff flat above and, to the north, a kitchen garden and a tennis court which had seen little use in recent years. There was no swimming pool, although younger members of the family often speculated that beside the tennis court would be the ideal location.

Leaving the window, with some reluctance, Frances unpacked their suitcases, stowing their clothes in tall cupboards which ran one length of the room. The twins were already installed in, and bouncing on the beds of, a smaller bedroom, originally a dressing room, which connected with the main bedroom. Beyond this was a bathroom with the original Victorian brass taps and fittings and an enormous enamelled bath standing magnificently on griffin-clawed feet. The floors, as throughout the house, were polished marble scattered with old, well worn, and in places quite dangerous, oriental rugs.

She heard a knock on the door and Charlie's voice, exaggeratedly hushed to indicate that the Aunts, who were only now awakening from their afternoon siesta with tea and Breton gallettes, taken to their rooms on neatly-dressed trays by Bridie, must not be disturbed.

'Frances.'

'Yes, Uncle Charlie.'

'I'm just slipping out for an hour. If there's anything you need ask Bridie when she has got the Aunts up and I'll see you on the veranda for drinks at the usual time.'

'Six thirty?'

'On the dot.'

Charlie's 'slipping out for an hour' at this time of day was a time honoured and universally understood ritual. He would drive, in the little 'house' Renault used by Dhani to take his wife or Bridie shopping, to a bar on the seafront at Juan-les-Pins. Drinks were served at the Villa Victoria, as they always had been, at 6.30 pm and never a minute before. Charlie found this wait tedious; he approved completely of the discipline of British licensing hours which gave one something to look forward to – the magic moment

Frances and Richard

when the tea towels came off the pumps – and he would not have contemplated having a drink between the hours of 2.30 and 5.30 pm. But by 5.30 in the evening, when London pubs were opening, and with a full hour to go before opening time at the villa, his throat became disagreeably dry and he craved the cooling balm of an ice-cold beer, or two, or maybe even three on a 'Three Beer Night' when the weather was particularly hot or the company in the bar particularly jolly.

He would sit in the relaxed ambience of the bar chatting with the proprietor or waiters, sipping his Kronenbourg or Adelshoffen and idly watching the girls with their long brown legs and short white shorts as they came off the beach and wandered back along the front to their pensions or apartments. It was an important and relaxed time of day for Charlie. However, he currently had a problem.

There were two bars on opposite corners of the Rue des Isles – the Neptunia and the Tropique. For many years he had patronised the Neptunia but then, on his arrival for Christmas 1994, had found it boarded up with an 'A Vendre' sign prominently on display. He had therefore moved his custom over the road to the Tropique where, over the past year, he had developed the same easy rapport he had enjoyed with the Neptunia staff for so long. His demi-pression, ice cold, with the glass misty and beaded on the outside, was placed on his table with a bowl of black olives immediately he entered, sometimes before if the waiters saw him squeezing the little grey Renault into a nearby parking space. They would keep an eye on his table and, when he was ready for the other half, he would only have to twitch an eyebrow, like a seasoned bidder at an auction, for his requirement to be recognised and satisfied with the minimum of delay, no matter how crowded the bar and its outside pavement tables should be.

The problem had arisen last November when, one evening, he noticed the Neptunia had reopened and, a few nights later, had made the fatal mistake of slipping in for a quick one for old time's sake. He had assumed that the proprietor and staff would have changed with the waiters he had known in other jobs scattered up and down the coast. Not so! As soon as he crossed the threshold his hand was seized first by Gerard and then by Michel with delighted cries of 'Bonsoir, Monsieur le Colonel, Ca va? Ca va?' A cold beer was placed on what had been his regular table without his asking and Gerard and Michel returned to their usual places at the bar, smiling and watching their returned prodigal in confident anticipation of a resumption of the old, time honoured, nightly routine.

Meanwhile at the Tropique, Madame looked at the wall clock, frowned and wondered what had happened to Monsieur le Colonel. So, what was Charlie to do? He had turned the various options over in his mind and had eventually decided he would have to split his custom between the two. There was not the time, nor would it be prudent, to visit both bars every evening so he had decided upon, and settled into, a routine of patronising each on alternate evenings.

He could not be seen by either one entering the rival establishment so, depending on whose night it was, he would approach either from the east or from the west, parking well up the front on the appropriate side, then scuttling furtively up the pavement and into the bar of the day. He had followed this routine since November last, like a bigamist trying to conceal the existence of one wife from the other. Of course, it had only taken the staff of both establishments a few days to realise what he was up to and, after a brief period of cool and rather sulky retribution, they entered into the spirit of the game to avoid mutual embarrassment. They would turn their backs if they saw him scurrying along the pavement on the opposite corner or skulking behind a potted plant in the rival establishment, and would exchange incredulous yet sympathetic glances with their colleagues with the occasional sigh or murmured 'Oh zut alors! Les Anglais!'

On this evening it was the turn of the Tropique. This was the time of day when Charlie did his best thinking and resolved his most knotty problems so, having settled at his usual table behind a pillar, which he believed concealed his presence from the other side, he reviewed the situation. Frances, Richard and the twins had arrived safely and tomorrow he would collect Sylvia and Emma from the airport. The family, or that part of it

Frances and Richard

which was to be involved in this decision-making process, would then be complete.

Frances was not actually his niece but he referred to her as such as he had never really understood the intricacies of cousinship. Frances was the daughter of Dr. Stephen Tyler who was the son of the late Captain John Tyler, RN, who had married Charlie's Aunt Florence. Captain Tyler was killed in action, commanding a light cruiser in 1943 and, from the end of the war until her death in 1984, Aunt Florence had spent much of her time at Antibes with her sisters, Mattie and Kate, and their mother, Lady Florence Morton-Stewart, who had died at the villa in 1968.

Frances had always been a boisterous girl and age and motherhood of twins did not, thought Charlie, seem to have mellowed her to any great extent. She knew what she wanted and usually got it. A gifted artist, she had worked before her marriage as a junior designer in the art department of a west end advertising agency in which her future husband, Richard Curtis, was Media Director.

Richard, a quiet and unassuming man with a passion and extraordinary talent for distributing his clients' advertising budgets across the most cost-effective media, was bowled over by the noisy little blonde from the art department with her heavy makeup and outrageous clothes. They had married in 1978 when Frances was 20 and, two years later when Richard made his move to form his own agency in Marylebone, Curtis, Broadbent and Associates, Frances came with him as Creative Director, a position which she filled with considerable flair and skill until the birth of the twins five years later.

Richard's agency flourished with the bountiful budgets of the Thatcher boom years and he and Frances moved from their flat in South Kensington to a six-bedroomed Victorian house in Richmond with a narrow garden at the back for the twins. They ate out twice a week, took winter breaks in the Caribbean and wanted for little.

Then came the recession, which always hits the advertising industry first, and the agency had its first, sobering experience of serious bad debts. As rival agencies folded daily around them, and the motor showrooms filled up with repossessed Porsches and BMWs, Richard had a hard time keeping his firm solvent. Curtis Broadbent retrenched, letting go most of the staff they had taken on in the mid-80s, tightening up on their credit control and taking on new clients only after rigorous examination of their financial accounts. At the end of the day, the agency owed its survival to Richard's growing reputation as a media planner in a climate where advertisers were striving to retain market shares on greatly reduced appropriations.

Frances bitterly resented the necessary curtailment of their plans and lifestyle, blaming it all on the assassins of Mrs. Thatcher, and she waited impatiently for the promised upturn in the economy which would, once again, bring Richard the rewards which his ability and hard work merited. In the meantime, any family money which might come her way would not be amiss and she did not look kindly upon the Aunts' absurdly outdated and extravagant way of life if, as she suspected, it was eroding what was left of the family fortunes and the expectations of her and her children.

Yes, thought Charlie, Frances would need a strong restraining hand in the forthcoming discussions.

Rue des Revennes, Antibes

2. Lady Florence

By the time Charlie got back to the villa, the family had assembled on the veranda for pre-dinner drinks. It was a pleasant time of day when the social life of the house reconvened after the diverse individual activities of the afternoon. It was a time for exchanging the day's news and gossip, for dinner guests to arrive and friends to drop in for a drink and a chat.

Bottles and glasses stood on a huge, circular, polished brass Indian table at the end of the veranda and, before the family gathered each evening, Bridie or Manjulika would fill the ice bucket, replenish the drinks, open or close windows, and adjust red canvas sun blinds, according to the prevailing weather. The roof of the veranda was tiled, like the main house, and the glass sides all opened on sliding rails so, no matter how searing was the heat outside on the terrace, the veranda remained a shaded and airy place.

The aunts were sitting in their usual places – Aunt Kate in her wheelchair and Mattie in a little high-backed Victorian chair which had also been her mother's favourite.

It was a manifestation of the differences in their characters that Aunt Martha was always referred to in the family simply as 'Mattie' while Katherine was always dignified with the full and formal title 'Aunt Kate'. Though Mattie was seven years older than her sister she was younger at heart. Her face, creased with smiles and radiating affection and good humour, was at sharp contrast to Kate's immaculate but stiff and somewhat haughty appearance. Mattie's hair was dyed, very badly, an unnatural and outrageous gingery-brown, her hollow cheeks were daubed with rouge and speckled with black fibres of mascara which had fallen from over-decorated eyelashes. She smoked cigarettes incessantly, in a long black holder, the ash from which invariably found itself down the front of her dress rather than in the ashtrays which were distributed in abundance throughout the house for her use. Her clothes never seemed to fit her properly, always appearing to be caught up on one arthritic joint or another and her dresses, though regularly washed and pressed by Bridie, retained their fresh appearance only until they had received their first sprinkling of cigarette ash (generally within fifteen minutes of her emergence from her bedroom) which would later be augmented with spilled champagne, claret or soup – whichever of which Mattie happened to be partaking when she entered her next coughing fit.

Mattie would laugh and cough alternately, both with equal violence and often at the same time. Food, drink or cigarette ash, or a combination of all three, would go flying across the table and the debris of what was left would float down and settle on the front of her dress.

Aunt Kate, who would watch each of these performances with unconcealed disgust and disapproval, would always say: '*Really,* Mattie!' often adding: 'it's *such* a disgusting habit,' or 'what *would* mother say?' to which Mattie, looking up guiltily from beneath heavily-pencilled eyebrows, would reply: 'Sorry dear; just a little tickle.' It would not be long before something else would amuse her and the barrage of laughter and coughing would start again.

Sometimes Kate would anticipate these outbursts and would fix her sister with a censorial stare before it actually started. On such occasions, if she felt a coughing fit coming on, Mattie would avert her eyes and let nature take its course. If, on the other hand, she felt reasonable confident that she could control herself for the next several minutes, she would meet Kate's eye and enquire in a haughty tone: 'Something the matter, dear?'

Everyone adored Mattie. She was the object of constant teasing, in a gentle and loving way, which she enjoyed as much as the rest. She was always game for a laugh (and a cough) and eager to hear the latest jokes and family gossip. She was demonstrative in a way which owed more to her Irish mother than to her Scottish father – clutching children to her and smothering them with kisses as they struggled to be free. She loved a 'little drinkie' and her response when she was asked if she wanted another was part of the Mattie legend: 'No, no. no!' she would say then, as he that proffered turned to move on: 'Oh well, perhaps a very *tiny* one darling.' and would then watch without intervention as her glass was once again fully filled.

So well-known was this response, that children would mime it behind her back as she did it. If she caught them she would fein great outrage and summon them to her with cries of: 'Oh you *horrible* children; come here till I thrash the hides off you.' When they crossed reluctantly to her, she would grab them and subject them to another ordeal of laughing hugs and kisses until the next onset of a coughing fit enabled them to make good their escape.

Mattie enjoyed a special rapport with Charlie who, though trying hard to give it up, was the only remaining smoker in the family. She would latch onto his arm with a whispered: 'Let's go and enjoy a little ciggy together, darling.' as she glanced conspiratorially over her shoulder for any sign of Kate.

Aunt Kate had more of the Scottish than the Irish blood in her veins. She was morally upright, practical and dependable without any of Mattie's mischief. Both girls had been brought up, and lived until late middle age, in the benevolent radiance of a mother who unquestionably knew best and who removed from them the need for any onerous thought or decisions.

On their mother's death in 1968, when Mattie was 61 and Kate 54, one of them had to assume her mantle. Kate was her natural successor. Though neither of the sisters chose to face reality in its full sense, Kate was more businesslike and better able to grapple with the likes of travel arrangements and tradesmen's accounts; and so it had been for the past 28 years.

Aunt Kate did nothing to conceal the distinguished silvery-grey hair which was always perfectly assembled into a faultless 'granny bun' at the back of her neck. Though severely disabled with rheumatoid arthritis, her clothes always seemed to hang perfectly on her poor twisted limbs and swollen joints. She made no concessions to her infirmity. Sitting upright and stately in her wheelchair (or Bath chair as she insisted on calling it) with at least one piece of her mother's jewellery displayed to best effect,

Lady Florence

she invariable looked as if she was ready to receive royalty – which in fact she would have been without any further preparation.

Though her mother had been dead for 28 years, her aura still remained in every part of the house and governed the activities of those within it; and Kate, as earthly trustee to her memory, was determined that it should remain this way. There was not a day went past when Kate would not ask herself, on matters ranging from social behaviour to domestic trivia: 'Would Mummy have approved of this?' or 'Would she have done that differently?'

Although Kate had made, what she at least considered to be, major concessions to the changing standards of dress and behaviour over the years, (Mummy would have understood this), the younger members of the family knew better than to arrive late for dinner, or informally dressed. Neither would any man appear stripped to the waist in house or garden, nor any woman in a bathing dress.

Charlie embraced his aunts and settled down in a wicker chair with a long whisky and water. Tonight it was the turn of the Curtis family to bring the Aunts up to date with their news. Frances and Richard were sitting by Aunt Kate while Frances gave them a blow-by-blow account of the reactions of the twins' headmaster when she had approached him regarding an extended Easter break: 'Honestly, that's what he said Aunt Kate – 'As far as I am aware, Mrs Curtis, your sons could take another six months holiday without in any way slowing down their academic progress which has been completely static since they joined the school.' Pompous ass!' Frances added.

Aunt Kate was listening with appropriate gravity and sympathy while, at the same time, keeping a concerned eye on Mattie who, she suspected, was encouraging the twins to try a little drop of gin in their Coca Cola.

Difficult to believe they are sisters, thought Charlie to himself as his mind wandered back over the events of the past century which had led to these two old ladies leading their time-warp existence in the South of France.

Easter at the Villa Victoria

* * *

The 'Villa Victoria' had been built in 1880 by Captain James Stewart and his wife Victoria Morton. James Stewart came from a Jacobite family which had staked its fortunes in the gallant but ill-conceived attempts to restore the Royal Stewarts to the British throne in the risings of 1715 and 1745. His great-great-grandfather, Alasdair Stewart, had fought, together with one son, three brothers and seven cousins in the Prince's army at Culloden. After their crushing defeat, and the end to their hopes of evicting the Hanoverians, Alasdair escaped to Sweden on a fishing boat with other Jacobite officers and eventually rejoined the Stewart court in France. The family was stripped of its land and possessions in Scotland and Alasdair Stewart died, penniless, as a pensioner of France, some fifteen years later in Boulogne where a sad community of disaffected Scots and English gentlemen lived out their lives on the charity of their erstwhile ally. His elder son, James, had been pardoned by the Hanoverian government on account of having lost both his legs at Culloden. He only lived another two years. His younger son, Charles, had been too young to take part in the 'Forty-Five' rising and in 1762 took the King's Shilling and was commissioned into a new regiment, The Stewart Highlanders, which was being raised for service in the Indies.

From this time, every generation of the family had served with the Regiment and had contributed to its impressive roll of Battle Honours from the Napoleonic Wars, through the Crimea, the Indian Mutiny, countless Imperial campaigns and two World Wars.

In 1879 James Stewart was serving as a captain in the second battalion stationed at Cawnpore when he met and married Victoria Morton, daughter and heiress of the owner of three substantial tea estates in Darjeeling. Her father had been happy to see his fortunes passing to the Stewart family with two provisos: firstly that he should join the name Morton to his own when they were married and, secondly, that he should resign his commission and take his new wife, Victoria, who was rather delicate, to live in a part of the world which would be better for her health. James, who was not a highflier and had for some time recognised the fact that he was unlikely to rise beyond the rank of captain (promotion was very slow at that time), saw no difficulty with either proposal. Indeed, as a tribute both to his wife and to their gracious Queen, he insisted that the house they were building for themselves in the South of France should be called 'Victoria' in honour of them both.

Victoria after eight very happy years at the Villa, during which her husband lavished upon her every comfort and luxury which medical opinion suggested and the Morton fortune could well afford, died at the age of thirty-two. Their first son, James, had died in infancy and their second son, Charles (it had always been, and would so continue, that sons were named in this order) was sent home from France at the age of seven to embark upon the traditional pattern of education – preparatory school, Wellington and the Royal Military College, Sandhurst, before commissioning into the Regiment. Their daughter, Mary, who never married, lived at the villa her whole life, caring for her father until his death in 1909. She died in internment during the Second World War.

In 1904, Charles Morton-Stewart married Lady Florence Cargill, daughter of an Irish Ascendancy peer. They had two sons and three daughters who included Martha (Mattie) and Katherine (Kate). Unlike his father, Charles Morton-Stewart *was* a highflier and was commanding the first battalion of the Stewarts when he was killed, sword in hand, at the head of his men during one of the hopeless but gallant charges on the Somme in 1916. He was awarded a posthumous Victoria Cross and left a young widow, five children and a spinster sister as custodians of the Villa Victoria.

By this time, the Morton tea fortunes, though far from exhausted, were looking a bit thin for the servicing of the needs of a family which no longer had any contributing male members. Then in 1922, Lady Florence's father, after a lifetime of loving care and concern for his tenantry and servants, was burned out of the house his family had owned for over two centuries by the Sinn Feiners. He left Ireland for a small house in Wiltshire where he died, a broken man, two years later. As both her brothers had been killed in the war, Lady Florence found herself heir to both her father's remaining wealth and a warehouse of such furniture and effects which the army had managed to salvage from her burning ancestral home. The furniture was more of a problem than the money. She accommodated what she could at the Villa Victoria and a few small pieces at her flat in Knightsbridge, round the back of Harrods, where she stayed during her visits to London. Other relations took a few pictures and bits and pieces but the family was too diminished to absorb the remaining part of the contents of a great Irish mansion. The rest was sold at auction, to her great distress, and distributed among the homes of the upwardly mobile in the English Home Counties.

Of all the inhabitants of the Villa Victoria over a period of six reigns, it was Lady Florence who left her mark most indelibly on its traditions and routines. Throughout the inter-war years she ran the villa in the gracious and well-ordered style of an Irish country house but with the added sparkle which the hedonism of the Côte d'Azur lent to that era. She paid no heed to the American-inspired movement to change the Riviera 'Season' from winter to summer. She regarded with amused disdain the arrival of a new class of rich and glamorous people whose fame and fortune had been gained in the world of entertainment. Her reputation as a hostess was known the length of the coast and, although her guests would sometimes include members of this new theatrical nobility, she could never take them as seriously as they took themselves and their unusual customs and values were always the subject of much merriment and light-hearted gossip between Lady Florence and her patrician friends.

So, while Scott Fitzgerald immortalised the Plage de la Garoupe, within sight of the villa's upper windows, and Isadora Duncan performed her strange dances in her studio on Cap Ferat, life at the Villa Victoria continued with much the same relaxed formality and exclusivity as its residents had enjoyed half a century before.

When war came to Europe, Lady Florence resolutely refused the evacuation arrangements offered by the British Consulate and continued living at the villa with her sister-in-Law, Mary, her two unmarried daughters, Martha and Katherine, and four Irish servants. Her elder son, James, was serving with the Stewarts and the younger, Charles, with a passion for aeroplanes, had joined the Royal Air Force. A large Union Flag was flown daily above the villa until November 1942, when the terms of the armistice were abrogated as a result of the Allied landings in North Africa, and Italian troops moved across the border to occupy the French Riviera.

When Lady Florence had made it plain to the strutting Italian commandant that she had no intention of accepting him socially, he confiscated the Union Flag and had the flagstaff chopped down with an axe by one of his soldiers. He also requisitioned her Bentley for his private use. When, the following year, Italy changed sides and her troops moved back across the border, the Bentley was left dirty, damaged and with two deflated tyres outside the railway station at Cannes.

When German troops replaced the Italians in the autumn of 1943, the German commandant, von Richert, was a very different proposition. He was an officer and a gentleman of the old school and had the Bentley retrieved, repaired, cleaned and returned to the coach house at the villa. He apologised to Lady Florence, in perfect English and with some embarrassment, for not being able to allow her to fly the Union Flag again for fear of provoking the local officials of the Vichy government.

Two months later is was his sad duty to explain to her that she and her household would be transported to Uriage, near Grenoble, where they and other British residents were to be interned for the remainder of the war. Their accommodation was cramped and spartan but reasonably comfortable and the British internees amused themselves with the establishment of a fiercely competitive Bridge circle. Von Richert visited Lady Florence on two occasions: firstly to tell her that her elder son, James, had been wounded in Italy, where he was commanding the Stewarts in the advance north, but had been evacuated to hospital in England where he was doing well. The second visit was to inform her, with genuine sadness and concern, that her younger son, Charles, had been posted missing after a Bomber Command raid over Berlin. His body and those of his crew were never recovered. It was a bad year for the family: shortly after this stunning news, Lady Florence was ro learn, this time from British sources, of the death of her son-in-law, Captain John Tyler RN, when the light cruiser he commanded was torpedoed in the North Atlantic. Then three weeks before they were due for release from the camp at Uriage, her sister-in-law, Mary, died following a short and unexpected illness. She was aged 65.

Greatly aged and sobered by her succession of losses, Lady Florence returned to Antibes with Mattie, Kate and the staff after the liberation of France. With characteristic strength of will, she got the family settled in and the house restored to its old order, as far as post-war shortages and the deep sense of mourning which hung over the household would allow.

Lady Florence lived for another 22 years until her death in 1968 aged 84. But the Riviera was never to be quite the same again. The years of post-war austerity and financial controls effectively killed 'The Season', as she had known it, when between the months of November and April the villas along the coast had been filled with bright and interesting people who knew how to behave in public places and at the endless round of glittering social events which had been their way of life.

As mass tourism exploded along the Mediterranean coasts in the 1960s, the list of acceptable guests at the Villa Victoria became shorter and shorter. 'They are not *tourists*,' Lady Florence would say indignantly, 'they do not *tour*; they stay in one place where they lie in the sun like fat pork chops under the grill.' From June to September when hotels were overflowing with the new breed of visitors and the roads along the coast were jammed with foreign cars, the gates of the Villa Victoria would be firmly bolted and the family would seldom venture from the grounds. All social intercourse among what remained of the old Riviera society ceased during the summer months which were becoming increasingly known by local tradesmen and their like, to the intense annoyance of Lady Florence, as 'The Season.'

When the seething tide of sunburned clerks and shop assistants washed back across the face of Europe to office blocks and suburban houses in

Lady Florence

Britain, Germany, Holland and Scandinavia, the family would emerge once again and a sadly impoverished version of the old Riviera life would recommence.

So it had continued after Lady Florence's death, through the 1970s and 80s when package tour operators extended the term 'Riviera' to include the coast beyond the Esterels, so greater numbers of visitors could enjoy its magic from newly built hotels, apartment blocks, caravan parks and even camping sites as far west as Saint-Tropez. Prices on the coast remained sufficiently high to discourage the sunbathing and lager lout cultures that had infected Spain and Greece, but the Riviera had changed. With its topless bathing and pizza parlours, it would never again be the sophisticated and fashionable international colony it had once been.

* * *

After drinks on the veranda came dinner which, at this time of year when it was still quite cool in the evenings, was taken in the dining room at a George III gateleg table which, in its earlier days in Ireland, had seated twenty but for the more modest proportions of the rooms at the villa, four of its leaves had been removed and stored. It was laid with elegant Georgian silver with Dublin hallmarks and worn thin with two centuries of use, shining Waterford crystal and two superb flower displays from the garden arranged by Aunt Kate in white Spode bowls.

The Aunts were seated first at the centre of one long side of the table, a position they had for long adopted, partly because they thought it was more cosy and partly because they could not hear each other without shouting when seated at opposite ends. Before sitting down, the worst of the cigarette ash was dusted off Mattie's dress by Bridie using a short-handled feather duster, of the type used by saucy French maids in theatrical farces, which was kept in the sideboard for this purpose.

Two magnificent silver candelabra which, in earlier days, would have been tended by footmen in powdered wigs, were lit. White Belfast linen napkins were shaken out on laps and the meal commenced: Chanterelle mushrooms in a Pernod and estragon sauce with fresh ribbon pasta and a light and silky Sancerre. Then came the main course: Fricassée de veau avec petit légumes served from old Sheffield plate entrée dishes with the Stewart crest on their domed lids, and the copper shining through from a hundred years of enthusiastic polishing.

Two bottles of 1983 Lynch-Bages had been carefully decanted and stood in worn, Venetian glass decanters on a silver salver on the sideboard. Wine was too serious a matter with the Morton-Stewarts to admit of any concessions to style or antiquity and Charlie had, some years previously, persuaded his aunts to abandon the handsome but impractical crystal wine glasses in favour of a modern French design of clear glass, enabling one to examine its contents properly, and a tulip shaped bowl into which one could get one's nose to better enjoy the glories of the villa's cellar.

Richard, who had come to appreciate claret in the affluent years of the 1980s, and now considered himself something of a connoisseur, swirled his wine round the glass, observing the orange tinge at the edge, inhaled luxuriously through his nose, sipped, swirled the wine round his mouth and swallowed. 'Beautiful!' he whispered to Charlie, who had clearly been waiting for his reaction.

'But if course', shrugged Charlie, 'only the best for guests at the Villa Victoria. Eh Mattie?' he sought the confirmation of his aunt.

'No, no, no my darling,' she replied, 'well, perhaps just a tiny drop.' as she extended her glass to him.

Cheese followed the main course, in the French fashion, enabling the claret to be finished to best advantage, then fruit was passed round in a silver basket of exquisite design, crafted by Benjamin Smith in his London workshop in 1793 – the year that Louis XVI and Marie Antoinette were executed, the start of the Reign of Terror. Optional with the fruit was a glass of ice-cold, golden Barsac in whose lusciousness the craftsmen of the Château Climens had lavished their ancient skill in harnessing the decay of the 'noble rot' for the enjoyment and homage of a privileged few.

Lady Florence

Though port was seldom served these days, the ladies would still withdraw first, to drawing room or veranda according to the season, where coffee was served with petits fours and cognac, or single-malt whisky was available for those whose digestive tracts were still in business.

This was an informal family dinner at the villa. On more formal occasions, when guests were invited, Dhani, in a white jacket, would manage the wine, circling the table with bottles and decanters, discreetly observing the consumption of each guest and ensuring that everyone's glasses were kept at exactly their preferred level. At very grand dos, which were rare these days, an additional fish course would be served and Monsieur Verrechia, who had been a waiter at the Martinez in Cannes before his retirement, was alway happy to help out for the evening.

The Aunts would retire at about 10 pm leaving the others to talk, read and drink if they wished or simply to sit and gaze at the amazing panoply of lights, like the view from an aircraft flying low over a city on a frosty night, which spread out below them.

Tomorrow, thought Charlie, would be tricky – the arrival of Sylvia and her daughter Emma – Sylvia whose name was never mentioned in the family. 'One of the surest marks of a gentleman,' he had been taught by his father from an early age, 'is the ability to make people of all ranks and backgrounds feel comfortable in one's presence. Only rich yahoos get enjoyment from the awkwardness and unease of others.' The tutorial was always illustrated with the story of George V who drank the water in his finger bowl after his guest had done the same.

If only, thought Charlie, the introduction of a low-bred Irish woman to two old ladies with 19th century social values, whose favourite nephew had been 'trapped' by her into marriage, causing his disinheritance and rejection by the family, were as easy as drinking water from a finger bowl.

3. Sylvia and Emma

Charlie hustled the little Renault through the heavy midday traffic on the coast road to Nice. He had started off along the RN7 but, when the traffic had effectively come to a standstill at La Fontonne, he had cut down to the coast road where he had found it just as bad. He was getting anxious. It was not that he was worried about being late to meet Sylvia's flight, but he was getting increasingly concerned that the half-hour he had promised himself in the Pullman Bar beforehand, to strengthen and prepare himself for the meeting, might be curtailed.

In the event, the flight was running 20 minutes late so, in a comfortable chair, with a glass of whisky in his hand, he had plenty of time to prepare himself and reflect upon the ignominious life of his late brother James.

In the social group in which the Morton-Stewarts belonged, to say that a man had 'married a barmaid' implied simply that he had married beneath his social level. In the case of James and Sylvia it meant just what it said – Sylvia actually *was* a barmaid (not that Charlie had anything against barmaids; some of his best friends were barmaids).

James had been what earlier generations would have called a 'bounder'. He was intelligent but bone idle. At prep school he did the very minimum amount of work to enable him to scrape through the Common Entrance into Wellington in the bottom ten. Here he stayed firmly and comfortably in the 'B' stream, hardly flexing his brain, narrowly escaping expulsion on more than one occasion and, finally, passing into Sandhurst with much the same undistinguished result he had achieved in his Common Entrance.

With the increased off-duty freedom he enjoyed at Sandhurst he became worse. His father was constantly pestered for supplements to his allowance to fund his heavy drinking and regular expeditions to Reading to pick up shopgirls. He was in constant trouble, as were the girls who were foolish enough to succumb to his polished line of chat.

Sylvia and Emma

Had his name been other than Morton-Stewart, he would certainly not have been offered a commission in the Stewart Highlanders. The then commanding officer had been warned of his character deficiencies but, argued the Colonel of the Regiment, how could someone with an unbroken family tradition in the Regiment since its inception in he 18th century not, possibly, come right in the end? But James never came right. Throughout his service he was pursued from posting to posting by unpaid tradesmen and angry fathers. His fellow subalterns presented him one Christmas with a framed plaque of his family crest in which the dagger had been substituted with a horse whip.

Then in 1964, when James was 31, he announced his engagement to Judith Forbes, a nice girl whose father was a Gunner colonel. His family and friends breathed a sigh of relief – this would settle Jimmy down, they thought, and give him something to work for.

After a lavish wedding which her family could ill afford but felt they must put on in view of the distinguished family into which their daughter was marrying, Judith settled down in a determined effort to reform the unreformable. Her will was broken after the first ten months when she disturbed her husband *in flagrante delicto* with her best friend. They were divorced two years later.

James was not actually cashiered from the army – he resigned his commission in 1968 under a cloud involving the misappropriation of mess funds. The Regiment managed to hush it all up out of deference to a family which had served it well and, in particular, to Charlie, now a promising young captain who had inherited, it seemed, all the Morton-Stewart qualities of gallantry and honour which had contributed so much to the Regiment's high reputation.

There was no love lost between James and Charles. Although Charlie was seven years younger, and their careers had therefore only overlapped for some eight years in the army, Charlie had always followed in the notorious wake of his brother and suffered for it. People to whom he was introduced would say: 'Morton-Stewart? Are you related to that chap . . . yes, hmmm

. . . yes.' A chill would descend on the conversation and the other party would extricate himself from Charlie's company and rejoin another group which would start talking in hushed tones while casting surreptitious glances in Charlie's direction.

It's so damned unfair, he thought on many occasions, my father commanded this regiment in North Africa and Italy, my grandfather won the VC with it on the Somme, my family have had spotless service careers for two centuries; then along comes that evil so-and-so James and everyone refers to me as *his* brother as if he was the only Morton-Stewart worthy of note.

Between leaving the army and his death in 1994, aged 61, James went through a dozen or more different jobs each ending in exasperation or unpleasantness – tourist guide, salesman, estate agent's negotiator; the best job he ever had was as secretary of a golf club for nearly four years – the longest he had managed to hold on to any job.

In 1977, aged 44, he married 20 year-old Sylvia Ryan, an Irish barmaid at 'The Admiral Fitzroy' in the Old Brompton Road who, four months later, presented him with a daughter, Emma. On hearing this news, his father, old James Stewart, promptly changed his Will leaving James only the income from a small Trust Fund, and that only out of compassion for his unfortunate little grand-daughter to whom the money would pass after James's death and when she came of age. The balance of his estate, including his homes in Scotland and Antibes, were left to his younger son Charles. Old James would greet his friends in the street or in his club with the words: 'Now he's married a barmaid!' but few realised that he meant it literally.

Charlie attended his brother's funeral in 1994, on behalf of the family, which was the first and only time he had met Sylvia and Emma. He had been very touched by the widow's obviously genuine grief. But, he thought, she was a very attractive woman who, at 37, would almost certainly remarry and make a new life for herself and her daughter.

Over the ensuing months, Charlie started developing feelings of guilt about his sister-in-law and niece. Sylvia, after all, was not responsible for her husband's actions before she met him – the actions which had been such a blight and embarrassment to Charlie as a young man. Nor, he recalled, had he heard of any major scandals involving his brother since his marriage to Sylvia. Perhaps she had been what he had always needed and, although he never achieved anything in his many and varied occupations, and his drinking, by all accounts, had not moderated, perhaps Sylvia had settled him down and made him as responsible a member of society as his unprincipled nature would allow.

Charlie looked at his watch and finished his whisky with a gulp. The arrival of the flight from London had been announced. Yes, he was glad that, despite the family's disapproval, he had invited Sylvia and Emma to take their rightful places at the family gathering.

He recognised her as soon as she emerged from passport control and descended towards the baggage hall. He caught her eye and pointed with his finger to indicate where he would be waiting for her when she emerged through Customs.

Sylvia looked cool and naturally elegant in a beige linen suit which looked uncreased despite her journey. Her jet black hair hung to her shoulders partly concealing a brightly coloured scarf at her neck. She was 39 but, thought Charlie, looked 29; she was, indeed, a very beautiful woman. He had pondered in advance whether he should shake hands with her (he had only met her once) or embrace her like family which, of course, she was. He had decided upon the middle course – a formal French three-cheek kiss, where the lips never touched the face, which slightly confused Sylvia as she thought is was all over after the second phase and was withdrawing herself as Charlie was bowing forward into the third movement.

'Sylvia, dear.' he said with genuine warmth and a welcoming smile.

'Hello Colonel Morton . . .' she started.

'Enough of the Colonel business,' he interrupted, 'I'm Charlie, do you understand? Charlie, from now on.'

She accepted the invitation with a hint of startled embarrassment and, with her head very slightly on one side she replied: 'Charlie, OK.' He noticed as she moved her head that her hair was so soft, and so well cut, that it hung out vertically from the side of her face forming natural and perfectly modulated waves as it was lifted by her shoulder, the shining, jet black folds glowing with all the colours of the rainbow like a raven's wing.

Sylvia stood to one side to reveal Emma behind her. Last time Charlie had seen her, on a week's compassionate leave from Rhodean to attend her father's funeral, she had shown, despite the tear-stained cheeks and red, heavily-lidded eyes, promise of becoming a great beauty like her mother. She had. She was small, about 5 ft 5 ins but, unlike many short girls, the parts of her body had remained in perfect proportion to each other. Her hips were skinny, like a boy's, and her chest, beneath a tightly-fitting bright red top, showed only the slightest swelling as a concession to her gender. Her legs were long and slim, as were her arms, ending in perfectly shaped and sized feet and hands. She belonged to what Dawn French has described as the 'Incredibly Small Bottom Club' and there could be no doubt that many 19 year-old girls would have killed to look like Emma looked in jeans. She had inherited her mother's jet black hair which was cut in a short and fashionable bob (was that the right word, Charlie wondered), cut short with clippers in a concave ring around her neck and crowned with longer hair on top, the shape of a perfectly risen soufflé. It would not have suited every girl but it suited Emma with her narrow face and high cheekbones. She was looking at Charlie through enormous brown eyes under the longest and blackest lashes he had ever seen. There was a slightly apprehensive smile on her face as if she were not quite sure if she would meet with her uncle's approval.

'Oh my goodness!' said Charlie in quite genuine awe. He extended both his hands and took her delicate little hands in his. 'Let me look at you.'

'My goodness! My goodness!' was all he could say and Emma, taking this to mean approval, threw her slim bare arms around his neck and kissed him noisily on the cheek. Then she was smiling at him with the freshest, most radiant, most innocent, most debilitating smile he had ever seen on the face of a young girl. He suddenly realised Sylvia was laughing; she had become well used to men, sometimes roomfuls of them at a time, being instantly and hopelessly enslaved by one smile from her daughter's huge brown eyes.

On the journey back to Antibes, Emma sat in the back next to the cases all of which could not be squeezed into the small boot. Her excitement was intense; she tried to look in every direction at once anxious not to miss a single thing. She bombarded Charlie with questions: 'What's that? What's that?' and, before he had finished his answer, she would spot something else and interrupt him. 'Calm yourself, Emma,' said Sylvia laughing, 'let Uncle Charlie concentrate on the road.'

'But what's that great fort thing ahead?'

'That great fort thing is Fort Carre,' Charlie answered, 'you'll see it every day from your bedroom window.'

'Wow!' said Emma,'Scary!'

When they arrived at the villa, the rest of the family were about to sit down to lunch on the veranda but its start was delayed to enable introductions to be made and for the new arrivals to have a glass of champagne. Charlie introduced Sylvia and Emma to the Aunts who smiled politely and shook hands. Then to Frances, Richard and finally the twins. Sylvia felt a reserve from the Aunts – no more than she had expected – a slight coolness from Richard and a downright hostility from Frances who shook her hand briefly, without a smile, and enquired curtly: 'Good flight?' before turning to resume her conversation with her husband without waiting for Sylvia's reply.

* * *

'You were bloody rude,' said Richard later in their bedroom. 'You really made that poor woman feel unwelcome.'

'She is.'

'Well she shouldn't be. She's James's widow.'

'James's whore.'

'She's not a whore; they were legally married.'
'Yes, when she was five months gone.'
'Well, it's only by divine providence that *you* were not five months gone when *we* were married.'
'That's quite different.'
'It's not different at all.'
'It's always the same, isn't it Richard,' she said with anger and exasperation, 'you'll always take anyone else's side against me – your wife.'
'Only when you're in the wrong.'
'I'm not in the wrong.'
'You are.'
'I'm not.'
'On this occasion you are.'
'On *every* occasion I am.'
'I thought you said you weren't?'
'Oh, shut up.'
Richard retired to the bathroom to ponder, once again, on the logic of women in general and Frances in particular.

Inside the City Walls, Antibes — Photo: TANGOPASO

4. Settling In

The family were to be all together for four weeks and it had been agreed that the main purpose of the gathering, discussions on the future of the Aunts and house, should be left until they were halfway through their stay, when everyone would have had the chance to see how things worked and to identify potential problem areas – a bit like councillors on a 'fact finding' visit to some exotic place at the ratepayers' expense, thought Charlie, but it would also give the family a chance to get to know Sylvia and Emma a bit better and, he hoped, for Frances's antagonism to mellow.

Sylvia's behaviour was a model of what it should be under somewhat difficult circumstances. With the Aunts she maintained an air of deference without subservience, always ready to run little errands for them and to sit by them and talk to them, or simply listen, but never pushing herself forward or attempting to impose a familiarity which she realised would be difficult for them to accept.

With Richard and Frances her manner was more circumspect. She suspected that Richard was probably ready to accept her but, in support of his wife, felt that a certain reserve was incumbent upon him. Her attitude to Frances was polite but never effusive and she never attempted to initiate a conversation. Frances, for her part, made no attempt to treat Sylvia with anything other than restrained hostility. She would take things at *their* pace, thought Sylvia, it would be demeaning to try and assume any level of friendship, let alone kinship, until such time, if ever, it was extended from the other side. In the meantime, she knew she had an ally in Charlie who made no attempt to conceal his growing affection for her and Emma in front of the others. He would rise from his chair and kiss them both (no longer the formal, French variety) before they retired at night, and would ensure that they were never excluded from a conversation, or left sitting on their own in a corner. This, in itself, was creating a frigidity from Frances of which Charlie was conscious but ignored.

Emma, on the other hand, whose youth, it appeared, made her less culpable than her mother for having dragged the family down in social stature, had enchanted everyone except Frances who referred to her behind her back as 'Little Miss Tartybum'. Within days she was teasing the Aunts, to their great delight, being hugged and covered in ash by Mattie, chasing the twins across the garden when they became unruly and pummeling them until, choking with laughter, they pleaded for mercy. They had become her slaves, following her everywhere and seeking her out in house and garden until she turned on them and made as if to assault them, sending them flying at top speed in different directions pursued by mock-angry cries of: 'Go away you horrible little boys, you foul little creatures.'

Settling In

It was not long before Emma's presence also became known among little boys of more advanced years and a succession of young men, whom the Aunts had not seen for years, and in some cases did not even recognise, began to call in for pre-dinner drinks and to enquire solicitously after the Aunts' health.

'Oh, you're Billy are you? Mrs Featherstonhaugh's grandson?' asked Aunt Kate. 'Yes, Miss Morton-Stewart.'

'Haven't seen you for years.' 'No, Miss Morton-Stewart. Well, you know how it is. Grandma was most anxious to know how you were both keeping.'

'I bet she was!' thought Kate observing the young man's gaze transfixed by her giggling, mini-skirted great-niece, sitting in the corner and watching Billy from behind long, fluttering eyelashes.

'There are seven young men outside enquiring after Aunt Kate's health.' said Charlie one evening as he came onto the veranda to pour himself a beer. Emma sprang to her feet with a startled gasp, her eyes wide, her expression frozen in embarrassment.

'Only joking," Charlie said taking a pull of his beer, 'there's only three.'

For Emma, aware of, yet unconcerned with, the probationary position which she and her mother occupied within the family, the beauty of the villa and its gardens, the bustle, glamour and bright sunlight of the coast were sheer magic. She was living on a permanent high. She felt all the time as if she had just drunk her first glass of champagne. The days were not long enough to contain the succession of joyous moods and feelings she was experiencing. The young men she could take or leave. Since she left school she had been inundated with suitors and, while she enjoyed their attention, and the company of the growing band of admirers who fought for the right to escort her to the swinging young places in Juan-les-Pins and beyond, these outings were not the mainstream of her joy. She was intoxicated by the magic of the Côte d'Azur mixed, it must be said, with a new feeling which was arising within her and which she had not experienced before – the secure sense of belonging to a family whose blood, and background and love she was beginning to feel she shared. Sometimes, completely unprovoked, she would rush at a startled Charlie, or Mattie, fling her arms around their neck and kiss them. Then, like a Will o' the Wisp she was off to do something else.

And as she was taking joy from her surroundings, so was she giving it. The whole house had acquired a new aura of happiness and vitality. Her youth, her energy and the sheer delight she was experiencing was infecting everything around her. She was a woman yet, still, very much a child.

The staff, also, had taken her to their hearts. She would mimic Bridie's brogue and descend to the kitchens and pick at Manjulika's pots on the range until she was laughingly shooed out of the kitchen by the little brown cook. Dhani would stand and watch her, smiling and chuckling to himself, as she chased the twins through the garden and, on evenings when Emma went out with one of her young admirers, he would sit up until she returned, patrolling the boundaries and watching the road for signs of headlights which would signal her safe return. On the veranda or in the drawing room, Charlie would also wait up, idly reading the *Nice Matin* and sipping a single malt, looking periodically at his watch and listening for the sound of her footsteps on the terrace. He would try not to make his presence obvious as he did not wish her to feel that he was fussing over her; and yet he was never comfortable until he knew she was back safely.

'Sure, it's as if the child had been here for ever, chust, been here forever.' Bridie said one afternoon as she sat at the kitchen table drinking tea with the Limbus.

'Yes,' said Manju, 'it's as if she belonged here.'

'She liven up this dreary old house.' Dhani added, grinning and rocking his head from side to side in the characteristic manner of the Indian sub-continent.

'And that mother of hers,' Bridie continued, 'so quiet and so helpful to all of them and her treated by Miss Frances like a piece of dirt, chust, like a piece of dirt. It's chust not right, chust, it's chust not right.'

Settling In

'No, no, it's just not right,' Manju agreed gravely, 'it's just not right.'

As each glorious Riviera day rolled through its clear, starlit night into the next, life at the villa continued in its established routines but with a new lightening of heart. Apart from Frances, the reserve fell away and they became a family; and even Frances was perhaps marginally less offensive than at first.

Aunt Kate, who had always been custodian of the family history and traditions, found in Sylvia a ready, and genuinely interested listener to the fund of facts and anecdotes it gave her so much pleasure to relate. Moreover, Kate was often surprised with the knowledge she already had, having assumed that during her marriage to James, such things would not have been discussed.

'Emma's great-great-grandfather was summoned on two occasions to Queen Victoria's Court out here, you know. she gave him a gold tie pin which Mattie has in her jewel box upstairs.'

'Really?' said Sylvia with genuine interest, 'was that when she was staying at Hyères?'

'No, Cimiez dear. She was only at Hyères for one year, I think. My grandfather went in 1896 and then again in 1897. On one occasion, I can't remember which, he was presented to the Emperor Franz Josef and the Empress; and Mr. Gladstone was there with some State Papers for the Queen.'

'How fascinating,' Sylvia said, 'and didn't someone tell me that he had to send back to Scotland for his uniform?'

'Yes, dear. How clever of you to know that.' Kate said with surprised delight, 'It was made clear to my grandfather that he should attend in his full Highland uniform. Queen Victoria was very fond of everything Highland, you know. So a servant had to be despatched to Scotland to get it out of mothballs. There was great concern that he might not get back in time. You've heard of Sarah Bernhardt?'

'Of course.'

'Well, she was there too, to give a private performance to the Queen. The

Easter at the Villa Victoria

French loved her, you know – the Queen I mean – except one year when there had been some trouble on the Nile at a place called Fashoda and there was a lot of anti-British feeling in France. The British government advised her not to go to the Riviera that year, but the old Queen was having none of that! She loved her time in the South of France. But the government did insist that she booked a suite of rooms at Bordighera, in the name of one of her ladies-in-waiting, so she could make a quick dash across the Italian border if things turned nasty.'

Sylvia was enthralled. What a privilege it was, she thought, to hear these stories, passed down by word of mouth through a family whose members had been protagonists. And what a delight it was, thought Kate, to be able to pass them on to someone who was so clearly interested.

'She travelled down by the Royal Train each year, you know, seven or eight carriages.'

'Seven ot eight carriages?' gasped Sylvia in amazement.

'Yes, dear. You see it was not just the enormous staff she brought with her, there were a lot of Indians, you know, but she brought all her own glass, china, silver, linen – everything. The train had to be stopped for half an hour in the morning so the Queen could dress.'

'Good gracious!'

'Yes, and she brought Irish stew in insulated flannel bags which they ate on the train; and the ladies-in-waiting were always grumbling because the food was so much better in the ordinary French restaurant car. She never accepted the existence of Monaco, you know, as a separate state. Although all the crowned heads of Europe would visit her on the Riviera, she would drive through Monaco in her carriage, like an ordinary tourist, and ignore the Prince when he was in residence. They sent her flowers and presents but she returned them all unopened.'

'Gosh! She wouldn't get away with that nowadays, would she?'

'No, dear. And you know the 'Battle of Flowers' in Nice? Well, the old Queen would always take an active part in that and what she liked most of all was to pelt all the French officers with flowers.'

Settling In

'Heavens! No wonder we're so popular with the French.'

'Well, darling, (Gosh! Promotion in the field thought Sylvia) we were Jacobites, you know, and the French were always on our side, fighting against the English.'

'The Auld Alliance.' said Sylvia.

'Yes, dear (oops! lost my stripes) but the French have always been the natural enemies of the English – and ours, of course, since we took the King's Shilling. But there has always been a mutual respect between us and the French. We've never really liked each other much, but we've always admired and envied certain aspects of each others culture. The French were very brave in the First World War, you know.'

'But they collapsed in the Second.'

'Yes, darling, (repromoted) but they were an exhausted nation. Their losses and suffering had been so great in the First War, they were far greater than ours, you know, and ours were bad enough. The French just hadn't the spark left in them for another sustained fight with Germany.'

'Aunt Kate,' Charlie intervened, 'you are boring the pants off Sylvia and it's time for a glass of champagne.'

'No she's not,' said Sylvia, 'I could happily listen to her all day.' And she meant it.

'Darling!' said Kate with real affection. She took Sylvia's arm in her two twisted old hands and squeezed it. 'Let's have a little glass of champagne together and I'll tell you about the famous courtesan who my mother entertained here one day.'

La Colombe d'Or, Saint Paul de Vence   Photo: WHISPERTOME

5. Dinner at La Colombe d'Or

'Do I look all right Uncle Charlie?' asked Emma, prinking and pulling faces in front of an 18th-century Dutch inlaid mirror in the drawing room. She was about to go out for the evening and Sylvia stood beside her, patting down a wisp of hair which had sprung loose from the soufflé.

'Stand still, child.'

Charlie looked up from his book and appraised his niece in her party clothes.

'You are the most beautiful little witch on the entire Côte d'Azur . . .'

'Shush, Charlie, she's quite big-headed enough.'

'Trés, trés chic,' Charlie continued, 'outrageously attractive, eminently fanciable . . .'

Dinner at La Colombe d'Or

'But,' Emma interrupted, turning sideways to the mirror and pouting prettily, 'aren't I a bit 1920s up top?'

'Only barmaids have enormous bosoms.' Charlie replied and immediately recognised his gaffe. 'That is, . . . what I mean is . . .'

'What you mean,' said Sylvia laughing at his embarrassment, 'is that *some* barmaids, not *all* barmaids, have enormous bosoms.' She squeezed his shoulder affectionately as she passed behind his chair to show that no offence had been taken.

'I'm a little worried about that child.' she confided to him when Emma had departed. 'She seems rather too keen on some new boyfriend she's met and, frankly, I don't like the sound of him at all.'

'Why not?'

'Well, I gather he's much older than her; he owns one of those yachts out there,' she nodded towards the rows of craft moored in the port below. 'I don't know which one; and he's Italian.'

'Oh dear!' Charlie said gravely.

'She wants to bring him here to meet us.'

'Probably the best thing; then we can look him over.'

Emma sat opposite Paulo Faggioli as they finished dinner at La Colombe d'Or, outside the gates of the ancient hill town of Saint-Paul-de-Vence. The hotel was a linchpin of the Riviera legend and had been patronised by the household names of each successive generation since the area had emerged as the most glamorous and exclusive holiday area in the world. It was here that Zelda Fitzgerald threw herself downstairs because her husband was paying too much attention to Isadora Duncan. The walls of the corridors and public rooms were hung with priceless works of modern art – Picasso, Bonnard, Derain, Miro and Matisse – many of them, so the story went, presented to the Patron by then struggling artists in lieu of the bed and board they could not afford. Picasso said of the hotel: 'It was my kind of hotel; no name outside, no concierge, no reception, no room service and no bill.'

Dinner was served at tables, beneath a vine-covered arbour, in a large, cool courtyard giving open views across the steeply-sloping land to the south towards the coast. Ancient fig trees, hung with lights, entwined their branches over the courtyard where waiters bustled to and fro to service impeccably-laid tables with spotless white napery. The courtyard of La Colombe d'Or at dinner time was undoubtedly one of the most romantic places on the Riviera and Emma felt completely in tune with its atmosphere.

At one table on her left was a British cabinet minister, whose name she could not, immediately, bring to mind. At a table over by the doorway into the hotel sat a famous British actor whose name she did remember. He must have been in his sixties and was dining with a young girl who one might have taken for his grand-daughter were it not for the intimate way in which they were exchanging mouthfuls of food and pinching each other's cheeks.

Paulo had been a magnificent escort. He had such Latin style; such *machismo*. Emma found the young men who took her out in London, and those who had been jockeying for position since her arrival in Antibes, juvenile and boringly predictable. She had been out with young men from a variety of different backgrounds over the past two years and had categorised them in her own mind.

First, there were the 'Grunters', generally from the lower end of the social spectrum who, from watching too many Clint Eastwood films, believed that the way to turn a woman on was by looking at her through slitted eyes, with a permanent scowl (hard men don't smile) and by talking in short, staccato grunts. This was generally enhanced by a swaggering, cowboy-style walk (as if they had wet their drawers) and a belief that their manliness was best displayed by drinking too much.

Next there were the 'Chippers', the 1990s reincarnation of the 1950s 'Angry Young Men'. They believed that the way to a woman's heart was to become broody and resentful upon learning that she came from a more privileged background than their own. The evening's conversation would be scattered with snide, class-orientated insults and disaffected socialist whining and would end with grand sulks when their invitation to continue

Dinner at La Colombe d'Or

the conversation over 'a coffee' was declined. (A coffee what? Emma wondered. A coffee bean? A coffee cup? A coffee ice-cream?)

Then there were the 'Braying Asses' – young men from the City who knew that the way to impress a girl was to show her how self-confident you were. This was achieved by talking in an over-loud voice and being rude to waiters. The more they drank the louder they became and the more amusement they derived from even the unfunniest remark. This resulted in an awful, grating, braying laugh which got louder and louder as the evening progressed until waiters began to frown and other diners to turn round and look annoyed. It was most embarrassing.

Emma had decided she really preferred the company of older men whose conversation was far more interesting, who were more attentive, and wanted to listen to what *she* had to say rather than the incessant sound of their own voices.

Paulo was recognised by waiters and barmen wherever they went. He knew what was good on each menu and what to avoid. He knew which wines to drink with each course and could afford the best. He was so suave and sophisticated; he had such style and self-confidence.

As they had approached the restaurant, an elderly man had been struggling to park his car in a tight space at the kerb. He was making a bit of a mess of it which necessitated Paulo stopping and holding up the heavy traffic behind them. Being France, the horns started sounding but Paulo remained calm and unperturbed at the pressure and anger building up behind. When the old man eventually got his car tucked in and signalled his thanks, Paulo just stared at him for ten seconds then, with the grace of a matador displaying himself to the crowd, he raised his hands and clapped stylistically at the old man's eventual success. Who but a Latin, thought Emma, could administer a reprimand with such cruelty and such style?

During the meal he had the waiters bustling around him, attentive to his every need. Once, he clapped his hands, like a Spanish nobleman, to summon the Sommelier. No offence was taken; it was the way he did it and the sheer authority of his presence.

'Em-ma,' he said. He protracted her name to such an extent that it made it sound like 'Enema' which made Emma want to giggle. 'You like-a to go somewhere to dance-a? Or you like a leedle, how you say, nightcap-a on my leedle boat?' Emma opted for a dance-a. Their relationship was not yet ready for a visit to the leedle boat – a monster 90 foot motor yacht with accommodation for twenty people.

The eastern area of Juan-les-Pins, known in the family as 'Werewolf Alley' was where young people went for their evening entertainment. The bars, cafés and discotecs were packed to capacity with the pleasure-seeking young of all nations; clubs with names like 'Bim-Bim', 'Bam-Bam' and 'Zit-Zit' aggressively sought their market share with gaudy, flashing neon signs and samples of their house music blasted over the crowded pavements through loudspeakers above dimly-lit doorways.

Paulo knew all the latest dance movements, bobbing and swaying with the precision of a ballet dancer to the surprise of many of the young people who were initially affronted by the presence of one so mature in their midst. Then the word went round the club in whispers that he was a famous film producer (nobody could remember his name) and that the beautiful girl with him was obviously an up-and-coming starlet en route to the casting couch.

When the music changed to slow and smoochy, Paulo drew Emma close to him and began to get heavy: 'Em-ma,' the astringent smell of his designer after-shave was almost overpowering her; she was gasping for air over his shoulder like a stranded fish, 'You ave such pretty little ears-a,' she flinched as he bit one, 'and you ave the most beautiful eyes-a I ave ever seen.' She remembered the old patter they used to have at school and wanted to giggle again – 'Your ears are like flowers – cauliflowers; your eyes are like pools – football pools.'

When Paulo dropped Emma home at 1.30 am the gate was opened by a small brown man with a wicked-looking curved knife in his hand, who opened the door on Emma's side and fixed Paulo with a curious and rather disturbing stare. Under this scrutiny, he abandoned his plan to kiss her passionately, turned his car round and withdrew.

Dinner at La Colombe d'Or

Dhani watched the retreating tail lights until they were out of sight. He had no time for Italians remembering the old soldiers' prayer for the three constituents of a perfect service life: 1. British officers to lead them; 2. American food and equipment, and 3. The Italians to fight.

Charlie watched from a darkened window in the dining room as the little brown figure barred the gate and walked back to the house swinging his kukri and muttering to himself. A tear came to his eye as he remembered part of Viscount Slim's deeply touching tribute to the Gurkhas:

> 'Bravest of the brave,
> Most generous of the generous,
> Never had a country more faithful friends than you.'

* * *

'The fart,' said Charlie to the twins after his second glass of champagne, 'is the centre core of the humour of People Like Us.'

'For heaven's sake, Uncle Charlie,' Frances admonished him, 'must you make them any more vulgar and repulsive than they already are?'

'They are at an age when they should understand such things.' Charlie said dismissively; 'Working class humour revolves around the size of people's genitals – men's willies and women's bosoms, or 'boobs' as they like to call them. Every night on the television one has to endure dirty little nudge-nudge, wink-wink jokes about genitalia. Gentlemen do not find this brand of humour amusing.'

'Nor do ladies.' mumbled Frances.

'Breaking wind, on the other hand, is almost invariably entertaining. A nobleman of Queen Elizabeth I broke wind in the Queen's presence and was so embarrassed that he went into voluntary exile for several years.'

'So he damned well should.' said Frances.

'And when he returned to Court several years later, the Queen, remembering the incident, greeted him with peals of laughter and the immortal words: 'My Lord, I had forgot the fart'.'

Mattie was giggling. 'Tell them about Great Aunt Sade, dear; Aunt Sade who broke her leg farting.'

'Really, Mattie.' said Aunt Kate disapprovingly.

'Honestly, Uncle Charlie,' said Frances, 'don't you think it's time this unpleasant little seam in the family's repertoire was closed down?'

'Not at all; it's part of our tradition.' He poured himself another glass of champagne. 'Well, your great-great-grandmother's family in Ireland, like all well-bred people, found humour in flatulence. My grandmother's aunt, Lady Sarah Cargill, who was always known as 'Aunt Sade', was at a very grand ball in Dublin. She was in the process of going out to powder her nose or something and, seeing a group of her immediate family clustered round the doorway, and feeling one coming on, thought she would amuse them, *en passant* as it were, by letting it fly as she passed through the door.'

The twins collapsed in hysterical mirth.

'But the floor of the ballroom was highly polished and, as she raised her leg to execute the deed with maximum drama, she slipped head-over-heels and broke her leg. From thereon, she has always been known in the family as 'Aunt Sade who broke her leg farting'.'

By now the twins were racked with helpless laughter which, being infectious, especially when accompanied by liberal quantities of champagne, was making everyone shriek with laughter too.

'Well, you know about the Queen and General Gowan?' Richard volunteered, accepting another glass of champagne.

'Go on.' said Charlie.

'It was during the State Visit of President Gowan of Nigeria in the early 1970s. He and the Queen were driving up The Mall in an open carriage when one of the horses broke wind. 'Oh, I do apologise.' said the Queen to her guest and he replied: 'Oh, I thought it was the horse'.'

'A story of doubtful authenticity,' said Charlie, 'but great fun just the same.'

It seemed that every member of the family was now determined to tell their favourite farting joke as the champagne went round again. Mattie

Dinner at La Colombe d'Or

recited from '*Sumer is icumen in:*'

> '*Ewe bleateth after lamb, cow loweth after calf,*
> *Bullock starteth, buck farteth, merry sing the cuckoo.*'

Aunt Kate quoted from a 10th-century Irish poem translated from the Gaelic:

> '*There's a woman in the country, I do not mention her name,*
> *Who breaks wind like a stone from a sling.*'

Even Frances, now entering into the spirit of the occasion, related stories of how Sir Rex Harrison, the famous actor, was notorious for breaking wind on stage and would frequently reduce the rest of the cast to a state of uncontrollable giggles in the middle of a performance, as he tried to cover up his indiscretion by hammy stage coughing and throat clearing.

The twins attempted, in succession, to tell a joke which involved a parrot, a duchess, a bishop and some sealing wax but had to abandon the attempt as neither could speak coherently for laughter.

When Emma came into the room and looked upon her family rocking with helpless laughter, tears streaming down their faces and three empty champagne bottles on the table, her face registered astonishment.

'What have I missed, what have I missed?' she cried jumping up and down in excitement.

'You've missed the champagne, darling,' said Aunt Kate, 'and your uncle educating the twins about gentlemen's humour.'

'*Gentlemen's* is the right word for it.' said Frances.

Easter at the Villa Victoria

6. *Paulo Faggioli*

People often wondered why Charlie had never married. He was pleasant looking, though not even his mother would have called him handsome, he had achieved his life's ambition of commanding his regiment, he was good company, gay in the old sense but not the new, well-bred, honourable, impeccably-mannered and kind to children. He had a comfortable private income on top of his army pension and, as would have been said in bygone days, he had further expectations.

It was something which, since his retirement from the army a year ago, and for the first time in his life, Charlie had begun to wonder himself. He wondered about it now as he sat in the Tropique and settled into his first cool beer of the evening.

It was not that he did not like women; he had enjoyed two *grandes affaires de coeur* in his life and many minor skirmishes. The factor which had overwhelmingly contributed to the downfall of them all was, of course, the Regiment. Charlie could never do things by halves, it was all or nothing, and there had never been any question in his mind, from the earliest age, that the Regiment was his destiny, indeed his entire *raison d'être*.

It was impossible for a foreigner to understand the passions and the incredible latent power generated by the British regimental system. And, within this system, there was no section which demonstrated and perpetuated its virtues more effectively than the Highland Regiments.

Before 1882, when the Cardwell Reforms had started the process of amalgamation, and people were less mobile than in later years, British infantry regiments were truly territorial – not in the sense of being part-time, reserve soldiers, but in the sense that each 'County' regiment drew its recruits mainly from a closely defined catchment area – the county whose name the regiment bore. Thus, the soldiers in each regiment tended to know one another and felt the need, by their conduct in peace and their performance in battle, to uphold the honour of, not only the regiment, but of their own county, town, village and even family, in which communities they knew their personal achievements would ultimately be judged, and the memory of them preserved. It was a powerful incentive to do a good job.

As the regiments continued to amalgamate over the next 100 years, the traditions and Battle Honours of their constituent parts were absorbed and preserved by the new regiments but, in the more populated parts of the kingdom, with large recruiting areas and the population becoming more mobile, the original territorial element was largely lost.

This was not the case in the Highlands where population was thin, communities widespread and a fierce pride in the martial traditions of the Highland soldier survived the successive waves of anti-army feeling which each prolonged period of peace inevitably provoked. In the Highlands, the Regiment was a living part of the community. Most families had at least one member who was serving, or had served, with the Colours. The Regiment was a part of them and they were a part of the Regiment, sharing in its triumphs and its tragedies, preserving and perpetuating its achievements and traditions.

Throughout the great days of Empire, and through two world wars, the Highland Regiments had made a contribution and sacrifice grossly out of proportion to their numbers within the overall population of the nation. It had always been hoped that this, along with the unique regard in which the Regiments were held in Scotland, would be taken into account during the ritual axings of the army to fund the welfare budget. It was not to be.

Charlie's ambitions in the army had always been purely regimental. He had no wish to become a general, nor even a full-colonel. The summit of his ambition was to command the First Battalion of The Stewart Highlanders, as his father and grandfather had done before him, preferably in war, and he had achieved this ambition during the Falklands Conflict in 1982. It has to be said that most army officers, without the benefit of Charlie's not inconsiderable private income, could not afford the luxury of such limited service ambitions.

What he had failed to think about seriously was that, after relinquishing command of the Battalion, even after the few years he had spent 'winding down' in a rather dreary job at HQ Scotland, in Edinburgh, he would still have a major part of his life ahead of him. He had never forseen this hiatus. As a young man he had never envisaged that there could be any form of life after he had achieved his goal. His grandfather, after all, had died at that point which his whole life had led up to – the moment of command in battle, with the frenzied keening of the Pipes and the screams of a Highland charge in his ears. Would that he might have passed on, Charlie thought, at a moment of such supreme ecstasy and fulfilment.

His father, of course, having reached the summit of his ambition, the same as Charlie's, during the Second World War, had lived on to the age of 77. What had he done, Charlie wondered, for those final 30 years. He had seemed happy enough – shooting, fishing, tottering to and from his club, berating his elder son and encouraging his younger. But he had had a loving wife and a family to care for him and, more importantly, his involvement with the Regiment lived on through the careers of initially two, and latterly one, of his sons.

Charlie, being an all-or-nothing person, had never been able to find a point of compromise between his commitment to the Regiment, which was total, and a personal life of his own outwith the confinements of the Battalion. He loved his jocks with a passion and understood their strengths and weaknesses with an insight that few officers could approach. From the time he was a subaltern, through every level of command, his section, platoon, company and, finally, battalion had to be the best. And it invariably had been.

'It is *your* privilege to serve *them*,' his father had taught him, 'not *theirs* to serve *you*. Every jock, no matter how lazy, wilful, objectionable or deceitful he may seem, has some good in him and it's your job, as his officer, to get it out of him and harness it for the good of the Regiment.' Charlie remembered clearly one evening in particular, shortly after he had been commissioned. He had been sitting with his father on the bank of Loch

Brora as they packed up their rods and removed their waders. A silver flask of Clynelish malt was passing back and forth between them and the midges were getting troublesome.

'I'll tell you, Charlie,' his father had said, 'the secret of a perfect fighting unit and, as a bonus, the way to total fulfilment as a man: you must *love* the little swine; you must guard them from outside dangers and from themselves, you must wipe their noses, arbitrate in their quarrels, sort their personal problems and always put their comfort and welfare before your own. You must be ready to lie, cheat or steal for them and, if necessary, lay down your life for them. And when the moment comes that they *know* this, that is the moment that *you* will know they are ready to do the same for you.'

And when that moment had come for Charlie, as it had, on a bleak, rain-sodden moor in the Falklands, he had remembered his father's words and had known that, at that moment, the Stewart Highlanders would follow him to the centre of hell and back. And with that knowledge had come the explosive euphoria of total fulfilment and the realisation that he had reached an apex of human experience which few men ever knew and, from which point, the rest of his life must be lived on lower ground.

But how, Charlie wondered as he caught the waiter's eye to bring him another demi-pression, could he have been so stupid as to make no mental provision for the years ahead. He had no sons to give to the Regiment in whose activities he could continue to live; he had always assumed that brother James would provide enough sons to lead the entire Scottish Division. He had certainly tried hard enough.

But, there again, what did he mean now by 'The Regiment'? With the collapse of the socialist monolith in Eastern Europe, the government had entered upon yet another, massive, finance-driven pruning of the armed services which had become known as 'Options for Change'. Despite the disproportionate contribution made by the Highland Regiments in Britain's wars, despite their vital importance to the fragile communities in the north, despite their current buoyancy in terms of training and recruitment, despite a public outcry in Scotland and the advocacy of every person and institution with a sense of justice and fair play, the government would not be swayed from its decision to amalgamate The Stewart Highlanders with The Urquhart Highlanders into a new regiment to be called 'The Western Highlanders'.

Of course the army was resilient and resourceful and Charlie had no doubt that the new regiment would shake down, as other forced marriages had done before it, and that the traditions of its constituent regiments would be carried forward by new officers and new soldiers in a new regiment of which Scotland and Britain would be justly proud.

But the Stewarts would be gone and the world could never be quite the same again.

* * *

The sun had sunk low in the west, the Old Town lay bathed in a terra cotta glow and the family assembled on the veranda to meet Paulo Faggioli. Emma, in a simple red dress which showed off her boyish figure to its best advantage, awaited, not without a degree of nervousness, the arrival of her special beau. He was taking her to dinner at 'Le Bacon', arguably the finest fish restaurant in the world, at the Point de Bacon on Cap d'Antibes, a couple of miles down the coast.

'What does he actually *do*, dear?' asked Aunt Kate.

'Oh, he's something to do with the fashion industry in Milan.' Emma replied with that evasive casualness used by the young to avoid questions they do not wish to answer. A humming from the electric gates, the scrunch of car tyres on the gravel and Paulo's car drew in.

Knowing the small amount they did of Faggioli, the family had not expected to like him, but nothing had prepared them for the sight which assaulted them as Paulo Faggioli mounted the stone steps of the terrace and approached them on the veranda.

He was aged, they guessed, about 45 with a rugged, sharp-featured Latin face which had obviously received the benefit of every means known to man to conceal, if not retard, the effects of advancing years. His black, and already thinning, hair fell in curly strands, in lengths quite inappropriate to his age, to a point just above his collar. He wore tight, white cotton trousers designed, presumably, to emphasise what he imagined was the still-athletic appearance of his hips and backside. His white silk shirt was unbuttoned to a point roughly midway between his Adam's apple and his navel, revealing a forest of coarse, black hair in which nestled a gold medallion suspended round his neck on a leather thong. The cuffs of his shirt were turned up in a single, purposeful fold, as if they had been ironed, or even sewn, into this position, to display two more growths of black hair on his forearms, a gold chain bracelet and the most vulgar, multi-function, gold wrist watch that the trendy Milanese designers thought they could get away with. On the third finger of his right hand was an enormous gold ring in which were set red and green stones which were probably rubies and emeralds.

'He's surely not taking you to 'Le Bacon' dressed like that, is he darling?' asked Aunt Kate.

'Hush. Aunt Kate.' Emma replied reproachfully.

'Good grief!' muttered Frances when she first saw him, 'Where has he parked his ice cream van?'

Paulo swaggered onto the veranda leaving in his wake an aroma like the fragrance hall in Harrods on a wet afternoon. His face was composed in a mildly supercilious, yet amicable, half smile, one dense black eyebrow held slightly higher than the other. His walk and his stance showed practised poise and complete self-confidence.

Emma presented him first to the Aunts, whose hands he kissed in the correct manner with a graceful bow and without his lips actually touching their hands, and then to the rest of the family. Charlie was so taken aback by the grotesque appearance of the fellow that he was initially lost for words and was grateful to hear Sylvia begin a formal exchange of pleasantries. The Aunts, also, were speechless, never in their lives having seen such a person as a guest in their house. Bridie, bustling back to the kitchen having deposited two trays of canapés on the veranda, vented her horror on Manjulika.

'I'm surprised at them letting someone like that into the house. He looks as if he's come with the fish, chust, he looks as if he's come with the fish.'

Dhani sat in his corner listening but he did not smile.

When Charlie enquired what he would like to drink Paulo asked for a Martini.

'Do you mean gin and French vermouth?'

'No, just a sweet Martini with a tweest of lemon.'

'Italian vermouth with a twist of lemon, right.'

For the twenty odd minutes that Faggioli was on the veranda before whisking Emma off to 'Le Bacon' in a cloud of 'He-Man' after shave, he moved from one group to the next, striking a succession of graceful and macho poses and, to the relief of the assembled company, doing most of the talking. Within this time he had mentioned his beautiful apartment in Milan, his beautiful villa in Amalfi, his business interests throughout Europe, his leedle boat, his personal friends in the Italian government and his connections with the Tuscan nobility – all with an air of reticence which suggested that he was only, modestly touching the surface of his worth and achievements, the true depth of which he would be embarrassed to reveal.

'Charlie,' said Sylvia later, her face showing anxiety and distress, 'will you speak to her?'

'Yes, of course.'

'Tomorrow?'

'Yes, the sooner the better I think.'

An air of pensive disbelief hung over the dinner table that night and there was less conversation and laughter than usual.

Juan les Pins Photo: JWIESKI

7. A 'Three-Beer Evening'

Mattie sat at the window in her room, a faded, heavy-covered folder open on the little work table in front of her. In her hand was a sepia photograph, creased and dog-eared with much handling, of a young officer in the stiff, service dress cap of the Great War period.

Mattie had been so much hoping that she could have supported Emma in her friendship with Faggioli, despite the disapproval of the rest of the family. Had he been vaguely presentable, she could have formed a new, conspiratorial level of the love which already existed, and was growing all the time, between her and her darling little great-niece. They would have shared a new secret bond from which everyone else was excluded and Mattie knew, from her own experience, the importance of one true ally, in whom one could confide, when the family had decided that a liaison was unsuitable.

Of course, with Faggioli it was out of the question – the man was a poseur of the worst kind. How dare he come to her house with his effeminate, greasy hair and dressed as if he were attending a bookmakers' convention. Charlie would have to get rid of the man – and quickly.

With Peter it had been quite different. Although he was the son of an impoverished country parson, he was a gentleman and knew how to behave. It was not his lack of money that had set Mummy against him – it was his lack of a future. At the time that Mattie had fallen hopelessly in love with him, and he with her, he had not been expected to live for more than a couple of years.

She had been the same age as Emma is now, Mattie recalled as she looked at the photograph. It was 1926 and the Featherstonhaugh's villa on the Cap was full of bright young things from London – relatives and friends of relatives. Peter was among them. Oh, what heady and romantic days and nights they were, she remembered with a sigh of pleasure; two or three times every week there was a party or a dance at one villa or another. They would Charleston on flower-bedecked terraces, twinkling with fairy lights, to the music of live jazz bands, with a backcloth of the deep blue Bai des Anges and the night scents of Mediterranean gardens drifting through open windows. Women in beautiful dresses and fashionable headbands and men in white dinner jackets with scarlet cummerbunds would circulate in the drawing rooms and promenade in the gardens. It had been so easy to fall in love on the Riviera in 1926.

The next time she met Peter, a few days later at the Lancasters' house in Cannes, he explained that he could not dance anything too energetic as he had a spot of bother with his lungs. Later she learnt that he had been gassed in the trenches in 1917 and was considered by the doctors fortunate to be still alive. Mummy had been gentle but quite firm: yes, he was a nice but deeply unfortunate young man and Mattie must realise that she must break her involvement with him immediately before she became too fond of him. But it was too late, she was already too fond of him and could conceive no future without him.

For five, wonderful weeks she saw him almost every day she could, always in the company of others and always furtively lest word of their continuing liaison should get back to her mother. There were elaborate picnics on the rocks at the Pointe de Tir Hoil, motor drives along the coast and to ancient inland hill villages, bathing parties on the Plage de la Garoupe which, at around the same time, was immortalised by Scott Fitzgerald as the playground of the Divers in 'Tender is the Night'. On one occasion there was dinner in the courtyard of La Colombe d'Or, under the fig trees – possibly at the same table as Emma had sat with Faggioli.

And throughout this intense but hopeless romance, it had been her Aunt Mary who had been her confidante, who had listened to her with kindness and sympathy. And it was Aunt Mary who had clutched Mattie to her bosom when she heard that Peter had collapsed on the steps of the Château Grimaldi and had died two hours later in the hospital at La Fontonne. And it was Aunt Mary who had comforted her and tended her through the months of black despair that followed, when hope and happiness had dropped off the edge of the world leaving a senseless void which could never be filled.

Yes, thought Mattie as she closed the folder and tied its pink ribbon, she would be Emma's Aunt Mary should she ever be needed, but not in respect of that barrow boy Faggioli.

* * *

Richard had been on the phone to London for over half an hour which had delayed their departure to the shops. A 100,000 run of a four-colour leaflet for an important client had been printed with the wrong telephone number. There was apparently no time to rectify it – the leaflets were required for a trade fair in Hanover in three days time. As was usually the case in such situations, nobody was to blame. The studio claimed that the change to the telephone number was included in a list of final corrections which had been faxed to the printer six days before the job went to press. The printers claimed not to have received the fax and yet, miraculously, the other changes on the same list had been made.

'It's not on,' Richard had said, 'to expect the client to accept a sticker. They're paying a lot of money for the job and it should be perfect. Get onto the printers and tell them they must correct and re-run the job and deliver, at least in part, in time for the first day of the Fair. We'll argue about who's to blame and who meets the cost later.'

'I thought you were supposed to be on holiday,' grumbled Frances as they eventually got away, 'can't they manage on their own for just a few weeks?'

They were headed for a huge supermarket on the outskirts of Antibes where, they had been told by Manju, they would find the most competitively-priced champagne and there were often special offers. It was their intention to take a couple of cases back to the UK with them. 'You get a taste for the stuff staying at the Villa Victoria.' Richard had said. 'It's absurd extravagance drinking champagne every day,' Frances had replied sharply, 'it's only meant for high days and holidays.'

They were stunned by the sheer scale of the supermarket which was bigger than anything they had seen in the UK. There were 76 checkouts behind which was a broad, tiled walkway with shops and boutiques on the other side. A centrally-placed control room on the walkway was in contact with the tills and a squad of girls in pageboy outfits, on roller skates, with headphones and beepers, would fly up and down the walkway, weaving perilously between shoppers and trolleys, to sort out problems and queries at the checkouts.

The range of goods on display was mind bending. The fresh fish counter alone was worth a trip just to see. Richard calculated that the length of the three-sided counter was about 120 feet. There were eleven assistants serving behind it and about 40 different varieties of fresh fish on display. There were six different grades of oyster and seven other types of hard-shelled

A 'Three-Beer Evening'

crustaceans which he did not recognise. There were mountains of mussels and piles of succulent scallops. There were live crabs, lobsters and spiny langouste; there were langoustine and eight different grades of prawn ranging from the small cooked and peeled variety up to enormous, 5-inch long crevette royale, two of which would make a meal. Many of the varieties of fish he recognised: two different types of sole; turbot, conger eel, three types of trout, tunny, mackerel; whiting; three types of cod, fresh sardines, anchovies, filets of raie and, of course, many different types of salmon both whole and fileted. There were also many fish he did not recognise: three types of rouget (red mullet), lotte, loup de mer (sea bass), pageot, colin, colinot, three types of daurade (sea bream), pagre, sar, chapon and saint pierre. There were trays of octopus, squid and rascasse for bouillabaisse – the Mediterranean fish stew. The counter operated on a system by which you took a ticket and waited for your number to be called. Then, stretching away into the distance, were self-service counters with pre-packed and priced trays of the more common filets – cod, sole, whiting and salmon. And this was just the *fresh* fish section! The frozen fish counters were away to the right, Richard noticed, beyond which a crowd of male shoppers had gathered to admire a troop of lithe girls who were modelling underwear on a catwalk in the central aisle.

As they wheeled their trolley back along the walkway, watching the bustle at the endless row of checkouts, a roller-skating girl in a red pageboy outfit, the beeper on her chest summoning her urgently to a problem at some distant outpost, cut diagonally across their path at high speed.

'That would be a good job for Little Miss Tartybum,' said Frances, 'she could really wiggle her skinny little bottom in that outfit.'

'I don't know why you have to be so unpleasant about her,' Richard replied, 'she's a sweet kid and she's done you no harm.'

'Oh don't say you've gone all goo-goo about her too,' Frances said scornfully, 'she's a self-centred little tart, just like her mother.'

'That's grossly unfair, Frances . . .'

'Have you seen the way that Sylvia looks at Charlie? The way she's always sidling up to him?'

'I'd say Charlie does more sidling up to her than the other way round, and a good job too; with you around the poor girl needs a friend at court.'

'What do you mean *girl*? The woman's forty.'

'Thirty-nine actually.'

'What's the difference?'

'One year.'

'Oh, shut up.'

* * *

At 5.30 that evening, Charlie sidled up to Sylvia, who was flicking through a magazine in the drawing room.

'Fancy a pint?' he asked.

'Oh yes, let's get out of here before Frances catches us.'

In the Neptunia, whose turn it was, the waiters, with true French professionalism pretended, initially, not to recognise Charlie, in the same spirit as an Edwardian madame would have cut dead her most valued client if she met him on the street with a lady who might have been his wife.

'So, this is where you disappear to at 5.30 every evening?' Sylvia said.

'Well, yes, or that one across the road.' and he explained the complications of his rota. She listened with growing disbelief then laughed.

'Oh, Charlie, who but you could get yourself into such a pickle. What does it matter if they see you going into the other bar? You can drink wherever you please.'

What an attractive laugh she has, Charlie thought, not in the least raucous or hysterical. 'Yes, I know but . . .'

'But,' she interrupted, 'you're a creature of habit and a very loyal person and you'd go to great lengths to avoid offending or upsetting anyone you like.' She raised her eyebrows seeking confirmation.

She's perceptive, too, he thought. 'Well, yes, I suppose that's it more or less. But that's enough about me, tell me about yourself, Sylvia,' he changed

A 'Three-Beer Evening'

the subject, 'how did you come to be mixed up with a lunatic family like ours?'

'Not much to tell, really.' she replied, 'I was born and brought up in a village in county Donegal, on the shores of Lough Foyle. My parents had a small hotel – well, *hotel* I say – it had four letting rooms which were very seldom let and the income came mainly from the public bar trade.'

She really is very attractive, thought Charlie.

Sylvia had two sisters and three brothers, all of whom had to leave the village when their time came as there was little employment locally and, although her parents had never put pressure on any of them to leave, it was always understood that the income from the pub could not support them all indefinitely, and the family was too proud to allow any of its members to slide into a life on welfare.

Sylvia had found the local boys bovine and lacking in any form of ambition and purpose and therefore had little social contact with her peers after leaving school. She avoided the dreadful Saturday night dances, which invariably ended in drunken fighting. She had acquired a reputation of being 'stuck up' and 'too good for the likes of us.' As she undoubtedly was, thought Charlie as he caught the waiter's eye for two more beers.

The young people in the village in which she lived were backward and unsophisticated and Sylvia was never infected with the primitive urge to get married and start breeding at the earliest possible opportunity which still often prevails in such communities. There were such wonderful opportunities for women nowadays, the evidence was in every newspaper one picked up: there were women managers in some of the major industries; there were women company directors; there were female officers in all the armed services and there were women in every profession. The western world, at least, was at last recognising that women could contribute far more to the management of the world than they had previously been allowed to and the weight of public opinion, backed by a growing structure of legislation, was beginning to ensure that they got the chance.

Sylvia could not, therefore, understand why, in her village, at this exciting moment in the achievement of equal opportunities, every girl from the age of 15 thought and talked of nothing other than 'catching her man' and what she would wear on her wedding day. The sad evidence of this lemming-like compulsion was all around her – young girls who might have had such fun, and achieved so much, their youth stolen and prematurely aged, surrounded by wailing children and dirty washing, locked into an endless life of drudgery, and often abuse, in a dreary council house.

Sylvia did not intend to sacrifice her youth and, when a friend wrote to her from London that there was a bar vacancy in the pub where she was working, Sylvia packed her suitcase and was on the night ferry from Larne.

The huge, busy London bar was a big change from the little pub in Donegal but she knew the trade and was not afraid of hard work. It would do for the moment, she had thought, until she had looked around at career opportunities and decided which path she was going to take. Meanwhile, the pretty Irish barmaid with her long, black hair, ready smile, and gentle way of talking became a great favourite with the regulars at 'The Admiral Fitzroy' among whom was one James Morton-Stewart, former army officer and currently bookmaker's clerk. The other barmaids had warned her against him.

'And you know the rest, Charlie.'

'No, not really.' said Charlie. It was definitely a 'three-beer evening' and he glanced at his watch to make sure that they had time for the third before summoning the waiter.

'Forgive me for asking this, Sylvia, it's really none of my business and just tell me to shut up if I'm out of order,' she looked intrigued, 'James was, well, he had a certain reputation . . .'

'You mean he was the biggest ram in London?'

'Well, yes.'

'That he was; I know what you're asking, Charlie.' What a beautiful, beautiful, smile she has, he thought. 'On the day I agreed to marry him, and that's the way it was, Charlie, don't ever let anyone tell you otherwise, I told him that if there was ever the slightest suggestion of another woman,

A 'Three-Beer Evening'

I'd be packed and out of his life the same day. No 'ifs' no 'buts', no warnings, no second chances. It was the only condition I made.'

'And was there?'

'There never was. And I'll tell you something else while we're on these intimate subjects . . .'

'I'm sorry, Sylvia, I really have no right . . .'

'It's all right, it's all right, I'd like you to know,' she held up her hand to silence him, 'I loved Jimmy (the Jameses in the family had often been called 'Jimmy' or 'Jim' or sometimes 'Jemmy' but never, ever, 'Jamie'). I loved him and did everything in my power to make him a good wife; and there hasn't been another man in my life – not before nor since.'

Charlie was stunned by the intimacy of this revelation and he knew that she spoke the truth. There was a palpable honesty about this woman of which he was becoming increasingly aware as he got to know her. But the better he knew her the more guilty he felt about the way the family had neglected her and her daughter. How, he wondered, could he ever be forgiven for having ignored their existence all these years. On human grounds alone, it had been inexcusable but there was more to it than that: at the age of 56, and with the time now to do it, Charlie had begun to think; and with thought came doubts or, if not doubts, at least some lightly-pencilled question marks against some of the social preconceptions which had governed his life thus far. Charlie was a man of simple and honest principles and he was becoming a little confused.

Port Vauban and Fort Carre Photo: COMQUAT

8. Machismo

Emma sat on the grass at the foot of the garden, her feet curled underneath her, looking up through swaying palms and rolling lawns bordered by exotically-coloured flowers to the cool white stucco of the house beyond. Rendered stone pillars on either side of the front entrance, with its glass-panelled door and protective, outer wrought iron screen, supported a large balcony surrounded by a stone balustrade with urns of scarlet geraniums on each corner. Two of the principal bedrooms opened onto this balcony and the other bedrooms on the first floor had smaller, wrought iron balconies supported by ornately-worked angle brackets. On the top floor, originally servants' quarters but now mainly given over to the paraphernalia and junk of a century of occupation, some, but not all of the windows had little balconies. A stone balustrade, matching that of the principal balcony above it, ran between the pillars bounding a raised terrace at the front door, on either side of which curved stone steps descended to the drive.

Machismo

The windows of the villa were tall and narrow, in the traditional Mediterranean style, and had hinged, louvred shutters, painted a pale lime green, which opened back against the wall on either side of the windows. In the ground-floor rooms, protection from the sun was augmented with bright red sunblinds which wound out on metal, concertina spars from concealed cassettes above the windows. In the mornings, when the sun shone fiercely on the south-east face of the house, the shutters were kept closed to protect the antique furniture and paintings within but after 3 pm, when the sun had passed round to the west, the shutters were folded back and the windows opened to give an uninterrupted view of the coast and beyond.

It was all so indescribably beautiful, Emma thought. If she had only known about this place when she was at school she could have more than parried some of those snooty girls who were always holding forth about Ascot and the Royal Yacht Squadron.

The past two weeks had been the most romantic and pleasurable of her life so far. She felt an energy and vitality she had not known before. The people she met were so interesting, so sophisticated. They were always happy and smiling and did not go all broody, resentful and intense. Well, Paulo had become a bit intense of late and she was getting rather tired of his groping advances at the end of each otherwise pleasant evening out. The trouble was that she was running out of excuses for not going back aboard the leedle boat – a course which she knew would be unwise.

She giggled to herself at the memory of Charlie's avuncular lecture the previous evening. With much throat-clearing he had told her he wanted a little talk with her. 'Oh, you're not going to get boring are you Uncle Charlie?' she had replied. He had rabbited on about background and breeding and age differentials: 'The bloody man is almost *my* age, for heaven's sake.'

She had listened with a sweet smile and her head on one side which she had learnt was guaranteed to disarm angry men. 'But Englishmen are so shy and awkward, Uncle Charlie,' she had said, principally to wind him up,

'Latin men have such poise, such machismo.'

'Let me tell you about machismo, darling.' he had said. 'In shy, awkward old Britain we have a different way of looking at things. We tend to measure 'manliness' not by swaggering, self-confidence in bars and cafés, but by how men behave when the chips are down. We're not very keen on loud-mouthed bragging – preferring to judge men's courage by what they *do* rather than what they *say* they're going to do.'

He's putting me down, she thought. How tiresome.

'Now listen to me while I tell you about your grandfather. When he arrived in North Africa with the Stewarts in 1940, they were part of General Wavell's army of less than 35,000 shy and awkward British and Commonwealth soldiers, pitched against the strutting and self-confident might of the Italian 10th Army commanded by Marshal Graziani – a man you would undoubtedly have admired,' there was a twinkle in his eye, 'for his valorous words and overwhelming machismo.'

'Well, at the end of the battle, Wavell's shy and awkward soldiers, outnumbered by more than four to one, had swept the courageous and manly Italian army into the sea taking 130,000 prisoners, 1,200 guns, 400 tanks, and 450 aircraft at a cost of less than 2,000 casualties.'

'Good grief!' said Emma, genuinely amazed.

'So you see, my pet, why in shy, awkward old Britain, Latin bragging and machismo has always been one of our favourite jokes.'

* * *

No one was ever really sure exactly what had happened the following night. It is possible that Emma, intoxicated with the laughter, the music and the lights of a very glamorous party in Golfe Juan, had simply drunk far more than was wise. It was probable that Paulo (or Lothario as the family now called him) had deliberately plied her with more cocktails than he knew she could take. It is unlikely, though family tradition would probably adopt this version, as it made a better story, that he had actually spiked her drinks.

Machismo

What is known is that around 1 am, Lothario approached the gangplank of his leedle boat, moored on jetty 14 in Port Vauban, Antibes, with Emma, very much the worse for wear, hanging half around his medallion-hung neck and half supported by a hirsute arm, with an outsize gold wristwatch, around her waist.

As he paused at the gangplank to get a better grip of her, a small, brown figure arose from the shadow of a mooring bollard and blocked his way.

'I take Missy now.' was all it said.

'How dare you!' blustered Faggioli, summoning up as much authority and raising himself to as great a stature as his present undignified attitude would allow, 'Get out of my way. How dare you, you . . . you . . .'

There had been a movement like a springing leopard, an outraged scream followed by a loud splash and the small brown figure was carrying Emma's waif-like form, as if it were a feather pillow, to the little Renault parked at the end of the jetty.

With the resilience of youth, Emma had risen next morning with only the mildest of headaches and had opened her shutters in time to see a sleek, white motor yacht slip from its mooring at jetty 14 and streak across the port with much braggadocio and needless revving of engines.

From the terrace outside the front door, Charlie and Dhanibahadur also watched its theatrical departure. A craft, thought Charlie, only marginally less vulgar than its owner.

'Slip up bad, Colonel Charlie, slip up bad.' said the little brown man gravely.

'What do you mean Dhani? You did a spectacular job.'

'Forgot cut hair.' he said, his face now wreathed in smiles as he made a slashing motion with the palm of his hand.

Easter at the Villa Victoria

9. The Cargills and the Hogans

On the top floor of the villa, a long corridor ran from north-east to south-west connecting, at the east side with the staff flat above the coach house and, at the other end, leading to a staircase which gave access to the attics above. Off this corridor were nine rooms which had originally been box rooms and servants' bedrooms in the days when the house supported a full complement of chamber maids, parlourmaids and footmen. Now they housed the Aunts' archives. In massive mahogany wardrobes, still called 'Almiras' as they had been known in India 100 years before, hung Lady Florence's coats and dresses dating back to the time she had been a girl in Ireland. Beautiful silk, chiffon and lace evening dresses hung beside faded print, ankle-length summer frocks, mid-calf flannel suits, pleated linen skirts and heavy, rough tweed top coats. There were drawers full of underwear, interleaved with lavender sachets, piles of hat boxes, seven or eight tiers high, and rows of shoes representing the span of fashion from the pointed-toe satin ballroom shoes of the Edwardian era to the flat-heeled suedes of the postwar years. In a separate cupboard hung furs and stoles with foxes' masks, their glass eyes still bright, and in pull-out trays were accessories – silk bows, ostrich feathers and flappers' headbands from the 1920s.

In the next room, similar wardrobes, with the same smell of camphor, contained the nostalgic relics of long-dead gentlemen. Tweed suits, light-weight duck suits, riding breeches, tail coats, dinner suits, kilts in Stewart tartan hung by loops on specially-spaced bars, and scarlet, gold and khaki uniform tunics with long-unpolished brass buttons. Rows of polished leather boots stood to attention on their wooden stretchers and metal helmet cases, their black paint flaked and scarred, containing solar topees and regimental head dress, stood ranged along one wall. Bundles of leather-covered and malacca canes, some with tarnished silver tops, riding whips, crops and polo sticks stood in a corner and on a shelf in one of the wardrobes were several swords with their scabbards and frogs – the basket-hilted swords of the Highland Regiments. In the drawers and trays there were piles of stiff-fronted dress shirts immaculately laundered but now yellowed with age, diced stockings, chilprufe and aertex underwear, rows of black and white dress ties with Moss Bros and Gieves labels, coloured woollen garters, leather belts with silver and brass buckles, a pile of scotch bonnets, some buckled, patent leather evening pumps and several sporrans with their straps and chains.

Sylvia stared around her in speechless wonder. She had no idea that such relics had been preserved; it was a collection which any museum of costume would have died for. Two days previously, Aunt Kate, after consultation with Mattie, had suggested to her that she might like to see 'some of our little treasures' on the top floor. The Aunts had never had such an interested and sympathetic audience as Sylvia and she, for her part, was fascinated by every little snippet of family history and every little anecdote related to her. Nor was she unaware when the visit to the top floor was mooted, of the very special privilege which was being extended to her.

The journey to the top floor was not easy. Both Aunts, each determined not to miss a trick, insisted in taking part in the expedition. A patent lift arrangement enabled Aunt Kate to ascend unaided, in her wheelchair, to the first floor, but to reach the second floor involved being lifted bodily in her chair by Dhani and Manju with Bridie flapping around below and issuing instructions. It was a reasonably smooth operation, Sylvia noted, suggesting that Aunt Kate's visits to the top floor were fairly regular events. When they reached the top, the Limbus returned downstairs and Bridie wheeled Kate along the corridor with Mattie shuffling behind. Clipped to one arm of her wheelchair, Aunt Kate had a huge chatelaine's ring of keys, some tagged with little linen labels marked with black Indian ink, from which she selected one for each door. As she struggled to turn the first key with her twisted fingers, Sylvia started to her aid and then thought better of it. It is something she likes to do and something she *can* do, she thought to herself, and anyway, it's all part of the drama.

The third room they entered contained rows of cabin trunks, huge, zinc-lined wooden cases and handmade leather suitcases with shipping company labels recording generations of Imperial travel. 'SS *Oriana*, Bombay, not wanted on voyage', 'SS *Jervis Bay*, Marseilles'.

'*Jervis Bay*?' said Sylvia, recalling a fragment of history from her schooldays, 'wasn't she an armed merchantman that was sunk by the '*Admiral Scheer*' after a very gallant fight?'

'Yes she was, dear.' said Aunt Kate, 'we came back from England in her just before the war.'

Mattie was pulling out a leather suitcase in a brown canvas cover which appeared to be one of a set of four. She opened the cover to reveal a crocodile case in perfect, unmarked condition, preserved partly by its canvas cover and partly by the care and professionalism of the porters of a bygone age who saw nothing demeaning in the job they were paid to do.

'My brother, James, Emma's grandfather, had these made from crocodiles he shot in India.' Mattie said. 'They would leave the skins with the tannery before they went back to England on leave and the cases would be ready when they returned.'

Sylvia lifted one up, marvelling at the quality of the work with its nickel fastenings and leather-reinforced corners. The weight of the empty case was more than that of an equivalent-sized modern case – fully packed. It might even stand up to the Heathrow baggage handlers she thought.

The next two rooms contained cases, metal deed boxes and dusty box files of family papers – letters, photographs, old Wills and legal documents some of which, Mattie told her, dated back to the 17th-century. There were rolls containing officers' commissions, mentions-in-despatches and citations; there were bundles of invitations to Royal and Viceregal receptions and dinners, and there were portfolios of watercolours of varying subjects, painted by successive generations of ladies of varying talents. Kate and Mattie kept plucking items out to show Sylvia, greatly excited at the opportunity of sharing with someone who cared the significance of the ephemera of which they had, for so long, been the sole custodians.

The Cargills and the Hogans

'This was the first of the invitations which our grandfather received to attend the Queen at Cimiez.' Kate said, holding out an embossed black and gold card with the Royal coat-of-arms.

And that was the uniform he wore that you saw in the other room.' Mattie added.

'This was the medal that a brother of our great-grandfather won at the Battle of Sobraon in the Sikh War of 1846.' said Kate blowing the dust of a leather medal case. 'He was only nineteen and died defending the Regimental Colour.'

'You can see it today in Canterbury Cathedral, dear,' Mattie added, 'the Colour he was holding when he was killed. There's not a lot left of it, mind you, it's very threadbare with age.' Sylvia held the medal in her hand and read the names on the bars recording the distant battles in which this young man had fought – Sobraon, Aliwal, Ferozeshuhur. She pictured him standing in the dusty heat of the Indian plain, surrounded by the brutality of battle, and wondered at a system which could inspire a boy, who should really still have been at school, a boy who had probably never known the love of a woman let alone reached an age where he could marvel at the beauty and innocence of children, to give up his life before it had properly begun for an inbred notion of duty and service to Queen and Country.

There were locks of hair from babies; there were silver lockets with very faded miniatures of much loved mothers, wives and children; there were printed obituaries and service sheets from the burials of long-dead relatives. Sylvia's mind was numbed by the volume of it all and the sadness, the passion and the joy which these dusty files recorded and preserved. Later, she would only remember a small part of the things that the Aunts told her on that first day on the top floor and the mass of family memorabilia which they showed her.

There was one particular thing which, above all the rest, remained in her memory: a scrap of paper torn from a ship's log book in mid-ocean, on which a sympathetic ship's officer had written the latitude and longitude of the spot where a dearly loved child had been buried at sea. Treasured through their lifetimes by grieving parents, and preserved by successive generations who could not find it in their hearts to destroy it, this little scrap of paper was all that remained to record the existence of a child who had laughed and cried and played in the sun a hundred years before.

* * *

'Uncle Charlie,' said one of the twins, 'why don't you make a pop when you open a bottle of champagne?'

'Because only vulgarians make a noise about it; like half-witted racing car drivers in jockey caps who shake the bottle and spray it all over each other.' Charlie would not concede that baseball had any place in British culture and would therefore refer to the caps worn increasingly by working class youths, (often back-to-front) as 'jockey caps'. 'Come here and I'll show you how to open champagne like a gentleman.'

'Off with the foil and this wire paraphernalia; then, a clean white napkin over the top.'

'Why?'

'So that if some moron has been shaking the bottle and the cork comes flying out, it doesn't put somebody's eye out. Then, holding the cork firmly through the napkin, you turn the *bottle* gently until you feel the cork beginning to rise; then you let it come under its own pressure until just before it comes clear of the bottle, then you press it firmly back towards the neck as it comes out. Voila!' there was a restrained hiss of gas and Charlie held up the bottle to reveal the fine and tantalising mist rising from its decorked neck. 'Always remember, it should sound like a duchess breaking wind.'

'How does a duchess break wind?' asked a twin.

'Like a bottle of champagne being opened properly.' Charlie replied.

'Oh, for God's sake, don't start that again.' said Frances.

* * *

The Cargills and the Hogans

If, when Sylvia had been looking in wonder at Lady Florence's dresses on the top floor, she had detected in Bridie a certain dampness of eye, it was easily explained. Bridie Hogan had joined Lady Florence at the Villa Victoria in 1951 at the age of 17, straight from Ireland, and had served her with love and loyalty for a further 17 years until her death in 1968. She then transferred her care and affection to Miss Mattie and Miss Kate who, she knew, could never have managed without her. She was now 62 and had been with the family for 45 years.

Her father had been a small tenant farmer on the Cargill Estate in County Cork where the two families, the Hogans and the Cargills, had lived lives of mutual service and respect for many generations – indeed, as far back as the Hogan family bible chronicled their history and their verbal traditions could be retrieved. Hogan daughters would go into service in the Big House and sons who were surplus to the requirements of the farm, would find positions in house, home farm, gardens or stables. Bridie's grandmother had been cook at the Big House and her great uncle, George, Head Keeper – both positions of enormous trust and responsibility, which had rightly carried considerable prestige and status in the local community.

Each family was dependent upon the other and saw no anomaly in their differing lifestyles. They saw themselves as an extended family, united in a common purpose, and each took an equal pride in producing the fastest horses, the fattest pheasants and, indeed, the finest children who, within their respective spheres, would do credit to the extended family. There was no rejoicing greater than that of the Cargills when one of the Hogan children with interests other than rural pursuits would make it good in the outside world and win the acclaim of his peers. Frequently, the Big House would quietly, without any show or fuss, fund the further education of a clever Hogan child or, instantly, and with the full influence of its position, arrange a needful operation or course of medical treatment.

Such activities were not regarded as largesse by either side but merely as the normal indulgence of a loving head of family. The Hogans saw nothing demeaning in serving the Cargills, and rejected with anger and resentment the proposition of the dark-browed activists of the early part of the century, that there was a difference between subservience to a rural master, that one knew and loved, and subservience to a faceless industrial consortium in an unfamiliar city. The Cargills, they were told, were not Irish but lackeys of the dirty English who had grown rich riding on the poverty of the Irish people. The Hogans, and many like them, had difficulty in identifying these oppressors from their own experience, and felt equal outrage at the injustice to their masters and the trivialisation of their own positions and achievements. Bridie's uncle Danno had one night cleared the village pub of these brooding men with his great red fists. Two nights later he was set upon in an alley and his face slashed repeatedly with a razor. He had borne the scars with unrepentant pride until his dying day.

By the time Bridie was born in 1934, the Cargills had been driven from the land and the gaunt ruin of the Big House stood in its once luxurious demesne now grazed yellow by sheep. With no employment, and the men removed to England and America in search of work and a future for their families, the meagre incomes of the farms were further strained to support daughters whose mothers, at that age, were running down corridors with piles of linen in their arms laughing and flirting with footmen. There was little joy in the village now,

The Hogans had wept when the Cargills left Ireland but their links had never been broken. Letters were exchanged and discreet pensions arrived regularly by mail. Cheerless cottages were brightened by the arrival of Christmas boxes from England, and later from the South of France, and relays of servants crossed the seas to serve the family in exile. Bridie Hogan, perhaps the last of the line, saw nothing degrading in the work she had done all her life and of which she was extremely proud. Her authority and status were endowed by the background of the family of which she was an integral and respected part. She knew that a lack of respect and concern for their servants was the surest mark of the *Nouveau Riche* who had not been brought up to the responsibilities of employment. They, too, were the hardest taskmasters, determined to extract maximum value from those who served them with little regard for their feelings or dignity. She eschewed the modern tendency to try and mitigate the concept of service and servants, indeed the words themselves, aware that nine tenths of the world's population were in service to someone else however fancy their title or perceived importance. To Bridie a ratcatcher was a ratcatcher and a servant was a servant.

Her views on all matters were snobbish and reactionary. She spoke frequently of 'The Old Days' meaning, more exactly, the days of her grandparents when social order was more clearly defined and when people knew their place within it. If something upset her, she would air her views with a violence and passion which the Aunts, on occasions, would find quite alarming but she was easily mollified by the gentle words and understanding which were her due, and which the Aunts had been schooled from birth, by their mother to provide. 'Irish servants don't brood and sulk like English servants,' she had told them, 'they just blow off like a volcano but it's soon over and done with and quickly mended.'

Bridie was acutely censorial of guests who she did not consider to be 'of the right type' and would make her disapproval known (witness her behaviour with Lothario) with clumsy and noisy service and by ignoring anything addressed to her. 'I'm not hearing you,' she would say under her breath as she strode purposefully in the opposite direction, 'chust, I'm not hearing you.' After the offending guest's departure, she would register her contempt by bustling officiously around the room in which the Aunts were sitting, puffing up cushions as if they had been infected with something contagious, clattering cups and glasses as she cleared them away while all the time mumbling under her breath: 'Lady Florence would turn in her grave, chust, she'd turn in her grave.'

Bridie's sturdy figure was well known in the shops and supermarkets in the area where the assistants had learned that to give her exactly what she wanted was less stressful than being subjected to a tirade in almost unintelligible French. Thus, when Madame from the Villa Victoria did not fancy the last piece of ham on the bone, a new joint would be started for her without argument. She enjoyed an excellent relationship with the Limbus, who had a great affection and respect for her and had learned, and studiously guarded against, the situations which got her wound up.

Bridie, as part of the family, knew what this gathering was about, and had seen the need for it growing over the past couple of years as Miss Kate had become completely chairbound and Miss Mattie increasingly frail and forgetful. She realised, of course, that any decision affecting the Aunts would affect her too, but this was of no importance to her. Such was the relationship of mutual trust between Hogans and Cargills, which had transcended the wars and domestic upheavals of the past turbulent century, that Bridie knew, without question, that her own future would never lack for comfort or security. Nor would the Limbus'. Once she had reassured them when they had expressed to her a mild apprehension regarding their future: 'You needn't worry, dears; you're working for gentlefolk not johnny-come-lately upstarts. In families like ours we always look after our own, chust, we always look after our own.' And although she was naturally concerned about the decisions which might be made at this gathering, she was sublimely confident that Colonel Charlie would do whatever was best for all concerned.

The Old Fisherport, Cannes *Photo:* GUY LEBÈGUE

10. The Nature of Privilege

The thing that had always struck Frances about those old people's homes which she had visited in the UK was the ever-present smell of urine and the airless, overheated atmosphere in the rooms. It was as if there were never enough staff to keep pace with the incontinence of the residents. There was nothing like this at 'L'Orangerie' in Cannes.

Set in a quiet street about half a mile north of La Croisette, and surrounded by the orange trees to which it owed its name, there was nothing to distinguish it from the prosperous and well-maintained private houses on either side of it. Not even a discreet sign identified the house as a nursing home for the elderly.

Inside was the smell of polish and flowers and although over-warm –

essential for the comfort of aged and immobile people – the air was kept fresh by the judicious chinking of windows which admitted sun-warmed air from the sea front.

Richard had been against this visit: 'Don't you think it's a bit high-handed to do this without consulting the others?'

'If we wait for the others nothing will ever get done. It's only sensible to have some facts and figures to hand when we come to discuss matters.' Frances had argued.

They were met by a middle-aged woman in immaculately-starched nurse's whites who took them to a small room which was evidently used as an office. 'Now, Monsieur-Dame, how can I help you?' she said in English. Frances explained that they were only examining options for two elderly ladies and were not yet in a position to discuss dates or final arrangements.

'Of course.' the nurse replied. She asked several questions about the ladies' health and requirements and confirmed that Kate's immobility would not be a problem: 'The house is fully equipped with lifts and ramps and there is 24:24 hour trained nursing cover. The doctor visits daily and reaches us in five to ten minutes in emergencies.'

She showed them one of the private rooms which was currently vacant. It was airy and comfortable. 'They can bring a few pieces of their own furniture if they like,' the nurse explained, 'or we can provide all things. Whatever you wish.'

Richard asked: 'Are all your . . .' he fumbled for the right word (inmates?, patients?, guests?). . . 'are all your residents French?'

'Some French, some English and we presently have two Americans and a Russian lady. But our guests' . . . (oh, that's the right word is it?) . . .'tend to be, how shall I say, well educated people . . . (well-heeled people, Frances thought) . . . and language is not a problem, most of our staff speak at least adequate English.'

'The ladies in question have fluent French.' Frances said dismissing this line of conversation. The nurse gave them a glossy folder containing leaflets and details of the home.

The Nature of Privilege

'What about costs?' Frances asked, 'Can you give us some rough guidance?'

'It is all in there.' the nurse indicated the folder. 'There are a number of options, of course, depending on the size of private room, the guest's diet, the amount of nursing care needed – things like that, but you're looking at something between 6,000 and 9,000 Francs . . .'

£800 to £1,200, thought Richard. Does she mean per month?

'Per week . . .'

Does she mean for both of them?

'For each guest.'

The twins had been left in Bridie's custody for the day so Richard and Frances decided to have lunch on the seafront in Cannes before returning to Antibes. They chose a bustling seafood restaurant with pretty tables laid out on the pavement under a striped awning. Richard ordered Crevettes Royale, enormous prawns which were a speciality of the region, and a bottle of chilled Fourchaume Chablis.

There were certain professions, Richard had learned, which were so stereotyped in the public perception, largely as a result of Ealing Studios films, that certain of its members always felt the need to perform their duties in a manner which was sufficiently overstated to ensure that the expectations of their clients would not be disappointed. You had, for example, the 'Cheeky Cockney Cabby' who treated you to a non-stop, one-man show of 'Cor blimey guvnor' humour as he hurtled you at suicidal speeds through the back streets of the metropolis. Then in the Highlands of Scotland, you had the 'Comic Ghillie' whose studied impertinence to sporting gentlemen from Surrey was passed down from father to son with the same thorough care that the art of removing a man's arm with a claymore had been passed down by earlier generations. Then here, the South of France, was the habitat of the 'Laid-back Latin Waiter' whose casual and slovenly service was always accompanied by intrusive and unfunny attempts at conversation. They had one now.

'Eengland, Piccadilly Circus, Margaret Thatcher.' he said as he scooped the spilled remains of the last customers' meal off the table cloth with his fingers. Then he laughed boisterously lest there should be any doubt that this was intended to entertain them. There was then a great performance as he placed a clean, white paper cover over the dirty tablecloth, pretending that it was to go over Frances's head like a bridal veil. This brought forth more loud guffaws. Richard returned a strained smile.

The prawns arrived, unshelled, on a huge bark tray with a separate bowl of mayonnaise and two finger-bowls with slices of lemon and rose petals floating on the surface. Each item was slapped down on the table in front of them with a gutteral cry of 'Eh, voila!' The tourists expected it. As they shelled and ate the huge prawns they discussed their morning's visit.

'The cost would be astronomical.' Richard said.

'Well, it must be a lot less than keeping them on at the villa. Anyway, there must be cheaper places.'

'In Cannes? I doubt it.'

Their friendly, couthy waiter had spilled a basket of bread on the floor and picking up each piece and dusting it off with exaggerated care, he replaced it on a clean, laid up table for the next customer. He gave a shrug and a stagy wink in the direction of Frances and Richard.

'How does that man keep his job?' Frances said with amazement.

'He probably owns the place.' Richard replied.

After lunch they took a walk down the Rue d'Antibes the main shopping street in Cannes and one of the most expensive and exclusive streets in Europe. They stared in wonder at the shop windows dressed with every luxury the western world could produce, and Richard told Frances that at Christmas time the display of lights rivalled that of any European capital. An aura of wealth hung over the pavements and the doorways of shops retained the heady scents of Chanel and Madame Rochas.

'They don't seem to have any hangups about wearing fur.' Frances said, noting the number of full-length minks though the April afternoon was mild by UK standards.

The Nature of Privilege

They drove back along La Croisette where afternoon strollers promenaded along the palm lined walkways in the shadows of some of the most glitzy apartment blocks and hotels in the world.

'There were two famous 19th century courtesans,' Richard told Frances, 'called Liane de Pougy and La Belle Otero, who was half gypsy. They frequented the casinos on the Riviera and engaged in a fierce rivalry. The story goes that, one evening, La Belle Otero appeared in the casino at Monte Carlo wearing an astonishing collection of jewellery so, the following evening, Liane de Pougy appeared in a plain white dress followed by her maid bedecked in even more jewellery than Otero had worn the previous night.'

'My God,' said Frances, 'a high society tart's put down.'

As they approached the Carlton Hotel, Richard pointed out the twin cupolas with their nipple-like peaks, one at each end of the hotel's magnificent facade. 'La Belle Otero had the last laugh,' Richard said, 'those cupolas are said to be made in the shape of her breasts.' Frances strained her neck to examine. 'Strange shaped woman.' she said.

'You know the old shape of champagne glasses, before flutes came in?'

'Like the Aunts used to use when we were engaged?'

'Just so. Well, they are supposed to have been fashioned in the shape of Marie Antoinette's breasts.'

'Really?' said Frances getting a bit tetchy at the way the conversation was heading, 'What an intelligent design concept.'

'Yes, one can think of a more practical basis but the French seem obsessed with women's bosoms.'

'Well, better than breaking wind, I suppose.' Frances replied.

* * *

Charlie sat in the Bar Tropique, wishing rather sadly that Sylvia was sitting opposite him, and continued his examination of the fundamental beliefs and unspoken taboos of his class. Let us dissect the subject of privilege, he thought, in a good, analytical, Staff College way.

1. A class system (call it what you will) in any society is inevitable and essential to the security and forward progress of that society. Put a hundred people of identical background and education on a desert island (he remembered his father saying), and within a month they will have established a class system. They will decide among themselves, instinctively and democratically, which people are best suited to perform each task necessary for the survival of the community which, as it develops, will naturally divide itself into hunters, gatherers, warriors and artisans. A leader will also emerge who enjoys the confidence and respect of the others.

2. To make the most efficient use of their resources, each group will do what it does best for the benefit of the community as a whole. While the leader, therefore, for example, is planning the grand strategy or administering whatever form of justice the community has decided is appropriate to its circumstances, his meat and his coconuts will be brought to him by someone else. No one would argue thus far, Charlie thought, but what happens when –

3. The leader dies and, because he has eaten less, due partly to the sedentary nature of his work, he is left with six coconuts more than his artisan neighbour. **Question:** Is it right that these six coconuts should become the property of his son who will thus, through no contribution of his own, start life with an advantage over the son of the artisan. Probably not, thought Charlie. But examine another scenario:

4. Two artisans live side by side, performing much the same work for, and receiving the same rations from, the community. Times are hard and food is scarce. Artisan A eats all his food and leaves nothing to his son. Artisan B tightens his belt and eats less, specifically to enable him to build up a little stock of coconuts to give his son a better start in life. He dies and

The Nature of Privilege

leaves two coconuts. **Question:** Is it then right that his son should not be permitted to benefit from his father's prudence and restraint? Certainly not, thought Charlie, yet this is what happens. Transpose it to the real world:

5. Artisan A spends all his income on his own comfort and pleasure – he changes his car every other year, has an enormous television set, spends a lot of time in the pub and bets on the horses. Artisan B has a five year-old car which needs a kick to get it started and saves his money (contributing extra tax to the exchequer on the interest) with the object of providing his son with a superior education which will enable him to get a better job, and lead a more comfortable life than his father. **Question:** Is it then right that Artisan A should resent Artisan B and should lobby to remove the means by which he can exercise his choice and improve his son's prospects? Certainly not, thought Charlie, yet this is the start of the classic class conflict. Back to the original scenario:

6. The leader dies with six extra coconuts. The community deems it unfair that the son should benefit from them, so they are forfeited and given out to drug addicts and one-parent families. The son of the leader and the son of the artisan therefore start life's race on an equal footing. Very right and proper. But, in the course of his upbringing, the leader's son was taught that it was unseemly to scratch his bottom in public and that it was unkind to mimic half-witted people. So although the two young men start life on an equal *economic* footing, the leader's son has acquired the rudiments of good manners and consideration for others, which sets him apart from his contemporaries who do scratch their bottoms and bait the village idiot. His 'difference' is resented by his peers who tend to ostracise him; but it is this difference which turns out to be the very quality which makes people vote for him at the next election.

7. So, thought Charlie, you could ensure through legislation that everyone started off with much the same opportunities in life, but you could not

inhibit parents' ambitions and sacrifices for their children, nor their perception of the importance of certain types of behaviour. So if, as the generations rolled on, men who did not scratch their bottoms sought out each other's company, this, surely was their right even if it attracted accusations of elitism.

8. But then you get the situation where two men apply for the same job; one a bottom scratcher who is ideally qualified and a non bottom scratcher who is less so. There would be a great temptation, if you had to share a place of work with him, to appoint the latter. This would be class prejudice, thought Charlie. The fairer, and ultimately more profitable, thing to do would be to employ the former and try to discourage him from his habit. This was what happened in the army. Young officers, nowadays, were selected solely on ability and potential. Then, if they were not gentlemen, which they frequently were not, they were taught to be gentlemen. The power of the British officer corps was so great that it could impose its standards of behaviour on young men from even the most lowly backgrounds. Education was the answer – education in place of exclusion or impediment.

Charlie recalled with some embarrassment and shame, the cruelty and arrogance of youth when he and his friends would refer to scholarship boys from humble backgrounds as 'Jally' Smith or 'Jally' Bloggs – Jally being the Wellington word for the trusty dormitory servants. His mother, who never came to terms with the growing influx of state school boys into the commissioned ranks of the army, called them 'Knobblenecks' as, she claimed, they could always be recognised before they opened their mouths, by their proneness to acne on the back of the neck.

As he had advanced through the service, Charlie had learned that state school boys, and indeed ambitious soldiers commissioned from the ranks, could become officers every bit as good as their public school counterparts – often a great deal better. They would usually embrace the officer's standards

The Nature of Privilege

of behaviour, and respect for tradition, with a zeal which could seldom be mustered by those born and brought up within the culture. Some of them never quite became gentlemen, of course, judged by the old criteria, but their sons would be sent to public schools and would pass for gentlemen and their grandsons would be equipped to mix in the best circles. This process of social mobility, Charlie had realised as he got older and wiser, was not only possible but was absolutely essential to the health and progress of the officer corps which could not survive without a continual cleansing of its blood with the robust and honest corpuscles of good yeoman stock. There was nothing new about this: many a Victorian general had risen from the rank of private.

Aware of this need, though he had never actually sat down and rationalised it in his own mind until now, Charlie, from the time he achieved his majority, had gone out of his way to encourage and assist the new class of officers to feel more comfortable within the social group in which they had been placed by their own abilities and ambitions. He would practise what today would be known as 'positive discrimination' – making allowances for them with which he would never have indulged those from his own background.

So why, Charlie now thought, should personal and civilian life be any different? If the officer corps needed this cleansing of its blood to remain healthy and progressive, why should families not require the same? The consequence of ignoring this need, after all, could be seen by the state of some of the country's oldest aristocratic families with their half-witted and wastrel scions. **Question**: Could it be that a marriage to a barmaid is something which every family like his should encourage and applaud instead of regarding it as the ultimate degradation?

Gurkhas   Photo: GURKHA BRIGADE ASSOCIATION

11. The Making of a Lahure

It was not that Dhani was unaware that he was driving a motor car of rare distinction. His disinclination for driving the Aunts in the Bentley stemmed from two principal sources. Firstly, the brakes. Although the car had covered less than 20,000 miles since it emerged brand new from the

The Making of a Lahure

dealer's showroom in Nice, on 20th February 1937, and this included some 5,000 miles of rough usage in the hands of the Italian commandant during its wartime requisition, the brakes were simply not up to the demands of the push-shove style of driving which was the norm on the Côte d'Azur in the 1990s. The engine was scarcely run in and the bodywork showed not a blemish nor any sign of decay. The luxurious upholstery was unmarked and still filled the car with the glorious smell of old leather. White-dialled instruments and shiny chrome switches sat tastefully in the polished walnut dashboard as confidently unconcerned with the admiration they inspired as a beautiful duchess in her box at the opera. The engine ran with a silky quietness, a slight but dignified whine from the transmission and a rich, baritone burble from the large-bore exhaust pipe which turned heads wherever the car went. But the brakes – they were something yet again.

The second factor which contributed to making Dhani's chauffering duties such an ordeal, was the Aunts' complete lack of understanding of the modern traffic system. 'Stop here Dhani.' Kate would demand imperiously in a nose-to-tail traffic flow moving at 60 mph, and Mattie would remonstrate with him for days for failing to turn right up a one-way street with three lanes of rush-hour commuters coming hell for leather in the opposite direction. 'We always went that way with Mummy,' she would argue in an injured tone, 'one gets a much prettier view of the cathedral.'

Because Dhani came from a disciplined background, and because he hated to cause anguish, however slight, to his employers, he would try, wherever possible, and within the context of risking all but certain death, to comply with their wishes. Thus, it was not uncommon during 'The Motoring Season' which, to the relief of the Antibes Police Department, was confined to a few weeks in the spring and autumn, to find the entire coastal traffic at a standstill, with tailbacks to Golfe Juan, while Mattie descended to purchase a box of Belgian Chocolates from a shop on the Boulevard Albert Premier; or the narrow streets of the Old Town gridlocked while Kate paused to admire the view from Les Remparts from which she had always admired the view since childhood.

Easter at the Villa Victoria

The French police, with an admirable tolerance for eccentricity, were usually very decent and accommodating. They had long since abandoned hope of communicating to the smiling little brown driver that there were certain regulations which had to be observed. It was easier, they had found, and restored order more quickly, simply to cone off the Bentley and direct the traffic around it. On one occasion, two motorcycle policemen had actually been detailed to escort it back to the Villa Victoria.

Today had not been too bad, Dhani thought. The Aunts were taking Sylvia and Emma to tea with Lady Wroughton and had promised to point out to them, on the way, some of the older houses on the Cap.

'Pull in here, Dhani.' Kate said as they passed magnificent and firmly-locked gates between imposing pillars. 'This was where the Tozer-Pykes lived. They always held a wonderful Spring Ball before they returned to England at the end of April. It was the last really grand do of the Season.'

'Can we see the house?' asked Sylvia.

'No, dear,' Kate replied, 'it is surrounded by its own grounds; you can't see it from the road.'

'And the Arabs have the house now.' Mattie added.

'Stop here, Dhani.' and the Bentley pulled in by white gates with a sign reading 'Villa Mistanguett'. Through a chink in the tightly-woven hurdles which surrounded the property, they could just catch a glimpse of a tall, white facade with pillared balconies, surrounded by palm trees.

'This was the Peels' house,' Aunt Kate said. The descendants of Sir Robert Peel the Prime Minister.'

'And founder of the police force,' added Mattie, 'hence the terms 'Bobby' or 'Peeler' for a policeman. The family had a huge cotton empire in Egypt when we used to come here as young gels. Such nice people.'

'But why the name 'Mistanguett'? Emma asked, 'wasn't she a famous music hall star?'

'Yes, darling,' Mattie replied, 'the house used to be called 'Chantercier'. Then the Peels sold it to Mistanguett, the actress, and she changed the name to her own. We didn't come here after that.' she added somewhat needlessly.

The Making of a Lahure

'Someone told us that it was one of several houses recently selected for King Hussein of Jordan, but he chose one of the others.'

After several more stops outside imposing entrances in tree-lined avenues, the Bentley drew in through the electric security gates of Lady Wroughton's house on the Avenue des Sables. Having seen the family safely disembarked and admitted, Dhani opened a toolbox on the Bentley's running board and removed two yellow dusters and a tin of Simoniz wax polish. When the family's tea had been served, he would be summoned into the kitchen through the back door where he would enjoy a mug of very sweet tea and a ham baguette while exchanging pleasantries and gossip, in a mixture of halting French and halting English with Helene, the housekeeper. In the meantime, he would remove the sticky finger marks left on one of the front mudguards by an over-enthusiastic nine year-old admirer that morning.

* * *

In a steep-sided valley in the foothills of the Himalayas, east of Khatmandu, Dhanibahadur Limbu had led a harsh childhood. In common with the other boys in his village, he had been expected to work from an early age – tending his family's straggling flock of sheep, meanly protected from the savage winds which strafed the hillside, with a few tattered clothes which had served his elder brother, with equal inadequacy, before him. Each day he would walk with bare feet along sharp, shale tracks to the local school – a journey of two miles each way. On his return, he would descend to the deep gorge at the foot of the valley to carry water back up the hillside to the rude, flint hut which was his home. Then there was wood and dung to be collected for the fire on which his mother, widowed by a Pathan bullet on the North-West Frontier, would prepare the family's meagre meal.

Their's was a culture of unremitting toil – a daily battle against hunger and a harsh environment which, over many centuries, had shaped the character of the Gurkha tribes into the gritty self-dependence which had won them the respect of the world.

Easter at the Villa Victoria

Only when the day's work was done and the smoke from the fires would curl up through the gathering darkness towards the snow-capped peaks above, would Dhanibahadur sit down and listen to the stories of the village elders. Then he would enter a magical world of parade grounds, battlefields, full bellies and a faraway white king.

Many, many years ago, he had been told by the Lahures, the white soldiers from across the seas had invaded their lands. The fighting had been fierce and there had been no winners and no losers. But such had been the mutual liking and respect, one side for the other, which had formed during the conflict, and such had been the similarity in their soldierly philosophies, that the war had led to an alliance in arms and friendship which had endured to this day.

Many years after this, the Lahures continued, the Indian sepoys of the Great White Queen rose up against their officers and British blood ran through the gutters of the sub-continent. Every Gurkha unit had stood by its oath of loyalty to the British and the Maharaja of Nepal, who had crossed the ocean to visit the Great White Queen, had personally led a contingent of the Nepalese army down into India in aid of their British friends. Many Gurkhas had died fighting with heroism beside British troops, and their loyalty and courage had been recognised with honours which had hitherto never been bestowed upon native soldiers. The special friendship was further reinforced with social privileges: Indian troops, the Lahures said, had never been allowed into British soldiers' canteens but Gurkhas had always been welcomed.

The bond had strengthened over another half-century of campaigning in many corners of the world until the first Great European War of 1914-18 when 200,000 Gurkhas volunteered for service and 20,000 fell in action. In 1923, over 100 years of comradeship-in-arms was marked by the signing of a Treaty of Perpetual Peace and Friendship between Britain and Nepal.

Now, the Lahures told the wide-eyed boys at the fireside, another great European War seemed likely and Britain would be, once again, looking to her Gurkha friends to swell their ranks in the coming conflict. Neither

The Making of a Lahure

Dhanibahadur nor his village contemporaries needed urging. From the earliest age, they had thought of nothing else but the day when they would be old enough to undertake the long trek to the British Army Depot to undergo the rigorous selection procedure which would determine whether they were good enough to be accepted for training as a Lahure, or would have to return, in despondency and shame, to the back breaking toil of village life.

At eighteen, standing with short-cut hair and stripped to the waist, Dhanibahadur had wept tears of joy when the Gurkha officer had called out the number which had been written on his chest with a wax marker, and told him he had been selected.

The training was tough and demanding but his hard life in the hills had prepared him well. With regular meals, he grew in strength and stature and rejoiced in every aspect of his induction as a soldier of the King. The drill, the ceremonial, the field and weapon training, the pride in uniform and bearing – all were fulfilments of his lifetime's ambition; everything matched up to, and indeed exceeded, the promises of the veterans upon whose words he had hung, around the village fires.

By the time he was ready for active service, the European War was well under way. He was posted to a battalion in North Africa which fought its way with gallantry and honour through the Italian campaign. At the Battles of Cassino, Tavoleto and Scorticata, Dhanibahadur's development from a proud and idealistic boy to a battle-hardened and ruthlessly proficient infantryman was completed. He was promoted to naik (corporal) in 1944.

After the War, the approach of Indian independence and partition brought a period of great anxiety and insecurity to Gurkha troops. Eventually it was decided that the Gurkha regiments would be split between the armies of Britain and India and, in a referendum known as 'The Opt' every soldier had the chance to chose which State he would prefer to serve. For Dhanibahadur there was no hesitation and great was his relief on learning that his regiment was to be consolidated into the British Army. He married a girl, Manjulika, from the next village to his own shortly before his regiment was posted to Malaya in 1948. Nine months later she gave him a son, Lalbahadur.

Over the next 18 years, Dhanibahadur was involved in almost continuous active service in Malaya, Brunei, Sarawak and Borneo during which time he was wounded twice, awarded the Military Medal and Distinguished Conduct Medal and was promoted to havildar, or sergeant as it had by then become known. During a long home leave in a peaceful lull in 1959/60, he noted with pride that little Lalbahadur was strong and sinewy and counting the days until he, too, could go for a Lahure. That day came in 1966, shortly before Dhani's demobilisation in Hong Kong when he received a letter from Manjulika telling him that the boy had been earmarked by the Galla Wala at a Hill Selection, had passed the rigorous final selection process, sworn his Oath of Allegiance to the Queen, and would shortly be leaving for the Training Depot.

About this time, employers were beginning to discover that the integrity and toughness of ex-Gurkha soldiers made them ideal for positions of trust in the security field. Dhanibahadur got a job as a security guard with a bank in Hong Kong where Manjulika joined him and obtained work as an assistant cook in a hotel kitchen. They lived happily in the Colony for the next 13 years, during which Manju learned good English and developed her skills as a cook, taking a succession of increasingly senior and well-paid jobs in the catering sector. On his 55th birthday, Dhanibahadur was compulsorily retired, but the President of the bank had acquired such a high regard for him that he approached him to see if he and his wife would be interested in the joint position as gardiens of his house in Antibes. Dhani had his army pension and they had saved enough in Hong Kong to provide for a reasonably comfortable retirement, but they were both extremely fit and active and jumped at this opportunity to extend their working lives. Moreover, they were concerned about the future of Hong Kong after the handover to the Chinese and welcomed the chance of employment in Europe. Sadly, the banker died eighteen months later and his house in France was sold but, providentially, at about the same time, they heard of a

The Making of a Lahure

vacancy for a couple with two old British ladies, in a house not far away, for which they seemed ideally qualified.

They were interviewed by a nephew of the old ladies, a major in one of the Highland Regiments alongside which Dhanibahadur had fought in Italy as a young rifleman. There had been an immediate and unqualified trust and affinity between the two men. Dhani and Manju moved into the flat in the Villa Victoria the next day and, over the ensuing 15 years, neither side had ever had cause to regret its decision.

Dhani smiled as he put a final buff on the wing of the Bentley. He and Manju were comfortable and fulfilled. They were loved and needed by the family they served and enjoyed the respect of the community in which they had settled. To their intense pride, their son Lalbahadur, had risen to the rank of Gurkha Captain and had commanded the Queen's Guard in London at Buckingham Palace. There was talk that he would shortly return to Nepal as a Recruiting Officer – that mystical figure which was respected above all others in the wind-lashed villages in the hills. During his recent service, with the seniority he had obtained, he could have had his wife and son, little Dhanibahadur, with him in married quarters. He chose not to, knowing that children brought up in the safe and comfortable environment of a military cantonment seldom acquired those qualities of toughness and self-reliance essential to a Gurkha soldier. Only the harsh existence of village life would form his character as it had formed his father's, grandfather's and great-grandfather's before him.

So little Dhanibahadur, aged 12, tended the sheep on a perilous hillside, carried water to the village and walked with bare feet to school each day, serving the harsh apprenticeship which would equip him for life as a Lahure in the service of the Great White Queen.

12. Curry Nights

Charlie's first attempt to convene a meeting to start off the discussions, which were the whole purpose of their being there, was held on Easter Day and was something of a failure. More than half of their four-week stay had passed and the family had settled into such a pleasant and relaxed routine that there was a noticeable reluctance to get down to business which might introduce friction and controversy into their harmonious lives. The Aunts themselves, he had decided, must be present; he would not feel right discussing these matters behind their backs. Afternoons were therefore out as the Aunts had to have their siesta and did not reappear until around 4.30 pm. This, theoretically, gave two hours until drinks time at 6.30 but meant that Charlie would have to sacrifice his cool beer trip to Juan – a prospect which did not fill him with joy.

So, it had to be in the morning. They would have to be finished, of course, by 11.30 as the Aunts would brook no interference with their morning champagne routine but, thought Charlie, if they could get started at 9.30 it would give them a couple of hours to talk and then the sessions could be continued each day until the necessary conclusions had been reached. He had announced this arrangement after dinner the evening before:

'I think it's important that we are all on parade at 9.30 as we have a lot to discuss.' he had said and assumed their concurrence from the mumbles and grunts he received in reply.

At 9.30 the next morning, Charlie, Aunt Kate and Sylvia had assembled in the drawing room but there was no sign of anyone else. Charlie sat staring at the blank pad on his knee and drumming with a pencil on the arm of the chair until, ten minutes later, a thunder of footsteps announced the arrival downstairs of Frances, Richard and the twins. Frances put her head round the door.

'You did say ten o'clock, didn't you?'

Curry Nights

'Nine-thirty actually.'

'Oh, well I won't be a tick. We'll just grab some breakfast.'

'We're really rather anxious to start, Frances.'

'Well, you don't expect us to go without breakfast, do you? . . . STEPHEN . . . put that bottle DOWN; that's not for breakfast . . . we won't be long, Uncle Charlie, honest.'

Charlie sighed and resumed tapping with his pencil. Sylvia, embarrassed by Emma's non-appearance and sensing Charlie's rising irritation, got up and headed for the door saying: 'I'll go and chase Emma up.' She met her at the door. 'We're all supposed to be in here, Emma. Where have you been?' she said reprovingly.

'You don't need me in on this do you?' Emma replied.

'It's the reason we're all down here child.'

'But I'm going to Cannes. Toby Chisholm is calling for me any minute now.'

'Then why didn't you tell Uncle Charlie last night? He made it quite clear that we were all expected to be here this morning.'

'Oh lawks!' Emma said despondently and sat down on the floor beside her mother's chair.

Frances hurried into the room with her mouth full and an enormous piece of bread and honey in her hand. 'OK, OK, I'm here, I'm ready now.' Richard followed her in looking sleepy, and sat down at the far end of the room.

Then Mattie appeared at the door, a look of bewilderment on her face. 'Why is everyone in here? Are we playing a game or something?'

'You know perfectly well why we're here Mattie.' said Kate who had known full well that she would have the opportunity of delivering this reproach, and had been looking forward to it. 'We are here to discuss *our* future. The family have come all this way to talk things through with us and you cannot even arrive on time.' She had been rehearsing something even more cutting but had forgotten the words at the last moment. Mattie sat down dejectedly.

Easter at the Villa Victoria

A shriek of pain from the next room, suggesting that one of the twins was attempting to maim the other, sent Frances flying out spilling honey on the carpet as she went.

'You're spilling your food, Frances.' yelled Richard after her.

'How come *she's* allowed to have breakfast and *I'm* not?' Emma enquired petulantly of her mother, 'I'm starving, I must have something to eat.' She ran from the room.

As Frances returned from placating the twins, she stepped accidentally on Richard's hand as he knelt on the floor, just inside the door, trying to remove honey from the carpet with a paper tissue.

'For heaven's sake!' he said in some pain and anger.

'Well, what are you doing down there on your hands and knees, hidden behind the door?'

'Trying to clean up the honey *you* spilt before someone treads in it.'

'Someone already has trodden in it.' said Sylvia calmly, 'There's another blob over there. Now just calm down everybody while I get a proper cloth and some water from the kitchen.' She left the room and returned shortly with a cloth and a bowl of soapy water. Frances tried to snatch the cloth.

'No, don't worry, I'll do it.' Sylvia said firmly.

'Why should *you* do it? Do you think I'm not capable of wiping a stain off the carpet?'

'Not at all, not at all,' Sylvia said placatingly, 'it's just that my hands are wet already and I'm practically finished anyway.'

By the time Sylvia had taken the bucket back and had returned to her seat in the drawing room, it was nearly 10.30. Charlie was bursting for a pee but was determined not to leave the room himself which would have diminished his own martyrdom. Seeing that everyone was at last sitting down and looking at him expectantly, he cleared his throat to start.

'Oh my goodness!' cried Mattie springing to her feet with creditable alacrity for an 89 year-old, 'I'd forgotten Madame Bourget's kippers.' She tottered towards the door. Emma sniggered; Aunt Kate scowled; Frances sighed and Charlie decided it was probably best not to try and conjure up

Curry Nights

any visual image of his aunt's latest little crisis. Indeed, he wondered, might this be the moment he could exit for a pee without any damage to the credit for forbearance he had amassed over the past hour. His mind was made up when a young man in a sports car drew up to the front of the house and tooted his horn.

'Oh, that's Toby,' said Emma, 'must go.' She made for the door, then thinking better of it, returned to where Charlie was sitting. 'Sorry, Uncle Charlie, I'm really sorry.' then brightly: 'What about tomorrow? I've nothing on tomorrow. Oh no! I promised Sophie I'd go over to them tomorrow. Well, sometime, Uncle Charlie.' She backed towards the door like a courtier leaving the royal presence. 'You fix it. You tell me when you want me. OK? Byee.'

'Right! That's it!' said Charlie theatrically, snapping his pad shut. He walked with dignity towards the door avoiding eye contact with anyone. Out in the hall his pace quickened as he made for the downstairs cloakroom.

* * *

Wednesday and Saturday nights had always been 'Curry Nights' at the Villa Victoria, augmented by periodic Tiffins (Indian lunches) at the whim of the current proprietors. In the 1880s and '90s the house was renowned among the 'Old K'hais' (old India hands) along the coast, and there were many of them. Invitations to curry dinners at the Morton-Stewarts were highly sought after. At such events, red-faced gentlemen would sweat over a good hot vindaloo, and their ladies would pick delicately at a uniquely excellent fish molee, while nostalgic memories of the hills and the plains were exchanged.

James and Edith Morton-Stewart had brought their own cook with them from India, and he managed to pass on much of his skills to his successor before his death. From thereon, however, the expertise which the house was anxious to maintain depended, to a very large extent, upon Edith's mother's Receipt Book.

Easter at the Villa Victoria

This was a large 13 ins x 18 ins stiff-covered account book with pages ruled in faded mauve ink, produced by Waterlow & Sons of London for Her Majesty's Government around the middle of the last century. It had a leather spine which had been worn away with 150 years of handling, exposing the thread-sewn signatures beneath. The covers and endpapers were of a beautiful, marbled design, and inside the front cover was a handsome printed label with the maker's name and the Royal coat-of-arms.

Edith's mother, Fanny, was married to a surgeon in the Bengal Medical Service who had, apparently, first used the book to teach himself in Hindustani the basic, everyday phrases which would enable him to perform his professional duties. Several pages of such phrases were listed and beside each, the munshi (teacher) had written the Hindustani translation:

> *Are you better than yesterday?*
> *Speak the truth.*
> *You are lying.*
> *Call the baboo.*
> *Every day when I come you are absent.*
> *Sit down.*
> *It is your own fault.*
> *Don't do so again.*
> *You must not fornicate with low-class women.*
> *Tell that man to return to his bed.*
> *etc., etc.*

When the surgeon had learned to use these essential phrases without reference to the book, or had abandoned the attempt, his wife, Fanny, had taken over the book for her own use. Page after page of immaculate copperplate writing recorded the secrets of her kitchen – Stewed Cheese; Lemon Syrup; Russian Fish; Kidneys in Batter; Stewed Sheep's Tongues; Meat Jelly; Sago Cream; Rissoles of Fowl; Devilled Duck or Teal; a Good Custard and Little Plum Cakes. There were detailed receipts for many North

Curry Nights

Indian dishes though the quantities of ingredients, as with Mrs. Beaton, usually required division by ten for modern requirements. But the centre core of her knowledge, which had been responsible for maintaining the excellence of Indian cuisine at the Villa Victoria a hundred years later, was her instructions for a basic curry powder which was recorded thus:

Haldi (Turmeric) 10 tbs.   *Dhania (Coriander Seed) 10 tbs.*
Jeera (Cumin Seed) 2 tbs.   *Khush-Khush (Poppy Seed) 2 tbs.*
Maythi (Fenugreek) 1 tbs.   *South (Dry Ginger) 1 tbs,*
Rai (Mustard Seed) half tbs.   *Sooka Miirch (Dried Chillies) 1 tbs*
Kala Miirch (Black Peppercorns) 1 tbs.

The Coriander Seed and Fenugreek must each be parched very carefully i.e. roasted like coffee berries before being pounded. The other ingredients should be cleaned and dried, each separately, and when pounded well, sifted. Weights having then been tested, the whole of the powders should be mixed, half a bottle of salt being sprinkled in by degrees during the process. The bottles, thoroughly cleansed and dried in the sun may then be filled and corked tightly down, the tops being securely waxed over. The flavour of this stock powder may be varied by the use of **Spices** *(cloves, cinnamon, mace, nutmeg, cardamoms, allspice of which a teaspoonful of one or at most two blended will suffice for a large curry.* **Green Leaves** *(Fennel, Maythi, Bajic, Lemon Grass, Bay Leaves, Karay-Pank and Kotemear (green coriander).* **Garlic and Onions, Green Ginger, Almonds, Cocoanut** *Powdered Almonds (sweet) with Cocoanut are very nice in proportion of 12 Almonds to 1 oz. Cocoanut. When Green Ginger is used it should be sliced very fine and pounded to a paste, a dessertspoonful being enough for one curry. The necessary suspicion of* **Sweet-Acid** *may be* *produced by a dessertspoonful of powdered or moist Sugar and the juice of a Lime or a spoonful of Vinegar. A tablespoon of Sweet Chutney and the juice of a Lime make a good substitute but a tablespoon of Redcurrant Jelly with one of Chutney and a little Vinegar or Lime Juice form the nicest combination for dark curries.*

*For **Fresh Paste** to mix with the stock powder take one small Onion, one clove of Garlic, one dessertspoon of Turmeric, one of freshly roasted Coriander Seed, one of Poppy Seed, a teaspoonful of Nepaul Pepper, one of Sugar, one of Salt and one of grated Green Ginger. Pound all to a paste. Also pound 12 Almonds (sweet) and 1 oz. of Cocoanut with a little Lime Juice to assist the operation. Then mix the two pastes and stir into them a teaspoonful of Cinnamon or Clove powder. A heaped up tablespoonful of this to one of the stock powder is sufficient. Additional **heat** can be obtained by those who like hot curries if red chilli powder be added to the above ingredients according to taste.*

Using these notes, a succession of Irish cooks maintained the status of the Villa Victoria as the best curry house on the Côte d'Azur until the departure of Hetty fourteen years ago. Every morning at 7 am Hetty had descended into the garden and leaped across a five-foot wide flower border on the east side of the villa. She had told Bridie when she joined the family that, when the day came that she could no longer perform this feat, she would know that death was near and she must return immediately to West Cork. One morning in 1981, a tear-stained face and a crumpled bed of cyclamens signified that the sad day had arrived. Hetty returned to Ireland to die and the Limbus moved in. It must be recorded that, 14 years later, Hetty was still very much alive and was daily performing a similar, if slightly less athletic, jump over a stream on her brother's farm, The flowerbed at the villa had, since her departure, been known as 'Hetty's Leap'.

Curry Nights

When Manjulika took over as cook, and underwent a rudimentary handover briefing on the preparation of the house curry, she knew she could do better. These, she realised were Anglo-Indian dishes of 150 years ago and today, with the ready availability of fresh foods, herbs and spices, she could present a much more authentic and interesting cuisine. Her first offerings were not well received – the Aunts and their guests were used to a certain kind of curry and did not want it changed. So Manju returned to the old recipe and gradually modified it, augmenting it with succulent little dishes of her own, until it was generally agreed that curry nights at the villa had never been better.

Today, she was preparing pieces of chicken which would rest overnight in a marinade of yoghurt and fresh spices. Bridie watched her as she pricked each piece of meat with a knife and brushed it with lemon juice.

'That strange Englishman from Nice was here again this morning,' said Bridie, 'and Miss Kate rummaging around in the attic, chust, rummaging around in the attic.'

'Always he sniff,' Manju replied, 'like he had a cold. Sniff, sniff, sniff.'

'I think it's a nervous habit, chust, a nervous habit.'

'I wonder if it some polish we use in the house, maybe him allergic to some smell.'

'Well, it's certainly not dust,' said Bridie decisively and defensively, 'not in this house, chust, not in this house.'

'Oh no, certainly not dust in this house, just, in this house.' Manju agreed, shaking her head from side to side as she dropped the last piece of chicken into the coffee-coloured marinade.

13. The Audit

Written on the top page of Charlie's pad, surrounded by childlike doodles of flowers and strange, exotic birds, was a summary of the enquiries he felt he must make:

> *1. **Health:*** *Present condition and prognosis – See Chouard – advice on Nursing Homes – How are they coping? How do they feel about things?*

> *2. **Care:*** *How are staff coping? Have they any plans of their own re. retirement? Hoist for Aunt K (for bed). Anything else needed?*

> *3. **Finance:*** *Analyse income and expenditure – Summarise investments and consult Harry Penn if necessary.*

Having found a parking space for the little Renault near the station, Charlie walked down the Boulevard Dugommier to keep an appointment with the Aunts' doctor. This was the medical area of Antibes where the brass plates of specialists in every ailment, and every part of the anatomy, bespoke both the French preoccupation with health and the high proportion of well-heeled senior citizens in the community. The preponderance of specialists in stomach and gastric disorders told yet another story.

Doctor Marcel Chouard was the Aunts' doctor and had been a friend of the family for some twenty years. His specialisation was the British residents in whose homes he was known and welcomed all along the coast. Dr. Chouard was an anglophile whose love of all things English had been fired by exhaustive reading of G A Henty and Biggles, as a boy, and P G Wodehouse in later years. Consequently, his perception of England was a little anachronistic – he believed that English families still dressed for dinner, spiked his otherwise perfect English with expressions such as 'dontchaknow' and was wont to startle new patients by addressing them as 'old bean' or 'old fruit'.

'Your Aunt Kate's condition can only deteriorate I'm afraid. All one can say is that she is mentally very strong and is coping with it well. The drugs I am giving her help considerably but they do need constant monitoring as they can have unpleasant side effects, dontchaknow.'

'And Mattie?'

'Well, Mattie is a great deal fitter than she deserves to be, but you have to remember she is 89 and cannot live forever.'

'What about the smoking and drinking?' Charlie asked.

'Pffff . . .' Marcel shrugged and exhaled noisily through fluttering lips in a most un-English fashion. 'At her age? It would probably do her more harm than good to try and give them up. I think at her age, as long as she keeps chugging on the way she is, a little of what she fancies probably does her good.'

'So what do you think, Marcel? Should I be considering a nursing home for them?'

'Why? If they are happy? Certainly there is no justification on medical grounds. Provided they can afford to stay on at the house and you do not foresee any difficulties with the staff, but, as I say, they are old ladies. This is the position as I see it now, dontchaknow, but things can change suddenly. I will continue to see them regularly, of course, and I have your telephone number in Scotland if there is any cause for concern. You know, I'm really very fond of them both, Charlie.'

'Well it's a great comfort to know that they are in such capable and caring hands. Thank you so much for all your attention.'

'Don't mention it, old fruit.'

* * *

Next, Charlie had interviewed the staff. Bridie, fearing that his enquiries as to 'whether she was beginning to find things too much' heralded a suggestion of retirement, became flustered and slightly hostile: 'Ah sure, they're no trouble at all, at all, chust, they're no trouble at all.'

'Well, is there anything you can think of, Bridie, anything I can change or arrange to make life easier for you? I am very conscious of all you have to do in the running of this house and looking after my aunts.'

'The house is run fine, chust, the house is run fine and Miss Kate and Miss Mattie want for nothing.' she replied, suspecting a hint of criticism in his enquiry, then, anxious not to miss taking advantage of such an opportunity: 'There is one thing, Colonel Charlie.'

'Yes?'

'That greasy gasoon who comes in to help Dhani with the watering. What sort of a person does he think he is with his long hair and his flowery shirt? Lady Florence would never have had a tinker like that anywhere near the house. I've seen him with his shirt off, too, with his sweaty chest, in full view of the house, chust, in full view of the house; Miss Kate or Miss Mattie would see him if they went to the window; and loitering around the back of the coach house smoking when there's work to be done; and Dhani never idle for a minute, chust, never idle for a minute. Lady Florence would never have had such a person in the house. There's no respect with tinkers like him. I've always had respect, Colonel Charlie, wherever I've been . . .'

'Of course you have, Bridie, and rightly so . . .' Charlie interrupted trying to stem the flow.

'There's no respect with him, sniggering and leering when he comes in for his tea; and sprawling with his greasy arms all over the kitchen; and he's after ogling at Miss Emma when she's down the garden, and him without two farthings to scratch his backside with, and his shirt off. It's not for the likes of him to be ogling at the likes of her; there's no respect with him, coming to this house and behaving like he was in his own tinkers' camp and smoking round the back of the coach house when there's work to be done, chust, when there's work to be done.'

The Audit

Charlie, wishing he had made his enquiry more specific, and feeling that little fresh evidence was likely to be forthcoming on the wayward habits of the garden boy, interrupted her gently: 'I didn't realise he caused you such distress, Bridie. Leave it to me; I'll have a word with him.'

Bridie left the room mumbling under her breath: 'There's no respect, chust, there's no respect, and him with his greasy hair and his shirt off.'

* * *

The interview with the Limbus was more simple and less vociferous. Charlie realised that to ask two people who had led such hard lives as Dhani and Manju whether their present, comparatively easy, duties were becoming too much for them, was somewhat gratuitous. But he did so just the same.

'Manju and me very happy here, Colonel Charlie,' Dhani replied, 'nothing wrong, no problems.'

'You see, Dhani,' Charlie explained, 'Miss Kate and Miss Mattie are getting very old and very frail and we have to decide if they are still able to stay on in this house, or if the time has come where we have to consider moving them to a nursing home.'

'Very old, very frail.' Manju said, 'All the more reason why they stay here. We look after them good, Colonel Charlie. We love them and we know what they like. At nursing home they not know what they like. They not happy at nursing home with strange faces, strange food, strange things all round. They been here so long. They used to this old house. They used to us and we used to them.'

Which, thought Charlie, was perhaps the most succinct and relevant argument he had heard so far in favour of retaining the status quo.

'Thank you Manju, thank you Dhani.'

'Thank you, Colonel Charlie.'

* * *

Easter at the Villa Victoria

This just left the financial aspect which Charlie had known from the start would be the most difficult and time consuming, but he had not realised, until he sat down with the Aunts' bank, tax and investments files, just how difficult and time consuming it would be, particularly for someone with only a rudimentary knowledge of book keeping and accounts.

He had bought himself a packet of multi-column analysis paper and set about, first, preparing simple income and expenditure summaries from bank statements, cheque book stubs and paying-in slips.

'I think you have everything there that you will need, dear,' Kate had said, 'but just give me a call if there's anything else you want.'

His first mistake, in common with many a novice book keeper, was over analysis. He headed up separate columns for 'Food', 'Wine', 'Household Cleaning Materials', etc., and soon realised that this would entail dissecting every supermarket till roll – a labour for which he had neither the time nor the inclination. He therefore scrapped his first attempt and coarsened his analysis to record broader areas of expenditure such as 'Insurance', 'Wages', 'Tax Foncières', 'Household Costs', etc. He started getting on a lot faster. His original intention had been to analyse the past three years, but, by the time he had finished the current year, and seen how long it took him, he decided that one year would be quite sufficient. The expenditure was fairly straight forward and at the foot of the final sheet he ruled two red lines and totalled the columns.

On the face of it, the income side was also relatively simple. The operating account for the household was with the Banque Nationale de Paris, BNP, at the Antibes La Fontonne branch on the eastern outskirts of the town. A regular, monthly credit from the Cannes branch of the same bank serviced the requirements of the account, supported by an annually-reviewed overdraft facility of, currently, 50,000 Francs which, it appeared, was seldom used. The operating account showed what bankers describe as a 'healthy, swinging balance' with the only evidence of a minor, seasonal cash crisis occurring in September when all the insurance renewals fell due. Previous years' statements confirmed that this was a regular pattern.

The Audit

The BNP account in Cannes appeared to serve as a collection account for share dividends and the interest accrued on seven different deposit accounts and trust funds. Here again, there appeared to be no cash crisis – indeed there was evidence of periodic surpluses where cash sums had been transferred back into one of the deposit accounts. Charlie, who was not an accountant, could not begin to understand why so many deposit accounts were necessary for the affairs of two old ladies. But he went through the statements of all seven and checked that the transfers to BNP Cannes came from interest and not from capital. He totalled the debits to these accounts and reconciled them with the credits to BNP Cannes. All in order.

He then examined the Aunts' tax file to ensure that there was no massive backlog of tax due. The annual returns had been meticulously completed and submitted by the bank's tax department, and the appropriate sums paid well before the due dates. Then he turned to the investments file and fanned through reams of contract notes to satisfy himself that there had been no selling of shares to augment income; but apart from routine housekeeping by their stockbroker, he could discover no sale of equities at all.

Charlie could remember quite clearly, about five years ago, Kate telling him that she was a little worried about their financial position:

'Things are so expensive nowadays, dear,' she had said, 'and there are so few economies that one can make. I don't know how much longer we will be able to continue living here, I really don't.'

As no further action was taken and Kate had not raised the subject with him again, he had assumed that from that time they had been nibbling into capital. And yet, his little audit had revealed no evidence of this – everything seemed in good order and their finances buoyant, positively buoyant. There was nothing on the financial side, therefore, which suggested the need for the Aunts to be moved out and he now felt better prepared to state this case at the family meeting to come.

Right now though, his mind was scrambled with contract notes, deposits and shirtless garden boys and could only be disencumbered in the serene surroundings of the Bar Tropique whereto he headed without further delay.

Easter at the Villa Victoria

Reflecting, over his first demi-pression, on the little tiff he had had with the family the previous day, Charlie justified his entitlement to be a little cool with them. Their behaviour had been inconsiderate if not irresponsible. This was not a holiday, it was a family convention to consider the very serious question of the Aunts' future. He had told them the evening before that their presence was required at 9.30 the next morning. This was not the army, where such matters are transmitted as orders, and obedience is taken for granted. This was a family of which he was, nominally, the head and in which his slightest intimation should jolly well meet with compliance. Perhaps he should have made them get down to business as soon as they arrived in Antibes, and not allowed them a fortnight of freedom in which to become undisciplined and feckless.

But why, he wondered, was he extending the cold shoulder to Sylvia? She had been there at the appointed hour and had done all she could to retrieve the situation. It was a communal punishment, he replied, the innocent must suffer with the guilty. He had been failed by the corporate body and the corporate body must be made aware of his displeasure.

He called for another beer. But she had been so sweet, so supportive. He recalled how she had taken charge, so tactfully, of the honey spilling incident (and how pretty she had looked, her raven hair ruffled as she scrubbed away at the carpet). It was she who had marshalled the family at dinner that night and arranged for them all to be on parade the following Monday, and had insisted upon a positive verbal response from each of them to ensure that there would be no misunderstanding.

Going in to dinner that night, he turned to her and gave her an enormous, stagey wink and received a radiant smile of understanding in return.

14. Herbert Pontefract

The next morning Emma, running from the kitchen to the dining room, a pain au chocolat clutched in her hand, collided with an American in the hall. 'Oh, I'm terribly sorry.' she said, dabbing at his lightweight jacket in fear that her breakfast might have come in contact with it.

'That's quite all right, little lady.' he replied with a gracious smile.

Good heavens! Thought Emma, do Americans *really* call people 'Little Lady'? She stepped back and surveyed him. He was tall with short fair hair, late 20s, and very good looking. What on earth can this man be doing here, she wondered, is he selling something? Standing beside the American was a small, balding man with wire-framed glasses and a crumpled suit whose regular sniffs seemed to indicate that he had no handkerchief.

'I'm Emma,' she said, extending a dainty hand to the American, 'and who are you?'

At this juncture, Aunt Kate, who appeared to have been showing the two men out of the house at the time of the collision, manoeuvred her bath chair between Emma and the American. 'They are just leaving.' she said.

The American, not wishing to appear discourteous, took Emma's extended hand over Kate's head.

'I'm Steve Fitzgerald, Hi!' The bath chair lurched again in the direction of the front door, breaking their handshake and driving the two men, like ewes before a Border Collie, towards the open door. It was quite obvious that Aunt Kate was trying to get rid of them and did not wish a conversation to develop. Unusually, for someone with such impeccable manners, she did not even introduce the sniffing man to Emma.

As he retreated across the terrace at the top of the steps to the drive, Steve turned and caught Emma's eye. 'Perhaps, sometime we could . . .' The bath chair lurched again, driving him on to the top step from where, emboldened in the knowledge that the chair could not pursue him down the steps, he finished his sentence: 'Perhaps we could meet for a drink, or a meal?'

'Great. Call me.' replied Emma in parlance which she felt would be understood by an American.

'Really, Emma!' said Aunt Kate crossly as she closed the front door and drove Emma before her across the hall, 'What forward behaviour. I'm quite shocked.'

What on earth was *that* all about? Emma wondered as she bit into her pain au chocolat.

* * *

'Henri,' Charlie called to the garden boy, 'un moment si'l vous plait.'

'Oui, Monsieur.'

'Do you like working here, Henri?' he continued, in French, of course.

'Oui, Monsieur.'

'Well, if you want to continue working here, you'll have to brass your ideas up a bit.'

'Oui, Monsieur?' said Henri looking mystified.

'When you address the housekeeper, you will not smirk, you will keep your eyes lowered and you will address her respectfully as 'Madame Hogan'.

'Mais, Monsieur.'

'You will wash your hair regularly and comb it before you go into the kitchen for tea where you will sit upright in your chair, your feet and knees together, your elbows off the table, and will eat your food with delicacy, without spilling crumbs on the floor or smearing butter on the table, and you will say 'Thank you' to Madame Hogan and Madame Limbu when you have finished.'

Henri's mouth sagged in amazement.

'When any member of the household passes you in the garden, you will avert your eyes and will not address them unless they address you first (can I really be speaking these words in Western Europe in 1995? Charlie asked himself) except for a courteous 'Bonjour Madame, Bonjour Mademoiselle, or similarly restrained greeting.'

Henri could not speak.

'You will not rev the engine of your motorcycle within a two mile radius of this house. You will cut the motor before you enter the gates in the morning and when you leave in the evening, you will not restart it until you have freewheeled silently down the hill for a distance of at least 200 metres.'

Henri had begun to tremble.

'When in sight of the house, you will not remove your shirt, yawn, stretch, whistle, sing, belch, fart, scratch yourself or behave in any other way that might be construed as unseemly, impertinent or vulgar. Do you understand me, Henri?'

'Oui, Monsieur.'

'Now, tuck your shirt into your trousers and away you go.'

'Oui, Monsieur.'

'And Henri,' Charlie called after the boy as he fled towards the mower shed, 'if you want a smoke, do not do it in any place where you are likely to ignite inflammable materials or can be seen by the housekeeper.'

'Non, Monsieur.'

* * *

The little sniffing Englishman who had, twice in the past week, been spotted within the walls of the Villa Darjeeling was, in fact, Herbert Pontefract and he was Christebys' man in Nice.

The achievement of such a position in a part of Europe as rich in the artefacts of a privileged society as the French Riviera, might be seen to denote a high degree of experience and competence. This was indeed the case with Herbert Pontefract.

Had his appearance and manner been more prepossessing, Herbert would certainly have held high office in the smart London auction room circuit. But he shuffled and sniffled and looked like a furtive pawnbroker and, though eminently well qualified, he simply did not fit in with the Knightsbridge antiques set.

The son of a Yorkshire cabinet maker, Herbert Pontefract had been brought up with fine furniture. From an early age in his father's workshop he had mixed with craftsmen and had learned to appreciate their skills. Such was his father's reputation that furniture was sent to him for restoration from all over the country, both from dealers and from private homes. Later, as an apprentice, Herbert had worked with his father on some of the finest antique pieces in the land. His father would never work to a price – there was a right way and a wrong way of doing everything and in the firm of George Pontefract & Son it was the right way, regardless of how long it took, or nothing.

Quality was paramount. They cared not how many hours were spent on a job as long as, when it went out of the door, they knew it was as perfect as their skills could make it. Often George Pontefract was embarrassed to reveal just how many hours it *had* taken them and the job was consequently undercharged. This, as in so many other small firms of craftsmen where quality tends to override costings, led the Pontefracts into financial trouble and, in 1968, the firm had to close down and George retired.

Herbert had no difficulty in finding employment. He had no wish to start up on his own and when he was offered a position with a dealer in Harrogate, who had sent work to his father for many years, he accepted it. His duties here were general and he became involved in buying and selling as well as restoration work. It was a small shop catering for the top end of the market and, over the twelve years that he worked there, he acquired a good working knowledge of silver, china and fine art, though, of course, his expertise in these fields could never approach his knowledge of English furniture which was his speciality and his passion.

On the death of the proprietor of the shop in Harrogate, Herbert moved down to London where he had a succession of jobs in the trade until his expertise reached the ears of Christebys who offered him a position at almost twice any salary he had previously commanded. He quickly became

Herbert Pontefract

an indispensable member of their London team. He could date a piece of English furniture with a glance, and after a quick inspection underneath it, or inside a drawer, could often name the craftsman, or school of craftsmen, who had produced it. He could instantly spot a clever fraud and could pass reliable judgement on any piece of restoration and assess its likely effect on market price.

The trouble was that, although he enjoyed the respect of his colleagues, he got on their nerves with his shuffling and sniffing, the latter being a nervous allergy which he could not control when in the presence of fine furniture. He could not be taken anywhere. As soon as he spotted a Regency chair or a George III sideboard, his nose would begin to twitch and the sniffing would start. His colleagues soon realised that his habits were as offensive to clients as they had become to themselves.

So it was that when the elopement of their manager in Nice with a male Romanian tennis player created a vacancy on the Riviera, a sigh of relief passed round the London Office and Herbert Pontefract was sent for.

Herbert's disinclination for working in the South of France was matched only by his wife's enthusiasm for it. She saw his appointment as a heaven-sent opportunity to exchange her dreary life in Penge for a glamorous and hedonistic existence in a part of the world known only to her, thusfar, in the pages of the Sunday colour supplements. During a euphoric shopping spree in the West End, in the immediate aftermath of the news, she had bought Herbert a pair of Bermuda shorts, a colourful silk shirt in a floral design and a Panama hat – mainly to mitigate the equally inappropriate wardrobe she had purchased for herself.

Once they had settled in to their small flat in a street off the Promenade des Anglais, she had come to realise that, apart from the heat, which she found oppressive, and the difficulties with language, life in Nice was not all that different from life in Penge – floors still had to be hoovered and meals cooked and she missed the coffee mornings with her cronies at which the characters of unpopular neighbours would be assassinated with suburban finesse. Naturally, she blamed the elusiveness of the life of glamour she had expected on her husband. If he was not so mousey, and so stick-in-the-mud, just think of the fun they could be having.

Herbert settled quickly into the routine of his job – there was seldom anything he couldn't handle and, on the rare occasions when he felt out of his depth, with a choice of eight scheduled flights daily between London and Nice, the appropriate Christebys expert could be at his side in no time. The domestic side of his life was less of a breeze. His return home each evening would bring on a fresh round of complaints and disaffected nagging and, even worse, when light and weather were opportune, harassment to don his shorts and coloured shirt and escort her to the beach.

He had succumbed to this coercion on a couple of occasions and had sat shivering on the sand, being pestered by North African peddlers and surrounded by groups of noisy teenagers, hyped up on alcohol or drugs. Gradually, Maud, for that was her name, came to realise that her dream of hedonism was an illusion and became increasingly bitter and vindictive towards her unfortunate husband. He, in turn, sought every possible excuse to remain late at the office and would often invent appointments at weekends – anything to get away from the hectoring of his wife.

He had a genuine appointment this Saturday. A young American had come into his office last week looking for 19th century Irish oils and he knew exactly where there were some. There were these two old biddies in Antibes for whom he had already sold a couple of paintings and who, he knew, had others. It was the one in the wheelchair who seemed to make the decisions and he had been to see her to establish if she would be open to offers subject, of course, to the usual commission scales for the introduction. She had confirmed that there were two pictures she would be prepared to sell, for the right price, and he had taken the American round there this morning, by appointment, to view them. He had clearly been delighted with them and would have made an offer there and then, but the old girl had come over all funny. She had suddenly cut the discussion short and had bundled them out of the house like uninvited guests. Most of Herbert's clients tended to be elderly, and he knew the ancients could be a bit odd, particularly if they were Irish, as he assumed these two old dears to be from the Irish paintings and beautiful Irish Georgian furniture which had set his nose off sniffing on each occasion he had been to the house.

He had telephoned Miss Morton-Stewart when he got back to his office. It had not been convenient, she had told him haughtily, to discuss business at that moment. Might he come over to see her on Saturday morning? He expected to be in a position to make her a handsome offer for both paintings on behalf of the American gentleman. Yes, she would see him, but would he kindly come to the tradesmen's entrance, ask for her personally and not engage in conversation with any of the staff or house guests.

Strange, Herbert thought as he put the phone down, sounds to me as if the old girl is flogging off heirlooms without telling the rest of the family.

* * *

Great Aunt Sade, when she was not entertaining her family by breaking wind in public, had been a prodigious landscape painter both in water colours and oils. In a family of artistic Victorian ladies, Sade transcended all of her generation in both volume of output and craft. Her easel had been carried from her barouche by her driver, and erected in every remote corner of County Cork and Kerry – on every rocky headland and lush valley; beside every towering mountain and spectacular ruin not to mention the street sites in Bandon and in Cork City.

Later in her life she had bought a house in Bedford Park, Chiswick, when it was an early artists' colony, and from here she launched similarly determined forays into the Surrey landscape, and it was partly from here and partly from her father's home in Ireland that Lady Florence had collected her aunt's vast portfolios of canvases after her death in 1903. The tragedy was that none of the family *liked* Aunt Sade's paintings which had become something of a family joke. There were so many of them. Every branch of the family hung at least one in some dark corner, purely as a gesture of solidarity, but offers of further canvases were always greeted with mirthful outrage: 'Oh, for God's sake no! Not another of Aunt Sade's paintings, please!'

Lady Florence, having spent many happy days of childhood with her aunt, was more sentimental and rejected the urgings of siblings and cousins to burn the lot after Sade's death. She took them to France with her when she was married, framed and hung a few favourites, and stored the rest in an attic.

Aunt Kate, as the self-appointed trustee of her mother's memory, resented the family's flippant judgement of her great aunt's accomplishments and guarded the portfolios with proprietorial zeal.

'So, the American is going to offer a handsome price, is he?' she said to Mattie after the phone call from Herbert Pontefract. 'Well, we'll just have to see how handsome is handsome. But he's only getting the two; we don't want to flood the market, do we?' She grinned maliciously.

'Shouldn't we tell Charlie about all this, dear?' Mattie asked anxiously.

'Certainly not. He's always been as scornful as the rest about Aunt Sade. But we'll show them, Mattie, we'll show them all, won't we?' and she tapped the side of her nose in a conspiratorial and most undignified fashion.

Fort Royal on the Ile Sainte Marguerite where the Man in the Iron Mask was imprisoned. *Photo:* MUSEESC

15. Les Iles de Lérins

The morning was sunny with a light to fresh breeze from the south-west – ideal weather for the day's sailing and picnic lunch which Charlie had planned for Sylvia and himself.

There was only one leisure pursuit to which Charlie was seriously committed. This was sailing. He had sailed in ocean-going yachts since childhood and had spent almost every Easter and summer holiday when he was at school sailing from the Hamble River with friends. He had competed in three Fastnets and countless cross-channel races and, by the time he went to Sandhurst, knew every haven in the Solent and on the Brittany coast intimately. He had an amazing feeling for wind and tide which made him a natural and expert helmsman and might well have placed him in the Olympic class, as a young man, had his regimental duties allowed the necessary degree of dedication which, of course, they had not. Had it not been for the family's army tradition, Charlie would certainly have made the navy his career.

Nowadays, he preferred the leisurely, gentle type of sailing to the cut and thrust of competition and, not justifying a boat of his own, nor wishing for the worry of its maintenance, he had acquired a quarter share, with three local yachtsman friends, in a 32-ft sloop which was moored in the marina at Golfe Juan, and which he used only for, perhaps, a dozen day sails in the course of a year. His co-owners had most of the use of her and arranged all the maintenance and paperwork – an arrangement which suited all of them well.

He had a pleasant feeling of excitement and elation at the prospect of spending the day alone with Sylvia. Bridie needed the little Renault for shopping so Frances, though thoroughly disapproving of their spending the day together, had reluctantly agreed to run them over to Golfe Juan and pick them up again from the jetty at 5 pm. Manju had prepared a packed lunch for them, Charlie had put two bottles of 'The Widow' and a six-pack of Kronenbourg in a haversack; it was 8.30 am and they were ready for the off.

Frances maintained a frigid silence on the journey, mumbling under her breath at the traffic to register how great an imposition this was. The only remark she addressed directly to them, as they pulled into Golfe Juan was: 'You know the twins would *love* to go sailing with you, Uncle Charlie.'

'And so they shall, Frances, so they shall.' Charlie replied, ignoring the reproach in her remark. Having removed their gear from the back of the Volvo, Charlie shut the tailgate. 'Thanks awfully for bringing us, Frances, see you here at five.'

'Have fun!' she said in an unpleasantly suggestive tone.

'Oh, we shall.' he replied.

'Now, Sylvia,' he said, taking her arm and striding towards a little bar in

Les Iles de Lérins

the opposite direction to the port, 'if there's one rule I've learnt in life, it's that a day's sailing must always be preceded by a little café-cognac.'

'But it's only 9 am!'

'Never mind, it's nourishing and fortifies one against the cold.'

'It's not cold.'

'Stop arguing, woman.'

Sitting at a pavement table outside the bar, big glasses of cognac and tiny cups of strong, black coffee in front of them, Sylvia pointed to a small stone memorial at the water's edge on the opposite side of the road. 'What's that?' she asked.

'That marks the spot where Bonaparte landed in France after his escape from Elba.' Charlie replied. 'Of course, it didn't look like this in those days,' he added, indicating the vast marina complex with a sweep of his arm, 'it didn't look like this ten years ago, either. There were just a couple of jetties then.'

After what seemed an endless walk along wooden-planked pontoons, they reached their boat, which looked, Sylvia thought, much the same as countless other yachts on the jetty. It had a sparkling white hull, a tall, aluminium mast and a dark blue mainsail cover. Sylvia, never having sailed before, was completely oblivious to the act of seamanship she was witnessing as Charlie sailed the yacht, without using the engine, out of the crowded moorings, through narrow channels between rows of tightly packed craft to the open sea beyond. They had just had the big mainsail up but, once outside the harbour Charlie said: 'Right, we'll get the jib on her now. Sit here and take the tiller. Just keep heading for that house on the hill there.' He pointed, 'See it?'

'Yes, but what shall I do?'

Charlie put his hands over hers. 'Push away from you, like that, and you turn to the left.' The bows swung to port. 'Pull towards you, like this, and you turn to the right. Simple. Now you see the burgee at the top of the mast?'

'The little flag thing?'

'Yes, well that shows you which way the wind is blowing. When I say 'luff up' push away on the tiller until her bows come up into the wind and that burgee is pointing astern. Then just hold her there till I get back. The boom will swing into the centre, so mind your head, and the sail will flap and make a lot of noise. Don't panic, just concentrate on keeping her head into the wind.'

Before Sylvia could protest, Charlie had gone forward to the bows and was clipping on a sail, which he had pulled up through a hatch on the foredeck, to the wire forestay which ran from the bow to the top of the mast. Her brow was furrowed with concentration as she tried to keep the bows pointing at the white house on the hill. Then he called out: 'OK, luff up.'

She pushed the tiller away from her and watched the bows swing round into the wind. The boom came into the centre where it rattled and clanked and the big mainsail flapped alarmingly. The burgee was pointing over the stern. There was a flutter of white as the jib went soaring up its stay, then Charlie was back in the cockpit.

'Well done! Now pay her off.'

'Huh?'

'Pull the tiller up and head back for the house on the hill.' There was the chattering of a winch as Charlie sheeted in the jib, the sails filled, the yacht heeled over at a perilous angle and they were sailing. The bows smacked into the waves sending clouds of white spray into the air on either side of the hull, the rigging was taught and straining with the power of the wind and a creamy white wake stretched out astern towards the harbour mouth which already seemed a long way behind. Sylvia felt an enormous sense of elation.

'This is fantastic!' she shouted above the howl of the wind. 'Why have I never done this before?'

'This is called tacking,' Charlie explained to her, 'we can't sail straight into the wind so we have to zigzag either side of it to work our way to windward. We have to come about now, onto the other leg of the zigzag. First, you shout out 'Ready About!' to warn your crew.'

Les Iles de Lérins

'Aye, aye Sir! Ready about!'

'Now, when you're ready, shout 'Lee Oh!', put the helm down and bring her through the eye of the wind and on to the other tack. You want to be heading more or less for that lighthouse.' He pointed to a tall, white finger off to starboard.

'Here we go then, Lee Oh!' she shouted and pushed down on the tiller. The bows swung through the wind, the boom came into the centre then out the other side. Charlie sheeted the sails in on the new side. 'Change sides,' he called and they both moved over to the weather side of the cockpit.

Charlie put his hand over hers to adjust the course. Every time he did this she felt a tingle of pleasure which she was reluctant to acknowledge to herself. 'Just keep her heading . . . just there,' he said. 'we must pass to the left of the lighthouse as we see it now.' He trimmed the sails a bit then sat down beside her. 'And the good news is that, when we're abreast of the lighthouse it will be time for our first cool beer.' His hair was tousled with the wind. He looks ten years younger Sylvia thought.

Once round the light, two cans of Kronenbourg were breached and they altered course for the Iles de Lérins. The sheets were eased and Charlie settled the yacht onto a broad reach to take them round the south side of the islands. As the Ile Saint Honorat dropped aft on their starboard quarter Charlie said sternly: 'The catering is a bit relaxed today isn't it?' and Sylvia, laughing, descended to the cabin for two more cans of beer. Another change of course and they were running before the wind towards the channel between the Ile Sainte Marguerite and the Ile Saint Honorat. The boat was upright now and the motion far less violent.

When they reached the centre of the channel, Charlie eased the yacht in towards the southern shore, furled the sails and dropped anchor. 'Time for lunch.' he said, 'What would you like to do? I can either get the dinghy out and we can go ashore for a picnic, or we can just stay on board.'

'Oh, let's stay on board.' said Sylvia, noting that people from several other anchored yachts were already on the island. She did not want other people intruding on their special time together. She unpacked the hamper and laid out their picnic in the cockpit while Charlie opened the champagne. She felt simply marvellous. Her skin was tingling with the wind, her lips were salty from the spray and she was happier than she had felt for a very long time. They ate, chatted and finished the first bottle of champagne. Sailing is glorious, she thought; the sunshine is glorious; Charlie's company is glorious; samosas and champagne are glorious; *everything* is glorious.

Do you think we ought to have a crack at that other bottle?' Charlie asked. 'Well, it's not serving any useful purpose stuck in the fridge, is it?' she replied. She said what a lovely boat it was. Charlie replied that it served its purpose but he did not consider it a 'proper boat'. What did he consider a 'proper boat' she asked.

'Oh, a wooden boat, I suppose, with varnished, carvel topsides and teak laid decks. These glassfibre hulls are tremendously practical and virtually maintenance-free but there's nothing like a wooden hull – it works with the motion of the seas; it feels good; it smells good. It's like an old house. I could never feel really at peace in a modern house with a damp course and double glazing. Old boats and old houses have a spiritual patina which soothes the soul.' He was far away, Sylvia thought, noting the distant look in his eyes.

'Yes, a boat with a long, straight keel and a deep rudder, a boat which will cross oceans, a proper boat which will turn into the wind and keep a heavy sea without assistance. None of this skeg and fin nonsense.' he said contemptuously, dismissing the results of forty years of state-of-the-art marine design. 'They were all proper boats when I was a lad,' he continued, 'the whole sailing world was different then. There weren't so many yachts around and there was room to breathe, and room to sail. Everybody knew everybody else and they were all such nice people. Cowes Week in the 1950s was like a big family gathering and the racing was fun. There was none of this push-shove yuppyism about the sport. It's all changed now, of course, the Solent today is like a great caravan park with people to match.' He's not unlike Aunt Kate in his way, Sylvia thought, he's living in the past; and nothing wrong with that.

Les Iles de Lérins

They sat on the deck in the sunshine enjoying the view, drinking champagne and getting deliciously tipsy.

'That,' said Charlie, indicating the Ile Sainte Marguerite with a nod of his head, 'is where the Man in the Iron Mask was incarcerated.'

'Really?' Sylvia replied. Her head was swimming pleasantly with the champagne. She was so happy and completely relaxed. She had been rather hoping that Charlie might have put his arm round her, or something – something to consolidate the feeling of affection for him which had been growing daily inside her since that first day at the airport and which, she felt, was reciprocated. But there was no sign of it and now she sensed a sudden tension in him.

'What's wrong?'

Charlie didn't reply, he was looking out to sea and up at the sky. The dreamy, little boy look had gone from his face which had suddenly hardened.'

'Get the lunch stuff below. Quickly. We've got to get out of here.'

By the time she had stowed the hamper in the saloon and returned to the top of the companion-way ladder, the wind was shrieking in the rigging and there was flying spindrift from the tops of the waves. Charlie had hoisted the mainsail and was up in the bows trying to haul in the anchor, but the power of the sudden storm was such that the cable was taut as an iron rod. He could not move it. He leaped into the cockpit and started the engine.

'We're going to push ahead with the motor to get the tension off that anchor cable. Take the tiller and keep her head pointed at that buoy. This is the throttle here.' he indicated a lever with a red knob at the side of the cockpit. 'Forward for faster. Listen for my commands.'

Charlie returned to the foredeck and heaved at the cable. Still it would not move. 'A bit faster.' he shouted. Sylvia inched the lever forward and heard the engine below her increase in speed. Still the cable wouldn't move.

'Faster still.'

At last she could see the cable coming in until Charlie shouted: 'Full throttle now and steer for the buoy.' The engine roared and the yacht thrashed its way through steep waves towards the eastern mouth of the channel. Sylvia, from the corner of her eye, saw signs of panic on the other boats at the anchorage. They, too, were trying desperately to weigh anchor and get out to sea. She saw Charlie swing the anchor inboard and lash it to the deck. The jib was going up the forestay, then Charlie was back in the cockpit beside her. He paid the boat off, the sails filled and the deck slanted to a crazy angle. The yacht gathered speed and, as they passed the buoy close to starboard, Charlie cut the engine. He trimmed the sails and settled the boat on a course for home. They were going like a train. The leeward gunwale was under the water and each time the bows smashed into a trough, the spray was flung back down the deck to the cockpit. They were both getting soaked.

'Oilies in the locker at the foot of the ladder.' Charlie shouted. The movement of the boat was so violent, and the angle of its heel so steep, that Sylvia had some difficulty in descending the ladder and getting back up again with yellow sou'westers and oilskins. It was just as well she did because, within a few minutes, the heavens opened and the rain was being driven horizontally across the surface of the angry sea. Suddenly, the land ahead had disappeared. She looked astern and there was no sign of the islands. Everything was obscured by driving rain and flying spume. They were alone on the high seas. Sylvia's anxiety turned to alarm. How could they find their way back to port?

Then she looked at Charlie and he was smiling reassuringly at her beneath the peak of his sou'wester. Then she knew that all would be well. She sat beside him and fluttering her eyelids theatrically through the salt spray running down her face said: 'My Hero!'

Charlie grinned, put his arm round her and squeezed her to him. So that's what it took, she thought.

The rain and the wind showed no sign of abating as the little yacht thrashed and corkscrewed its way through the gloom in the general direction, Sylvia hoped, of home. But Charlie's arm was round her and she was happy and content.

Les Iles de Lérins

'Haven't we got another beer?' he shouted in her ear.

'I'm not going down below in this.' she shouted back.

'You'd better take the helm then and I'll go.'

'No fear! I'll go.'

The storm blew over as suddenly as it had come upon them. The rain stopped, the wind moderated and backed, the sun returned and there, on their starboard beam, was the 'first cool beer' lighthouse and, in the distance, dead ahead, the tops of the masts above the breakwater at Golfe Juan. The mainsail had been reefed down and now Charlie shook out the reefs and raised it to the top of the mast again.

'Should dry out by the time we get back.' he said.

As he had shown no inclination to put his arm around her again, Sylvia grasped the brim of Charlie's sou'wester on both sides and, pulling it down over his ears like the flaps of a deerstalker, pulled his head to her and kissed him firmly on the lips. 'Thank you, Charlie,' she said, 'for one of the happiest days of my life.' Charlie felt too weak at the knees to reply.

As they walked back up the pontoon hand-in-hand, tired, still slightly tipsy but glowing with health and happiness, they noticed the Volvo parked on the road waiting for them. Sylvia hurriedly disengaged her hand from his, but he seized it back again then, as they crossed the road to the car, put his arm round her shoulders and drew her to him.

'Might as well give Frances her money's worth.' he said.

16. Les Sapeurs-Pompiers

At 6.15 every morning, including Sundays, Dhani would leave the house and walk down the hill to the baker's shop on the Avenue Jules Grec where he would buy the morning bread. He would reach the shop as it opened at 6.30 and, except when there were guests staying at the villa, the order never varied – one pain au restaurant, two baguettes, seven croissants and two pain au chocolat.

On his way, he would meet the dog shit men. Antibes was a well managed town with beautiful, flower-bedecked boulevards but, despite the regularly-placed signs depicting a small, defecating dog and warning of the penalties which owners faced if they allowed their pet to emulate its example, there was still a major problem. So, early each morning, little men with carts and shovels did their rounds of the residential areas. First, on the hill itself, there was Jacques who was rotund and jovial and would always exchange a jokey greeting with Dhani as he passed. Dhani might say: 'You're a bit behind this morning, Jacques.' or 'You've missed a bit there.' to which Jacques would reply with some couthy, provencal quip the full meaning of which Dhani seldom understood, but he would laugh amicably just the same.

On the Avenue Jules Grec was Pierre who was hunched and boney and always had a Gauloise hanging from the corner of his mouth. Pierre was not the jokey type but would always exchange a formal 'Bonjour, Monsieur.' with Dhani and would sometimes press a handful of change into his hand with a request that he should bring him back a packet of cigarettes from the tabac, two doors down for the baker's. Dhani was always only too happy to oblige.

About midway between the points where Jacques and Pierre were performing their duties, Madame Gevry would emerge from the apartment block where she lived, in dressing gown and carpet slippers, with her elderly poodle on a lead. She would look from right to left to establish which of

Les Sapeurs-Pompiers

Les Hommes de Ville was farthest from her before deciding which section of the freshly-swept pavement she would encourage her dog to foul.

On the other side of the broad, tree-lined avenue, roughly opposite the baker's shop, was the Sapeurs-Pompiers station with a long row of garages which housed the emergency vehicles of the Ville d'Antibes. At the time that Dhani collected the bread each morning, the duty watch was preparing for its breakfast and one of the pompiers would be despatched across the road for the bread. Consequently, Dhani knew most of the men with whom he would always exchange a friendly greeting. The pompiers also knew Dhani and knew of his background which, as men of action themselves, they were able to understand. They would point out his upright, quick-pacing little figure to new recruits and say: 'There goes a man of courage and honour who you should be proud to know.'

When, therefore, Dhani mentioned to the young man beside him in the shop that there was a matter in which he would appreciate their assistance, he was conducted instantly across the road and taken to the Section Officer who shook his hand warmly and enquired how they could help.

There was a pedestrian underpass beneath the railway station which provided a significant shortcut between the Boulevard General Vautrin and the town centre. It was used, mainly, by women going shopping, including Bridie and Manju on occasions, but was fast becoming a no-go area due to the activities of a bunch of youths who hung around the entrances and harassed women using the tunnel. Their latest sport, Dhani explained to the pompiers, was to rig up little explosive charges in the tunnel, using fireworks, which they would detonate when some unfortunate woman was halfway through. Dhani had tried to catch them on his own, he explained, but could not be at both ends of the tunnel at the same time. He needed a little assistance.

The Section Officer looked grave. It was really a matter for the police, he said, but he was sure that some of the lads would help when they were off duty. But as Dhani outlined his plan, pointing out that the danger of fire in the underpass from these home-made explosive devices was, surely, a matter for the Sapeurs-Pompiers, the gravity changed to mirth and the whole duty watch jostled each other to put forward their own detailed suggestions.

* * *

Charlie, lying awake in bed, heard Dhani unbarring the gate on his way for the bread. He had had a restless night reliving his day's sailing with Sylvia and the events which had occurred. It had been reckless stupidity, he thought with hindsight, to have cuddled her like that to provoke Frances, who was a vicious little bitch and would already, he had no doubt, have related the incident to the family, highly dramatised and in the most damning way possible.

Should he have done it at all, he wondered, never mind Frances? Was he being far too forward with his sister-in-law? Was he behaving like a dirty old man and running the risk of his family's contempt and, worse, of ruining what was becoming such a delightful friendship?

She had kissed him, of course, but was that just a playful action in the euphoria of a very happy day? They had both had a fair bit to drink. Was he confusing an act of demonstrative friendship with flirtation? There was no doubt he was very attracted to Sylvia and, in the short time he had known her, she had started to throw into question so many of the prejudices, he now recognised them as such, which he had previously imagined would lie undisturbed in some inactive corner of his mind for the rest of his life. He had no business being attracted to her, he told himself; he was 56, for heaven's sake, well past the age when this sort of thing was acceptable. He had always believed that people should grow old with dignity, and there was no dignity in losing one's composure over a woman at the age of 56. And why, he asked himself, should he even contemplate jeopardising the well-ordered and comfortable life he enjoyed with the intrusion of a romantic entanglement, with all the misery and discomfort which that entailed?

And yet, his heart started fluttering every time he saw the wretched woman. He found himself manoeuvring to be in the same room as her, to cross her path in the garden or the hall. He felt quite sure that her feelings for him were purely platonic. She seemed to enjoy his company and the slightly mischievous charade which Frances's disapproval of their friendship had instigated; but this was all it was. If he tried to make any more of it, he was in danger of making a fool of himself.

Why did God have to invent women, he wondered as he prepared to shave, couldn't he have devised some equally efficient but less tiresome means of populating the earth?

* * *

Mattie was also awake at 6.15 and worrying. She always deferred to Kate in all matters of import – Kate's mind had always been so much better than her own and, of late, Mattie was finding it so difficult to remember things. But she really did feel that Kate was not quite playing the game with Great Aunt Sade's paintings. Charlie had very kindly undertaken to review, among other matters, their financial position, and it seemed all wrong that Kate should be concealing from him the source of income which, over the past several years, had been the main thing which had enabled them to balance the books.

She could not quite understand what Kate's motives were. She knew, of course, that her sister wanted to redress Aunt Sade's reputation in the family as a flatulent, Victorian dauber who had produced a mountain of paintings which nobody wanted, but the sale of several pictures at astoundingly high prices had, she felt, already made the point. So why did Kate continue this game of secrecy? Perhaps she wanted to delay the grand revelation until all the pictures had been sold, and it would be recognised that Aunt Sade had restored the family fortunes for several generations to come. But there were mountains of the canvases in the attic, all inadequately insured, and she and Kate would both be dead long before such a plan could be fulfilled. It all seemed rather silly and obsessive, Mattie thought. She had told her sister so but there was no moving Kate once she dug her heels in.

It was against her upbringing to sneak, particularly on a sister, but she really wondered if she should not tip Charlie the wink. Perhaps, on balance, not, she decided – her life would not be worth living if Kate found out as she undoubtedly would.

* * *

At around the time that Charlie and Sylvia had been moored off the Iles des Lérins, Emma had been lunching with a group of friends at a pavement café in Werewolf Alley and had spotted Steve Fitzgerald sitting alone at a table on the other side of the terrace. She crept up behind him.

'Well, hello thay-ur,' she said in an abominable attempt at a Dixie accent, 'Can I ask you to join us for a little mint julep or some-thay-ung?'

'You certainly cay-un, may-um.' Steve replied with more authentic annunciation.

Though a bit older than most of the group, he had joined in their youthful banter in a relaxed and good humoured way. Emma learned that he worked in the American embassy in Paris and was spending a short holiday on the coast looking for Irish paintings for his parents, who lived in Boston and were of Irish descent.

'Well, you certainly came to the right place.' Emma said, remembering the number of Irish scenes which adorned the walls of the villa. 'Is that why you came to our house, to see Aunt Kate?'

Steve hesitated before replying, remembering the way that he and Herbert had received the bums' rush from Miss Morton-Stewart when Emma had appeared, and recalling Herbert's speculation as to the likely cause of her behaviour. Perhaps the old lady did not wish her niece to know what she was up to. He answered guardedly: 'I was just accompanying a friend.'

Emma frowned at what she considered, in view of his declared quest for Irish paintings, a very improbable explanation. 'Curiouser and curiouser.' she said.

Before they dispersed, Steve had asked her to have dinner with him the

Les Sapeurs-Pompiers

next day. 'I'd like that,' she said, remembering how American girls always replied to that question in the movies, 'but first, you'll have to meet my folks.'

'Might that not be a little awkward?' he asked, with visions of a furious Aunt Kate pursuing him down the drive in her bath chair.

'We'll just have to see, won't we?' Emma replied archly.

So it had been arranged that Steve would call for her the next evening and have a drink with the family before taking her to the Royal Gray in Cannes. Meanwhile, Emma had some squaring off to do with Aunt Kate.

* * *

'It's perfectly disgusting.' Frances railed.

'You're over reacting again, Frances,' her husband replied, 'there's nothing wrong with a friendly hug.'

'It was more than that. You didn't see them, and they were holding hands as they came along the jetty. You'd think Charlie would know better – stupid old fool.'

'You really can be very unreasonable, Frances. They are both unattached adults and you can hardly consider holding hands an affront to public decency, or a threat to the morals of the young.'

'Charlie is a gentleman. He should know how to behave. One doesn't expect anything better from her, of course – a common little Irish barmaid.'

'She's an extremely nice person, actually, and the fact that she was once a barmaid should not influence your opinion of her. She's part of the family now.'

'Not as central a part as she would like. Not content with snaring Uncle Jimmy and driving him to an early grave, now she's after Charlie.'

'That's a monstrous thing to say. It was not Sylvia that drove James to an early grave, from what I've heard of the old swine. She probably prolonged his life more than you'd care to know.'

'Nonsense!'

'And as to her chasing Charlie, as I've said before, if anyone is doing the chasing it's Charlie. And why the hell shouldn't he? Best of luck to him I say.'

'Yes, you would say that, wouldn't you? The chauvinist pigs must stick together, mustn't they?'

'Best of luck to them *both*, perhaps I should have said.'

'So you admit that she's as much to blame as he is?'

'What giant stride of logic brought you to that conclusion? I don't accept that either of them is to *blame*. Blame doesn't enter into it. They are simply two very nice people who seem to find pleasure in each other's company and, if there's anything more to it than that, it is nobody's business but their own.'

'Oh, you are wet, Richard.'

'By wet, you mean fair."

'By wet, I mean wet."

* * *

'Merci, Madame Hogan.' Henri said as he rose from the kitchen table after his tea, shirt tucked into his trousers, hair combed and perhaps marginally less greasy than usual. 'Merci, Madame Limbu.'

He backed respectfully out of the door with a little bow. 'Merci, Mesdames. Vous êtes trés gentile.'

'Oh, good gracious!' said Manju.

'Ah sure, we'll make something of that boy yet, chust, we'll make something of him yet.' said Bridie.

17. Steve Fitzgerald

'Darling Aunt Kate,' Emma said, putting her arms round the old lady and kissing her warmly on the cheek, 'you remember that young man who was in the house the other day?'

'The American?'

'Yes, darling.' she squatted on the floor at her aunt's feet looking up at her adoringly. 'Well, he's asked me to go to dinner with him at the Royal Gray this evening. He's such a nice young man and I know you'll thoroughly approve of him when you get to know him better. I bumped into him in Juan les Pins yesterday. I was asking him what he was doing here seeing you with that other funny little man.'

'And what did he say?'

'Oh, he wouldn't tell me. Quite refused to discuss it at all. Said it was entirely between you and him and nobody else's business.'

'Quite right.' said Kate, much relieved.

'Well, darling, I know what importance you place on correct procedure so I explained to him that I couldn't possibly go out with him until he had met my family properly and that he must come round this evening and have a drink with us first. Was that the right thing to do, Aunt Kate?'

'I suppose so, dear.'

'I thought so, darling. I asked myself at the time 'What would Aunt Kate want me to do?' He'll be here about seven. He's so much looking forward to seeing you again; said what a very dignified lady you were.'

Charlie, who had overheard this conversation, caught Emma's eye as she left the room.

'You wheedling little minx!' he hissed at her.

* * *

Easter at the Villa Victoria

> *Kilkenny*
> *Co. Cork*
> *Eire*
> *4th April 1996*

Dear Bridie,

I heard from the Agent yesterday and he says it would be quite all right for you to have the cottage if you should need it. He says he couldn't reserve it firmly for you without a deposit but there's not much chance that anyone else would want it. There's all those cottages by the Home Farm and them with no money to do them up and nobody wanting to live there anyway. The two cottages up by Pike's Wood are sold now (holiday homes of course) and Katie Brannigan died last week so there's another that will be available, I shouldn't wonder, she had no folk that anyone knows of. Mick wondered if you might not be better off with Granny O'Hara's place on the corner by Spear's Meadow? There'd be less to do to it and there's been folks from Cork that's been in it since last autumn so there's been fires lit. Mick says it's nearer the village to walk though I don't think there's much in it myself. So, that's another to keep in mind if you do have to come back.

I ran into Hetty in the market last week and she was asking after you. She's still jumping over the stream every morning, poor daft cratur, may the Lord help her. And Michael Donovan, him whose brother was in the Excise at Bandon, he's back from England and his wife expecting her seventh. The first boy was simple it seems and he's away to a home near Dublin, poor soul. Mick's a man short just now so I must go to help with the milking. Supposed to be sick but the word is he's got a fancy woman in Bandon and him two doors from Father O'Brien. Mick won't have him back if he's any sense.

Tell me if there's any more enquiries you want me to be making but I hope it won't come to anything now.

Your affect. sister, Mary

* * *

Herbert Pontefract sat morosely at his desk struggling to come to terms with the fact that there were no other jobs he could find, or invent, to further delay his departure for home.

It was their wedding anniversary tomorrow, which had been hanging over him like a black cloud for several weeks as, in a weaker than usual moment, under excessive pressure from Maud, he had agreed that they would have a celebration lunch, with champagne, at the Hotel des Etoiles in Juan-les-Pins. Herbert hated such places. He felt awkward and self-conscious in smart hotels – the sort of places he had sometimes had to go with his Knightbridge colleagues. It was not so bad if he was a guest when he could just roll with the flow and was not expected to take any executive action. But to have to manage such an occasion himself – to summon waiters, order wine and interpret menus he did not understand, whilst suffering the contempt of haughty head waiters and other guests – this was his grossest nightmare.

Then there was Rupert St. John Powell's visit next week, the thought of which was making an almost equal contribution to his misery. The old girl in Antibes had asked for a valuation of her complete collection of paintings. There were hundreds of them, he had seen them stacked up in the attic. Herbert, who was not an art expert, did not feel qualified to undertake such a major valuation on his own so had been forced to summon help from London. Help with 19th century oils meant only one thing – Rupert St. John

Powell, pronounced, he had been told, Sinjun Pole, who, in terms of loathsomeness, was head and shoulders above all his other tormentors at the London office. He would undoubtedly protract his visit for longer than the valuation justified, Herbert knew, so he could cavort around visiting chums and lording it with the Nice office staff and customers.

It was all he needed, to have that polo-playing ponce breathing down his neck for most of next week.

* * *

It was pointless trying to conceal it from herself, Sylvia reasoned, she was falling in love with Charlie and was in danger of making a fool of herself – indeed, she might already have done so. She'd had far too much to drink yesterday. If she had been more clear headed she would never have dreamed of kissing him like that or of taking his hand on the pontoon. It had been such a very happy day and, at the time, it seemed like the natural thing to do; she had wanted him to know how much she had enjoyed being with him. That business, though, in front of Frances, that was really crass – her position in the family was fragile enough without handing Frances ammunition on a plate. What on earth had possessed her to behave in such a reckless way.

It had been wonderful the way they had all, except Frances of course, made her feel so welcome and so much part of the family. It had come to mean a great deal to her; she had been very lonely since Jimmy's death. And now, if Frances put the boot in, as she certainly would, she could find herself ostracised and lonely again, after all the progress she had made.

But she recognised that the family's opinion of her, important as it was, was actually far less important than Charlie's. He was such a gentleman, he would never make her feel awkward or embarrassed but what on earth must he think of her now. She had sensed a very slight reserve in his manner towards her at lunch; was this the beginning of the end of the friendship she had come to value so highly, she wondered.

Steve Fitzgerald

She had loved Jimmy dearly in spite of all his faults. She had loved his sense of fun, his gentleness and the aura of stability and self-confidence which only a background like his could endow. Charlie was very like Jimmy, but without the faults. In place of Jimmy's impulsive irresponsibility, which, she had to admit, had been great fun, on occasions, Charlie's nature was cautious and concerned. He saw the best in everyone and continually made allowances for shortcomings in others. He was generous with that part of himself which he gave so readily to those he loved; he was loyal, fair and compassionate.

She realised now that she had started to fall in love with Charlie from that first day at the airport but it was only since yesterday that she had admitted it to herself. There had been odd moments when she had thought that be might be beginning to feel the same about her but she now realised that this had been presumptuous. He must have sensed her growing feelings for him and, because he was so kind and so gentlemanly, had not wished to hurt her by making her think that his own feelings were at a different level. It seemed quite clear to her now and she knew what would happen next: he would very gradually and very gently withdraw from her. There would be no outward change in their relationship, he would still be friendly and kind and attentive, and only the two of them would be aware that the limits of their friendship had now been defined and the magic thread had been cut.

Charlie would shortly be going out for his evening beer. If he asked her to go with him, which she prayed he would, she could perhaps find something to say to allay any fears he might have of her becoming a nuisance. Then they could, at least, perhaps, save a part of their friendship. But Sylvia's fears were confirmed as she heard him start the little Renault and head down the hill without even popping his head round the door. 'I've really blown it.' she said to herself. She felt her face flush and a knot in her stomach and was overcome by a deep sense of loneliness and sadness.

* * *

Charlie had a great affection and respect for Americans. He had come across quite a few in the course of his service career and had seldom met one that he did not like. He had always found them sensible, articulate, courteous and clean. But his pro-American feelings were founded on something more substantial than a casual judgement based on his own personal acquaintances.

Charlie hated ingratitude. The thing he liked least about the French was their, at best, reluctance and, at worst, refusal, to acknowledge the fact that Britain had saved their skins in two world wars. National pride was a fine thing, he wished that more of it was evident in Britain today, but national pride was in no way enhanced by a de Gaullist refusal to acknowledge national debt. Throughout his life, Charlie had wasted no opportunity to remind those who would denounce or lampoon the Americans, that Britain had itself, twice this century, been baled out by that great and generous-hearted nation.

What fascinated him most about the United States was the miracle of how such a vast collection of such polymorphic peoples could have compounded themselves into a nation at all – let alone a nation which had provided such steadfast world leadership since the demise of the British Empire. He valued highly the integrity of their foreign policy and their wisdom on the world stage. For Charlie, the Special Relationship had never wavered and he was proud, and thankful, to have America as Britain's friend and ally.

He was delighted, therefore, to learn that Emma's new friend, who was due any moment for drinks, was American, and genuinely looked forward to meeting him.

As Steve Fitzgerald came up the steps of the veranda, smartly dressed in lightweight suit, collar and tie, Charlie recalled the horrific sight of Lothario making the same entrance. Steve was pure blueberry pie – short haired, clean, with a manly bearing and an open, honest face. Good looking too, but without that nauseatingly effeminate air of self-esteem so often evident in good looking men. Charlie liked the cut of his jib. Here, he thought, was a much more suitable escort for his niece.

Steve Fitzgerald

Emma introduced him to the Aunts and then to Charlie. A good, firm handshake, a dry palm and he looks you straight in the eye, Charlie noted with approval. 'What would you like to drink, Steve?'

'May I have a beer, Sir?'

'You certainly may.'

Steve chatted for some of the time with the Aunts and Sylvia in a friendly, relaxed manner and impressed them all with his comportment. When he moved on to Frances, who had already fuelled her outrage over the Charlie/Sylvia situation with two very large gins, his reception was less amiable.

'What's your name again?' Frances asked, 'I can't possibly keep up with the names of all the men Emma brings to the house.'

'Steve Fitzgerald.' he replied.

'And you are from New York, I suppose?' she said dismissively.

'No, I'm from Boston, actually.'

'Boston. Isn't that where you wasted all that tea.'

'Well, if you consider the first move in the establishment of our nationhood a 'waste', yes, I suppose so.' Steve replied laughingly and was glad to be rescued from her hostility by Charlie who engaged him in conversation for some time until Emma came up and said: 'Am I going to get any dinner tonight, then?'

'Greedy little thing! Steve and I were having a very interesting talk.' then turning to Steve, 'Well, it was very nice meeting you, Steve. I do hope we'll see more of you.'

'Thank you very much, Sir. I hope so too.'

After Emma and Steve had left, the family went in to dinner and all were agreed what a thoroughly nice young man Steve was. Frances did not join in the acclaim and said, merely: 'What an *extraordinary* tie he was wearing – bizarre, even for a Yank.'

* * *

Later, over after-dinner coffee at the Royal Gray, Steve said to Emma: 'Seems a really nice guy that uncle of yours.'

'Yes,' Emma replied. 'he's a poppet; a bit Victorian at times but he's always been really sweet to Mummy and me. He protects us from Frances, too.'

'What's with that Frances?' Steve asked.

'It's all to do with class. You're an American; you wouldn't understand.'

'Try me.'

'Well, in the eyes of the family, my father married beneath him. My mother was a barmaid so she and I have never been accepted until quite recently. Frances is the only one who still gives us the cold shoulder.'

'How cruel, and how ridiculous.'

'Not really, it's the way they were brought up. Anyway, you have a class system too, except that yours is based on money – which is the one thing that has absolutely no relevance at all in ours.'

'Well, we have 'Old Money' and 'New Money' which I guess amounts to much the same thing.'

'Not really; money is money.'

'So, what does constitute gentility with the British?'

Emma thought for a moment. 'Well, Uncle Charlie says it's down to four things – Breeding, Manners, Education and Position. In the old days it was purely Breeding that mattered but, nowadays, you have to have two out of four to qualify.'

'And what about titles?'

'Oh, they don't enter into it. You have Lords whose fathers were grocers and you have ancient families who have never been offered a title or have chosen never to accept one.'

'Oh my!'

'Oh yes. That's the biggest buzz of all with some of them. Charlie was telling me about some great uncle of mine who was governor of some colony or other; he refused a knighthood because he said he was a gentleman already!'

'Well, well!'

'And there were periods when titles were sold for political donations and they were bought up by all the moneylenders and war profiteers; and nowadays, they give knighthoods to footballers and pop singers.'

'And what's wrong with that?'

'Nothing, I suppose. But you can see why many people think the whole system has been debased – a long-haired, drug-taking rock star receiving the same honour as a man who has given a lifetime of valuable service to his country.'

'Well, anyway,' Steve said, 'I think people should be judged on what they are and what they do, not on what their grandparents were.'

'Couldn't agree more. Mummy, from her humble, Irish background, is an intelligent, kind and beautiful person, and infinitely superior in every way to Daddy who, despite his breeding and background, was a bit of an old reprobate. The more I think of it, the more I think that he was damned lucky to get her to marry him. She deserved far better.'

'Someone like Uncle Charlie, perhaps?'

'Yes.'

Easter at the Villa Victoria

18. The Pontefracts' Anniversary Lunch

Mr. and Mrs. Pontefract made their entrance to the lobby of the Hotel des Etoiles at five minutes to noon. Herbert wore dark trousers and an ill-fitting beige jacket which he had bought, at Maud's insistence, and under some pressure as the shop was about to close, off the peg at Marks & Spencers. If he allowed his arms to hang down, the sleeves dropped almost to his knuckles and the shoulders assumed a strange camber which, together with his Panama hat, gave him the appearance of a minor racketeer of the 1920s. When buttoned, a medium-sized teddy bear could have joined him, without constriction, within its ample folds.

Maud, on the other hand, had optimistically selected a white, silk slub dress, with red polka dots, which was palpably a size too small for her. It wrinkled round her hips and constrained the movement of her legs. The ensemble was completed with white, high-heeled shoes, a white handbag and a wide-brimmed straw hat which would not have looked out of place at Ascot.

They were greeted by an attentive porter who directed them through a door onto the terrace when Herbert had announced their intention of having an aperitif followed by lunch.

'We'll have our aperitif here, Herbert.' Maud said, selecting a quiet table in the corner.

The Hotel des Etoiles had been built in the 1920s since when it had been in the ownership of the same family. In the centre of its south elevation, steps, flanked by miniature bay trees in tubs, descended to a wide terrace where dinner was served each evening, when the weather was clement, which was most of the time, at tables arranged along a stone balustrade, beyond which was the sea. The wall of the hotel overlooking the terrace was covered with a dense growth of bougainvillaea through which peeped the balconies of the premium-price, sea-view rooms. The area was lit at

The Pontefracts' Anniversary Lunch

night with white glass globes on wrought iron standards fixed on the balustrade. At the west side of the terrace, more steps gave access to a luxurious bar within the hotel.

'There's nobody around.' Maud said.

'Perhaps we're a bit early.'

'Someone will come, I expect.'

Having waited for ten minutes, there was still no sign of a waiter or of any other guests appearing on the terrace for their pre-prandial aperitifs.

'Go to the bar, Herbert, and get a waiter.' she said.

Herbert ascended the steps to the bar to find that it, also, was deserted and there was no sign of a bell or other means to summon assistance. On his way back to their table he heard the sound of voices from below the balustrade and, walking over to it, looked over the edge.

'Everyone's down here.' he called to Maud.

She joined him and looked over the edge. There, below them, was another level to which the whole life of the hotel apparently migrated at this time of day. A concrete platform, not unlike the deck of a luxury liner, stretched the length of the upper terrace ending in a long jetty from which bathing and water skiing was taking place. All along the deck, pretty tables with blue and white cloths, parasols and white cane chairs, were laid up for lunch for which a few guests were already preparing. At the end of the deck, where the jetty started, was a bar area under a huge, blue and white awning, where most of the guests appeared to be. A host of smartly-dressed waiters weaved in and out of the tables bearing trays of long, cold drinks to guests gathered in groups beneath the awning or recumbent on reclining chairs in the sun.

'Well, that's where we go.' said Maud, 'What are you waiting for?'

At the foot of the steps, which Maud had a certain amount of difficulty in negotiating due to the tightness of her dress, they were greeted by a smiling waiter. 'Bonjour, Monsieur-Dame, lunch for two?'

'We'd like a drink first.' Maud said.

'Of course, Madame. Please take a seat,' he indicated the bar area, 'and I will get the Captain for you.'

Easter at the Villa Victoria

The Captain, a title reflecting the shipboard atmosphere of the terrace, Herbert assumed, arrived and snapped his fingers for a waiter to bring them the bottle of house champagne they ordered.

'Would you like to order your meal now, Monsieur, or wait a little while?'

'We'll wait a little while, thank you.' Maud said abruptly.

'Of course, Madame, I will reserve a table for when you are ready.'

After the first glass of champagne, the elation which Maud was beginning to feel at having found, at last, the glamorous life which had eluded her for so long, was shaken by the arrival of a golden-limbed German girl, wearing nothing but the briefest of bikini bottoms, who slumped down, bare breasts wobbling in Herbert's direction, in the chair facing him.

'Turn your chair round, Herbert.' Maud hissed at him. Then, beneath the bathers' shower at the neck of the jetty, now directly in Herbert's line of vision, another long-legged beauty peeled off her T shirt and began to wash herself.

'Turn your chair, turn your chair.'

By this time, Herbert had revolved nearly 180 degrees with his back to their table and had got the leg of his chair caught up in the rush matting on the deck, so he could turn no further in either direction. So, when the girl from the shower, sans T shirt, came and sat on his left side, he therefore had no option but to turn his head sharply to the right giving him a severe stab of pain in the neck. It was only a matter of time before his new line of sight was corrupted by another girl removing her clothes and, spondylosis denying any further movement of his head, Herbert struggled to free the trapped leg of his chair from the mat. It came free suddenly causing him to fall back against the table with a crash, spilling the remains of Maud's champagne on her silk slub dress and attracting the attention of every waiter and guest in the bar. The shower girl, who had also had her drink spilled over her, leaped to her feet upbraiding Herbert in noisy Italian for his carelessness, leading the other guests to believe that he had molested her in some way. A circle of frowning faces and bare bosoms surrounded his table until the Captain appeared and, with the authority of a Kensington nanny,

The Pontefracts' Anniversary Lunch

defused the situation by placing their glasses on a tray and saying firmly: 'Perhaps Monsieur would like to go to his table now.' Clearly, Monsieur did not have a choice.

Herbert, hot, sticky and miserably embarrassed, ordered the fish of the day, though he was not fond of fish, partly because that was what Maud wanted and partly because it was the only item on the menu he could understand. The sommelier placed an eight-page carte des vins in front of him and waited indulgently, pencil poised. Noting that Monsieur seemed a little flustered, he indicated a section on page five and suggested:

'Perhaps, with fish, a Chablis?' Herbert's eyes scrolled through the prices to find the cheapest but they all seemed equally extortionate.

'Which would you recommend?'

'The 1990 Vaillon here is very good,' he pointed with his pencil, 'Domain Moreau, Premier Cru.'

'Right.' Herbert nodded his head.

'An excellent choice, Monsieur.'

The fish of the day was rouget – small, red, bony fish served whole in a rich Provencal sauce which rendered it virtually impossible to separate the meagre portions of flesh from the abundance of bones. As he struggled through it, Herbert thought of a good fillet of Grimsby cod, fried in beer batter and served with chips and mushy peas and wondered, yet again, how the French had acquired their reputation for cuisine.

'Delicious, isn't it Herbert?' Maud said, trying hard to convince herself that it was so. Herbert merely grunted.

Then she was choking on a bone.

'Are you alright, dear?' he enquired anxiously, 'Here, have a bit of bread; drink some water.' She tried but was still choking.

'Hit me on the back.' she spluttered and, as he thumped her several times between the shoulder blades, he became aware that other guests were looking at him again and frowning.

'Now he's assaulting his wife.' someone shouted.

The fish bone cleared and Maud pushed the rest of her meal aside. They had coffee, paid the enormous bill and left.

On the way home, with a rare touch of humility, Maud said: 'It wasn't really all that special, was it?'

'No, dear.'

'And all those brazen hussies with their bare bosoms. They wouldn't get away with it in Whitby.'

'No, dear. They wouldn't.' he replied.

* * *

That morning in the post, Charlie received two letters, both from retired Stewart Highlanders.

The first was from Colonel Alasdair Forbes, the Regimental Secretary, advising him that the Regimental Trustees had decided to commission a new history of the Regiment. The present history, which had been published in 1949, only told the story up to the end of World War 2 and, having been produced to a budget, and within the constraints of postwar economy, contained very few illustrations.

The Trustees felt it was now an appropriate time, with the forced amalgamation of the Regiment, to update the history to the present day whilst augmenting the text with more photographs, maps and diagrams. It would also be an opportunity to incorporate some revisionist thinking on certain of the World War 2 campaigns dictated by the better informed and more balanced knowledge which the passing of 50 years had brought.

They were looking for an author/editor with an encyclopaedic knowledge of the Regiment and Charlie's name had been put forward. Would he be interested?

The other letter was from 'Forty-Four' – Charlie's manservant in Scotland.

In the Highland Regiments where there were always many soldiers with the same surname, and often the same initials, it had always been the practice to differentiate between them by the addition of the last two digits of a soldier's army number. Thus you had Macdonald 36, Macdonald 03 and, in this case, Macdonald 44 or, simply, Forty-Four as he had always been known to Charlie.

Forty-Four had been Charlie's batman in the army and had been delighted to continue in effectively the same capacity when they had both left the service. They enjoyed an excellent rapport, regularly playing each other at squash and chess, but with their relationship never being threatened by familiarity crossing the boundaries of mutual respect.

Now, it seemed, their long time together would shortly have to come to an end. Forty-Four's father had been ill and had asked his son to return home and take over the family croft on the west coast near Kyle of Lochalsh. He would not, of course, leave the Colonel in the lurch, he said, there was no great urgency and he would stay on for as long as it took to make alternative arrangements. He hoped that this might be possible within, say, six months.

He would miss Forty-Four Charlie thought. He was a good man, proud of his Highland heritage, who had never succumbed to the pressures which assailed young Highland soldiers to act and talk like Glaswegians. The taunts of 'Teuchter', meaning a simple man from the hills, had never bothered him – that was exactly what he was, and proud of it. Charlie knew he must release him as soon as possible, it would not be fair to keep him hanging on with his father ailing and in need of him. Whether or not he should start looking for a replacement was not yet clear; when the time came, an approach to the Regimental Headquarters in Inverness to keep an ear to the ground for a suitable soldier due to leave the army would probably be the most effective course of action.

As to the Regimental History, there was nobody who knew more about the Regiment than Charlie and, although he had doubts as to his ability as an author, he thought he could probably make a reasonable go of it. Alasdair wanted his answer before the next Trustees' Meeting in six weeks time, so that was another decision he would have to make.

Easter at the Villa Victoria

* * *

At the passage de pietons beneath the railway station, the group of youths had had an entertaining afternoon. They had frightened two young girls with lewd gestures and suggestions, outraged an elderly patriarch with fascist salutes, and had just terrified a middle aged woman by exploding a home made bomb in the tunnel when she was passing through. Having seen her emerge and disappear in the direction of the port, to their jeers and catcalls, they descended into the underpass to relive their triumph and retrieve the tripwire which they used for detonation before preparing another surprise for the next unwary pedestrian.

As they returned to the entrance, a blast of high pressure water hit them square and true and knocked them flying on to their backs. As they struggled to their feet, it knocked them down again. They scrambled on hands and knees through the swirling water towards the other end of the tunnel. As they reached it, the circle of light darkened and another jet of water struck them down. The lights in the tunnel were switched off leaving them in total darkness with the water level rising around them.

Snivelling, bruised and soaking wet, they crouched, terrified, in the centre span of the tunnel until the flow of water subsided and the level began to abate. Then they crept towards the entrance again where their way was barred by a burly pompier. He grabbed each youth in turn and examined his face closely. 'Now, I know who you are,' he said, 'and I don't want to see any one of you anywhere near this underpass again. Do you understand?'

'Oui, Monsieur.' they whimpered in unison as they fled for their bicycles.

19. Political Correctness

Charlie sat in the drawing room, aimlessly turning the pages of *'Nice Matin'*, but taking none of it in, waiting for the sound of Sylvia's footsteps in the hall so he could ask her to join him on his evening excursion to the Neptunia.

Last night, in accordance with his declared policy of disinterest, he had gone without her, and had spent the next hour and a quarter wishing he had thrown caution to the wind and taken her nonetheless. He would not be so foolish tonight; he yearned for her company and the gladsomeness of her smile.

His eyes, ostensibly following a story about a traffic accident in Cagnes-sur-Mer, he was, in fact, reflecting on the hybrid nature of his nationality.

Charlie had always *felt* Scottish. As a boy he had put salt on his porridge, though he would have much preferred sugar, believing it to be the proper Scottish way, and had endured the sniggers and saucy remarks when he wore the kilt to chapel on Sundays.

He could trace his Stewart ancestors back through hundreds of years of Scottish history and had, of course, spent the active span of his life in a Scottish regiment. But, in common with most Scots families which had been involved in the management of Empire, the bloodline had become diluted by intermarriage over the years, The Mortons were English, the Cargills Irish and his mother's family, the Pikes, were Welsh.

Being a member of a service family, which was always on the move, and having been educated at schools in England where there were English, Scots, Irish, Welsh and Colonial pupils, Charlie, as had his father and grandfather, spoke without a regional accent. This was confusing to foreigners who would often say: 'But you do not have a Scottish accent?' to which he would reply: 'No, we don't all have Scottish accents.' or 'Well, my father was in the army and I was educated in England, you see.' This was easier and less embarrassing than having to explain that most Scots of his social class had no accent anyway.

In the community in the Highlands in which he lived, most people knew of his background and army service and accepted him, sometimes grudgingly, as a sort of Anglo-Scot. But outwith the Highlands he was always an Englishman. This did not distress him unduly – he was extremely proud of Britain's achievements in the world since the Act of Union in 1707, and particularly proud of Scotland's disproportionate contribution to them. On balance, he was proud of being British first, which deferred to his mixed blood, and Scottish second.

Though his love of Scotland, both as a country and a nation, was passionate, and he had never seriously considered living elsewhere after his retirement, he had become rather disillusioned with the modern Scot. While the rest of the civilised world had recognised the sterility of socialism, and its harmful effects on the weaker members of society, and had consequently rejected it, Scots, over the past twenty years, had been increasingly gulled by bitter, Central Belt politicians into embracing socialism in the guise of national feeling.

This, in turn, had led to a new wave of anti-English attitudes which Charlie, in common with all other informed and pragmatic Scots, found unreasonable and offensive. This was not the good natured and healthy antagonism one felt at Murrayfield when Scotland was playing 'The Auld Enemy'. This was a twisted and unpleasant bitterness – bitterness to English families living in Scotland, who were referred to derisively as 'White Settlers', though they were outnumbered 10 to 1 by Scots living and working in England who were accepted with hospitality into the communities in which they had chosen to settle; bitterness towards the 'English' (ie Westminster) parliament for its 'neglect of Scottish affairs', though Scotland consistently benefited from a greater share of government expenditure than either its population or tax contribution merited; bitterness towards the Highland landlords who, in the main, were totally committed to the wellbeing and prosperity of their communities and often worked their backs off, and plundered the family coffers, in an effort to provide employment and decent wages for their people.

No, Charlie thought with sadness, Scotland was not the nation it once was when Scots had made the going in every far-flung corner of the world and had led the way in every field of human endeavour – engineering, the law, medicine, education, the armed services and business. In those days, Scotland was respected as a vibrant, determined and innovative nation; today, he had observed with deep regret, she was noted principally for whining disaffection.

It was not cast in stone that he should spend the rest of his days in Scotland and now with Forty-Four's departure imminent, and new domestic arrangements therefore necessary, it would be a good moment for a move if that was what he wanted. Where would he go? What did he want and expect from the locality in which he lived?

His father who, Charlie thought, had probably felt much the same mongrel national status as himself, had retired to London. But he had the expectations of a wife to consider; Charlie had more freedom of choice. He enjoyed London in short doses, but was not sure that he wished to live there.

There was a time when he had enjoyed shooting and, as a Highland regimental officer, had never been short of invitations to the most prestigious grouse moors. But with age had come compassion for all living creatures and his matched Purdys had seen little action in recent years; he now preferred to watch birds than to kill them. The same applied to stalking and he had enjoyed some wonderful days on the hill in his youth; but he was getting too old to enjoy slithering on his stomach through wet heather. Fishing he could take or leave. His father had been a passionate salmon fisherman and Charlie had spent many rewarding days in his company, flogging the fast-flowing waters of the Northern Highlands. Now, if he fancied a day's fishing at all, which was becoming increasingly rare, he tended to prefer the bucolic tranquility of a Gloucestershire trout stream to the wild beauty of a Highland strath. Fox hunting had never been a part of his family's culture, except for the Irish branch who had lived for little else, so there was no field sport which need influence his choice of where to live.

He could, he knew, easily become absorbed with a sailing boat, a long-keeled, wooden-hulled boat such as he had described to Sylvia that day; but where would he keep it? That was the problem. There was no such thing as an isolated, peaceful mooring in the south nowadays; the south coastal waters were over-run with yachts as the roads were over-run with cars, and he did not, at his age, fancy the prospect of frostbiting in the colder waters of Scotland or the North of England. There was, of course, the Mediterranean – a completely different style of sailing but at least one could rely on decent weather to compensate for the overcrowded marinas and noisy power craft, which tended to stay well inshore anyway.

There could be, in fact, very tangible advantages to his selling up in Scotland and moving in to the Villa Victoria. He could take over from the Aunts all the responsibilities of managing the household which would relieve that problem if, indeed, there was a problem, which he was beginning to doubt, at a stroke. It was, moreover, a very pleasant and relaxed way of life out here. There was as much, or as little, social intercourse as one wanted, the house was eminently comfortable, with a trusted and experienced staff; he had his favourite little bars and restaurants and would undoubtedly develop others. The idea had a lot going for it. He would miss his army cronies, of course, but they could exchange visits and need not lose touch.

Charlie looked at his watch and frowned. It was five minutes to five and there was no sign of Sylvia coming down. He gave it another ten minutes before abandoning hope and departing for Juan.

* * *

Sylvia had decided to stay in her room until Charlie left for his evening beer to avoid a repetition of the previous evening. If he was planning not to take her again, and she was not there to ask, he could not have the

Political Correctness

satisfaction of not asking her (she was Irish, after all, and was entitled to indulge herself occasionally with a bit of Irish logic).

When she heard him leaving, she noted he was twenty minutes late – unusual for Charlie whose timing on matters relating to alcoholic intake was always meticulous. Could it be that he had been waiting for her? Why else would he have delayed his departure for so long? This thought alleviated, to some extent, her disappointment at being left behind again – albeit by her own design.

* * *

Mattie, not really understanding what Richard did for a living, but believing it to be something to do with printing and commercial art, thought that he would like to see her brother's collection of cartoons, cut from newspapers throughout his adult life. It was a very specialised and comprehensive collection she told him. Yes, he would very much like to see it, he had unwisely replied. Consequently, at drinks time that evening, Mattie appeared with two large scrapbooks.

Richard had only to turn the first few pages before realising what the Colonel's specialist subject had been. All the cartoons, and there were hundreds of them, were about cannibalism. Every bizarre and corny cannibal joke, which had tickled the nation's humour in bygone days, was included in the pages of the scrapbooks. Huge, black cauldrons containing missionaries or gentlemen in solar topees, watched over by smiling savages with bones in their hair, were represented in a dozen different ways on every page.

> *A savage reads a book he has taken from the missionary he is about to cook. It is entitled: 'How to Serve your Fellow Man.'*
>
> *Another asks his victim: 'What's you name, please, we want it for the menu.' or, more simply: 'Got a match?'*

On the next page, a native leading a trussed-up Englishman asks his wife: 'Hope you don't mind, I've brought the boss home for dinner.' and one, leading in a bound up scuba diver enquires: 'How about some sea food for a change?'

One Englishman in a giant frying pan, turns to his companion and says: 'Funny thing, I thought these chaps preferred us boiled.' and another, tasting the stock in which he is boiling: 'You have to hand it to them, Lovejoy, we taste superb.'

On the final page, a savage in a chef's hat tells the missionary in the cauldron: 'We got the recipe from a cartoon in the newspaper.'

'*Mattie!*' Richard said, having taken a large gulp of whisky and water, 'this has got to be the most politically incorrect document I have ever *seen*! You probably risk a jail sentence just for being in possession of it.'

'How do you mean, dear?'

'Well, nowadays, you're not allowed to lampoon any ethnic group. It's considered very bad taste.'

'As the cannibal said to the missionary.' Emma mumbled under her breath.

'But cannibals *did* exist dear. A cousin of my grandmother is believed to have been eaten by them.'

'Maybe so, but the nations concerned do not like to be reminded of the bad things they may have done in the past. It's not politically correct.'

'Is it politically correct, then, for people to be constantly denigrating *us* for the bad things *we* are supposed to have done in the past? Like trying to convert heathens to Christianity and shooting mutineers out of cannons for slaughtering our women and children?'

'Oh, perfectly so. In political correctness there is one rule for the British and another for the rest of the world.'

Political Correctness

'And is it politically correct to remind Germans about the holocaust?'

'Oh yes. There's yet *another* rule for *them*.'

'It doesn't seem quite fair, dear.' Mattie said plaintively 'I really can't see much difference between boiling Christians in cauldrons and roasting Jews in ovens; they are both equally reprehensible.'

'Well you see,' Richard said, 'the Germans, with centuries of civilising influence behind them, were much more informed and intelligent people and should have known better.'

'That's racist.' said Emma.

'Yes, probably. It's difficult to say anything nowadays which isn't racist.'

Charlie intervened: 'Political correctness takes a lot of flak nowadays, and rightly so. Some of its elements are quite grotesque and these are always the parts which people quote and ridicule. But, when all is said and done, PC started, even though it has now got wildly out of hand, as an honest attempt to discourage people from being offensive to other people.'

'But isn't that what people like us have always done, dear, as second nature?' Kate asked.

'Yes, *we* have, Aunt Kate, but the sad fact remains that the world is still full of intolerant, bigoted people who give not a jot for the sensitivity of others and miss no opportunity to burlesque and embarrass them.'

Frances was looking uncomfortable.

'When it was introduced,' Charlie continued, 'political correctness was about controlling the damage that such people inflicted upon their neighbours. We are approaching the 21st century now and, unless the world can dismantle its prejudices on race, creed, class, sex, what have you, and learn to work together to address the massive problems which confront humanity, I see little hope for the future of mankind.'

'Peoplekind.' Emma corrected him.

The Grand Hotel, Antibes *Photo:* AIMELAINE

20. Sporting Behaviour

The day of the second 'meeting' had arrived and the family was assembled in the drawing room. This time, everyone was present and on time.

'Well, now,' Charlie began, 'the purpose of our all having come down here together was to see if Aunt Kate and Mattie,' he smiled indulgently in their direction, 'were managing all right on their own or if there is anything we should be doing to help them. As we all know, they have lived here for most of their lives and, since Granny's death in 1968, have run the house with great competence – maintaining all the old standards and traditions so, firstly, and I don't want to sound patronising, obviously, but I think we, as a family, should all say 'Thank you!' to Aunt Kate and Mattie for keeping the Morton-Stewart flag flying in such a consistently stylish way for so many years.'

Sporting Behaviour

'Hear, hear.' There was a murmur of approval, a few claps, and the Aunts smiled with pleasure.

'Now, they would be the first to agree,' Charlie continued, 'that they are not as young as they were and, as we have seen over the past few weeks, a house like this does not run itself. There is a lot of organisation; staff to be looked after; accounts to be kept, and a never-ending round of maintenance, to the buildings and grounds, to be organised and overseen. There is a lot to do and, although we must all agree that everything is being done perfectly at the moment, we must ask ourselves whether it is fair to expect the Aunts to continue doing what they do indefinitely. So, firstly, let me ask them how *they* feel about things.' he turned to the Aunts. 'What are your general thoughts? Do you find that things are beginning to get a bit on top of you?'

'I don't really do very much, dear,' Mattie said, 'Kate is the organiser. All the credit for keeping the house going is hers.' Then she added in a lower voice: 'I'm only here for the beer!' Emma tittered.

Kate thought for a moment or two before replying:

'Well, I can't pretend that some things aren't becoming a bit irksome. I have such difficulty in writing now, you know.' she held up her poor, twisted hand and demonstrated how little movement remained in the joints. 'I get through everything, but it all takes me three times longer than it used to.'

'She has a lot of difficulty writing the cheques and letters now.' Mattie confirmed.

'And my memory is beginning to let me down; that's the other thing I find difficult. I can remember things that happened a long time ago, in fact it's strange, things keep coming back to me from years and years ago, things I had completely forgotten, and I remember them in minute detail. But I can't sometimes remember what happened yesterday, or the day before.'

'I can't remember what happened five minutes ago.' Mattie chuckled to Emma, who she recognised as her most appreciative audience.

'I think we can carry on as we are for a while yet,' Kate continued, 'some things *are* becoming a bit of a strain, I can't deny that, but I'd sooner struggle on than face up to the alternative.'

'Of giving up the house, you mean?' Charlie asked.

'Yes, dear. You see we're not so stupid as to think we're going to live forever, or that our health will improve, and the time will undoubtedly come when we simply can't manage any more and will have to give up the house and go into a nursing home. But we really would like to put that day off for as long as possible. We have been here all our lives, you see, and the prospect of having to live in a single room, surrounded by a load of other moribund old trouts, is pretty awful.'

'It needn't be as bad as all that, Aunt Kate,' Frances said, 'there are some really very nice places around.' She decided not to mention the enquiries they had made in Cannes which, in the present climate, might appear to the others to have been officious.

'I'm sure there must be, dear,' Kate replied, 'but there's no place like home and we have been here for so long.'

Charlie changed course: 'Now, I have been to see Doctor Chouard, with Kate and Mattie's consent, of course, and he sees no reason why, from a medical point of view, they should not continue here for the time being. Does he look after you well?' he asked them.

'Oh yes, dear.' they chimed in unison, and Mattie added: 'He visits us regularly and he always comes instantly if we need him.'

Charlie went on: 'Now, obviously, Aunt Kate and Mattie are very dependent on Bridie and the Limbus.'

'Oh yes, dear.' they chimed again, and Kate continued: 'They are simply wonderful. We couldn't possibly manage without them. I forgot to do the salaries in December and they didn't even mention it until I realised my mistake the next month. My memory again, you see; I've never done anything like that before. We simply couldn't manage without them.'

'Well, you won't have to,' Charlie said, 'I have spoken to them all and they are very happy with things as they stand and nobody is considering retirement or anything just yet. A couple of things we *will* have to talk about though, Aunt Kate: firstly a hoist to help them getting you in and out of bed and, secondly, if you want to continue your trips to the top floor, I think

Sporting Behaviour

we'll have to consider extending the stairlift up there.'

'Will that really be necessary, dear? We seem to manage all right as we are.' Kate said.

'Indeed, but the Limbus are not getting any younger either and I think it would be a sensible precaution. We don't want them dropping you down the stairs, do we?' he added with an attempt at levity.

'Heaven forbid,' said Mattie, 'we'd never hear the end of it.'

'Now, as to the financial side of things: again, with Aunt Kate's consent, I have been through their financial records and, although I do not pretend to be an accountant, it appears to me that everything is in order and that the household is operating comfortably within its income for the time being.'

'It wasn't a couple of years ago.' Mattie said. Kate glowered at her.

'What has changed then?' Charlie asked gently. There was silence.

'You will have to tell him, dear.' Mattie said to Kate.

'I sold seven of Aunt Sade's paintings – you remember? The ones that everyone wanted to burn after she died.'

'And?'

'And the interest on the money we received for them has bridged the gap. It's all there in the files you had. It's in the No. 7 deposit account.'

'Oh yes.' Charlie said.

'It's all there,' Kate said defensively, 'we haven't touched a penny of the capital. The pictures were just sitting there doing nothing and none of you would have even given them house room.'

'Aunt Kate,' Charlie said soothingly, 'nobody is questioning your stewardship in any way. It seems you are a better business person than all of us.'

'And a better judge of fine art.' Emma added, which seemed to please Aunt Kate better than anything which had been said before.

'But, Aunt Kate,' Frances intervened, 'how much did you get for the seven paintings?'

'A little over one and a half million, dear.'

'Francs?'

'Pounds. They were auctioned in London.'

A communal gasp went round the room and all eyes were involuntarily raised to the ceiling, looking up towards the attic which was known to be the repository of the rest of Great Aunt Sade's prodigious output.

'We must have the other paintings valued, Aunt Kate.' Charlie said in a hushed voice.

'It's all organised, dear. The man from Christebys in London is coming tomorrow so we will know exactly how we stand on that front.'

After a pause for everyone to recover their concentration, Charlie resumed his chairmanship. 'So it appears that, thanks to Aunt Kate's incredibly astute management, and the talent of our much maligned ancestor, there are no financial problems at the moment. Has anyone got anything else they want to say?' The company remained stunned and silent.

'Well,' Charlie concluded, 'it seems that, in spite of some growing difficulties with the paperwork and things, Aunt Kate and Mattie feel they are managing all right at the moment and there seems no point in discussing any radical changes at this stage.'

People started shifting position in their chairs preparatory to getting up and leaving the room when Mattie opened the conversation again:

'Kate makes light of her difficulties,' she said, 'but things really are beginning to get a bit on top of her, you know. Now if you, Charlie, were here all the time, wouldn't that be the answer to everything?'

'Well . . .' Charlie fumbled for words.

'You are retired now,' Kate said. 'you're a free agent, you can live anywhere you like.'

'You've no ties,' Mattie interrupted, 'you've no wife or children to think about and your precious Regiment has gone.'

They have been hatching this up together, Charlie thought to himself.

'Well,' he replied, and all eyes were focused on him, 'it's a funny thing, but I was mulling over the same thought myself, only yesterday. It's not quite as simple as it may appear, of course, I have been offered a job by RHQ (near enough to the truth, he thought) and I have a number of other commitments in UK but, let's say, it's not beyond the bounds of possibility. I'll have to give it some serious thought.'

The meeting over, the family dispersed and Sylvia was heading for the stairs when Charlie called her back.

'Now, I don't want you skulking in your room this evening. I waited for you last night and made myself late; had to rush my second beer; gave myself indigestion.'

'Oh dear!' she laughed.

'Here,' he pointed to the floor, 'Ten minutes to five; on the dot; no excuses. Now, off you go.'

'Yes, Colonel.' she replied with a theatrical salute.

* * *

'It's unbelievable,' Frances said to her husband, 'they have been sitting on a fortune, probably not insured, and think of the interest they would have earned over the years if they'd sold the paintings and invested the proceeds.'

'There wouldn't have been any proceeds,' Richard replied, 'were it not for your grandmother's sentimentality and Aunt Kate's prudence. They'd all have gone on the bonfire.'

'Frightening!'

'I think the money means far less to Kate than clearing Great Aunt Sade's artistic reputation.'

'That's the impression I got, too.'

'She'll have to be known now as 'Great Aunt Sade who restored the family fortunes'.' Richard said.

'And did you see Charlie's fleet footwork after the revelation? Can't wait to move in and spend some of the money.'

'Charlie doesn't need the money. He has more than enough for his own needs and, anyway, he was thinking about moving down here before this business came up.'

'So he says.'

'If Charlie says so, I'm sure it is so; he's an honourable man.'
'He's a fool.'
'Why do you say that?'
'Well, look at the way he's being manipulated by that tart Sylvia.'
'Don't start that again, Frances.'
'She stayed in her room last night so he couldn't take her boozing with him. Playing hard to get.'
'Don't be ridiculous.'
'Do you mean to say you haven't noticed how they're frigging around? They've had some sort of a tiff and are avoiding each other.'
'You have a vivid imagination, Frances.'
'There's none so blind . . .' she replied.

* * *

In the afternoon, Charlie, Emma, Frances, Richard and the twins played three-a-side cricket on the lawn. John bowled his father out and punched the air in triumph with both hands.'
'You mustn't do that, John.' Charlie said.
'Why not, Uncle Charlie?' the boy asked in surprise.
'Because gentlemen do not behave like that. It's not sporting.'
'Sporting?'
'Whatever game you are playing, you should never show any sign of triumph or anger – no matter how pleased or cheesed off you may feel. '
'That's a bit out of date, Uncle Charlie.' Frances said.
'Good manners and sportsmanship are never out of date.' he replied. 'They'll have to learn how to behave like gentlemen on the cricket field before they go to Wellington.'
'The way they're going at school they're never going to get to Wellington.' Richard said.
'Added to which,' Emma said, getting a stranglehold round Stephen's neck with one arm, 'they'll have to learn not to *cheat*,' she twisted him sharply to the right and he squawked, 'and tell *fibs*,' she twisted him to the

left and he squawked again, and *bully girls.*' another twist and squawk.

'They don't have girls at Wellington.' John said.

'Yes they do.' his mother corrected him.

'Do they, Uncle Charlie?'

'They do now; they didn't in my day.' Charlie replied, thinking to himself how very glad he was that they had not. His time at Wellington had been blissfully happy and he was eternally thankful that this sublime period of youth, with its manly disciplines and friendships, had not been complicated by the intrigues and jealousies that the presence of girls invariably generated.

And the whole question of sporting behaviour, he wondered, had that all changed as well? He was sickened by the way sport had gone with the advent of professionalism – the mincing nancy boys on the international tennis circuit with their tears and tantrums; soccer players with shoulder-length hair hugging and kissing each other (not that he had ever followed 'Oikball'; Wellington was a rugger school, thank heavens!). Having been brought up in the old discipline of sportsmanship, it offended him deeply to witness the behaviour that many players seemed to get away with nowadays; county cricket and rugby union were the only sports he could still watch with any degree of pleasure.

'Uncle Charlie,' Stephen's voice brought him back to the game, 'you're in.' Charlie hit a six clear across Hetty's Leap.

'And none of that punching the air in triumph, Uncle Charlie.' Emma cautioned him severely.

Easter at the Villa Victoria

21. *Rupert Saint John Powell*

To understand Rupert Saint John Powell's contempt for the working classes, it is necessary to examine his own background. His grandfather, Fred Powell, had been a small working builder in Camberley who, on more than one occasion, had been imprisoned for indecent exposure. So well known were 'Flasher Powell's' activities, that it had been the vogue for some time, in Camberley and its hinterlands, to talk about 'doing a Powell', or even to use his name as a verb – eg 'Powelling in the middle of the street'.

Flasher's son, Michael, a clever lad, kept his coat buttoned up, did very well at school and obtained a temporary wartime commission in the Royal Army Pay Corps. In the building boom of the 1950s, he developed the family business and made a great deal of money. A housemaid was employed at their smart, mock-Tudor house in Frimley, who was paid the barest minimum wage, was expected to do everything, and was, in general, treated with less consideration than Michael's father had received while serving time at Her Majesty's pleasure. The position became vacant every five months, on average. Also, in an attempt to disassociate himself from his father's notoriety, Michael added 'Saint John' to his surname, which was not entirely without pretext as his wife's mother, a boarding house keeper in Bournemouth, was a Mrs. 'John', and Michael's childhood had been spent in a council house next to the Church of 'Saint' Patrick and all Angels. What better provenance could one wish for? He also let it be known that he liked it pronounced 'Sinjun Pole'.

Rupert, his son, another clever lad, was sent to prep school, and then on to a minor public school where, on Speech Day, his father, the 'Major' (naturally he improperly retained his temporary wartime rank) would arrive in smart blue blazer with polished brass corps buttons and a neatly-trimmed military style moustache.

Rupert Saint John Powell

With an allowance from his father, and the veneer of a gentleman, Rupert went on to Sandhurst and obtained a commission in a smart cavalry regiment, which was very short of candidates at the time, in which he learned to ride and play polo and began to mix with people whose relaxed and patrician demeanour he tried hard to emulate. He also developed an interest in, and a good working knowledge of, paintings and fine art. He became ashamed of his father, with his temporary rank and pseudo military air, who was never invited to regimental dos. Nor did he ever take his new friends home.

What Rupert could never understand was why he never really gained the inward respect of his troopers, or enjoyed the same easy rapport with them, that his brother officers seemed to take for granted. He had no best friend to tell him that his men had no respect for him because he had no respect for them.

One day he forgot to remove his cap when entering the Sergeants' Mess. His Commanding Officer heard about it and sent for him.

'Who do you think are the most important people in this regiment Powell? he could never bring himself to use the 'Saint John'.

'Well, us, Sir? The officers?'

'Wrong.' Rupert was confused and silent.

'The Warrant Officers and NCOs are the most important people in this and every regiment. It is they who hold the whole thing together, it is they who tighten the nuts and bolts when they become loose, and they who cover for us and mop up the mess, when we cock things up. They depend upon our support but not nearly as much as we depend upon their's.'

'No, Sir.'

'You have the makings of a *reasonable* officer, Powell, I'll say no more than that, but there is one fundamental fact you've got to get straight in your mind: because a soldier doesn't use the same tailor as you, and eats in a different mess, it does not make him a lesser man. It doesn't matter what he does – he can be the RSM or a shithouse cleaner – if he works hard and does his job to the best of his ability, he is worthy of your respect.'

Easter at the Villa Victoria

'Yes, Sir.'

The CO continued more gently. 'Now, I realise your background is somewhat different from most of the officers in this regiment, and I make allowance for that.' Rupert coloured; was it that obvious?

'It just means you have to try all the harder. Now to fail to remove your cap in a Sergeants' or Corporals' Mess is an act of rank discourtesy and disrespect. Never let it happen again.'

In spite of this wise remonstration, 'Flasher' Powell's grandson never came to understand that special bond between officer and man, which created crack units and, in his anxiety for social acceptance, regarded all that was working class with increasing disdain. Like the tragic Eurasians of the Raj, he was never wholly accepted by either side.

He left the army in the first round of redundancies under the 'Options for Change' cuts and joined Christebys to put to good use his now considerable knowledge of paintings.

This promised to be an interesting assignment, Rupert thought to himself as his plane curved in to the coast and lined up with the runway at Nice Côte d'Azur Airport. An enormous, and hitherto unknown, collection of 19th century Irish oils and an opportunity to ingratiate himself with one of the oldest British families on the Riviera. He had looked them all up, of course, in Stud Book and Army List and knew enough of their background to be able to drop a few meaningful names. They might even ask him to stay – that would be a good one for the Knightsbridge wine bars: 'I was staying with the Morton-Stewarts in Antibes last week, you know, cousins of Lord Cargill, knew Charlie in BAOR, ha, ha, ha; been there since the year dot; practically *founded* the place, ha, ha, ha.' Yes, there would definitely be some mileage in that. The only trouble was he would have that awful little oik Pontefract hanging around. Still, he would soon find a way to get shot of him.

* * *

Charlie felt that he must say something to Sylvia this evening, once they were ensconced at the Neptunia, to reassure her that nothing had changed between them, that he still wanted them to be very good friends and that his behaviour in the boat the other day had just been a moment of champagne-induced foolishness which would not be repeated. And yet, did he really want to go this far? Did her really want to close the door on the possibility of their friendship developing into something more?

Sylvia, likewise, was thinking that she must say something to Charlie along the same lines but, again, wished she could think of some way of keeping options open for the future.

Once they were settled in the bar, and were halfway through their first beer, Charlie began:

'Sylvia.'

'Yes, Charlie.' (He looks serious. What's coming next? Is he going to tell me that, in view of my behaviour, he thinks it would be better if we didn't meet anymore?)

(She looks very serious. She probably thinks I'm about to make advances again. Perhaps this is not the moment to say my little piece.) 'It will be sad when this little holiday ends; it's been such fun.' he said instead.

'It's been absolutely marvellous, Charlie – the weather, the villa, the family, the wonderful outcome of the business about the Aunts' future. Were you serious when you said you were thinking of coming out here permanently?'

'I'm certainly thinking about it. There are a lot of factors to be considered, of course.'

'Of course.' (He's a bit more relaxed now. This might be the moment to say my piece.) 'Charlie.'

'Yes, Sylvia.' (Oh Lord, why is she looking so serious? Is she about to tell me that she thinks it would be better if we didn't see each other any more?)

(He's gone all serious again. He thinks I'm about to make advances, poor dear man. Perhaps it's not the time to say my piece.) 'What do you think about the current political situation in Eastern Malawi?' she said instead.

'Hadn't really thought much about it,' he replied, slightly puzzled, 'what do *you* think about the current political situation in Eastern Malawi?'

'Where is Eastern Malawi?' she answered. They both laughed.

'Does this mean,' Charlie said, 'that we are running out of things to say to each other?'

'Oh no. There's a lot I'd *like* to say to you, Charlie, but I'm not sure that you would like to hear it.'

'Oh dear! What have I done now?'

'No, no. Not unpleasant things.'

'Like what, then?'

She thought for a minute. 'Well, like how much I agree with everything you say.'

'Really? he replied in astonishment, 'nobody *ever* agrees with *anything* I say.'

'I do.'

'Give me an instance.' he said, conscious of the fact that he was fishing for praise, but was so elated by Sylvia's approval of any part of him that he could not help himself.

'For instance, last evening when you were explaining about political correctness. You, a fusty old reactionary colonel – the last person from whom I'd have expected to hear such words.'

'Fusty? Reactionary?' he called for another two beers, 'No, it's a movement born of consideration for others. Even if it has become pure farce, it was honestly conceived and merits a fair hearing.'

'And fairness is important to you, isn't it?'

'Above almost everything else.' he replied. 'You see, as a nation we have lost just about every sterling quality we used to have – we have become indolent, greedy and effeminate, but the one quality which has never been corrupted, and pray God it never will be, is our sense of fair play. It is the only thing which sets us apart from other nations. It is the thing, above all else, that foreigners admire in us, even if they don't understand it. Do you realise that in many foreign languages there is no such word as 'fair'?'

'I didn't know that.'

'It is something uniquely British. It is something which is evident in almost every one of us, in some form or another. It embraces integrity, compassion, tolerance and natural justice. It is our greatest asset and allows us one of our few remaining claims to morality. It is our sense of fair play which makes us queue in an orderly fashion – foreigners can never understand that – and stops us from castrating our defeated foes, and makes our legal system the envy of the world, and sends us leaping to the defence of every miserable little person, country or cause which we see as an underdog.'

'Goodness! You do feel strongly about it.' Sylvia said.

I do. If, in my life, I should be deemed worthy of having earned an epitaph, I would wish it to be 'Here lies Charlie Stewart, a fair man'.'

'I think you've probably earned it already, Charlie.'

'In which case, my cup of happiness is almost full. But not *quite* full because there are a few things I would like to say to *you*, Sylvia.'

'Like what, Charlie?' her heart was thumping with expectation.

'Like, it's definitely a three-beer night.' he said and summoned the waiter.

She laughed despite her disappointment. 'No, that's not playing the game,' she said reproachfully, 'I gave you a 'for instance' now it's your turn to give me one – a sensible one.'

'Put that way I can hardly refuse. Well, I love the forgiving and considerate way you have treated us after the shabby way we treated you for so many years.'

'That's water under the bridge, Charlie and, anyway, you personally, were always kind to us.'

'Not nearly as kind as I should have been if I'd known the sort of person you are. And . . .' he stopped.

'And? Go on.'

'You're fishing for compliments.'

'I am. Go on.'

Here goes, thought Charlie, I might as well be hung for a sheep as a lamb. '... and I love your company. I love being with you. I love the gentle timbre of your voice and the magical ripple of your laugh.' She placed her hand over his on the table, 'and the way you've just put your hand over mine.'

'Stop it, Charlie! Be serious. This is serious stuff. Go on.'

'Well, I love the gentle timbre of your voice ...'

'We've already had that; *and* the magical ripple of my laugh. What else?'

'Well, I'd just like to see a great deal more of you, Sylvia, if you feel you can put up with me.'

'I can.' she said.

She was smiling at him in a way that was making his heart beat so violently that he felt she must surely hear it on the other side of the table. Her eyes were moist and blurred, her dark hair waved softly in the breeze coming off the seafront. She really was amazingly beautiful. And there was something in the way she was looking at him, and in the pressure of her hand on his, that told Charlie, at last, that there was something more than just friendship in her feelings for him.

And Sylvia now realised the same. There could be no misunderstanding the way he was looking at her now and the way he placed his other hand on top of hers and caressed it gently. Charlie, she thought, you are falling in love with me just as I am falling in love with you and the sky has never been bluer, the sea breeze never more scented, the world never more wonderful ...'

'You're toying with your beer, Sylvia.' he said sternly, and she noticed that his glass was empty and she had hardly touched hers. She poured half of hers into his then clinked glasses with him.

'Cheers! darling.' he said.

'Cheers! my funny, fair old Charlie.' she replied.

As they went out hand in hand to where the little Renault was parked there was suddenly a new dimension to the world. All their previous worries about the other's feelings had been removed and had been replaced with an overwhelming contentment and joy.

Charlie said to her: 'Promise me one thing, Sylvia – no doubts or remorse in the morning. What's been said has been said and I will think just the same tomorrow.'

'And so will I, darling.' she replied.

The Theatre, Antibes *Photo:* AIMELAINE

22. Revelations

On her way to the bathroom the next morning, Sylvia flung a pillow at her sleeping daughter and, on the way back, pulled the bedclothes off her and said with a cordiality unusual for that time of the morning:

'Come on, sleepyhead. Out of your sack. Time to be up and about.'

Emma sat up in bed frowning and rubbing her eyes.

'Mummy! What on earth is the matter with you?'

'Nothing at all.' She drew the curtains allowing the morning sun to flood into the room. 'Just look at that morning,' she opened the window and breathed deeply, 'far, far too good to waste slugging about in bed.'

'*Mummy!* What's the matter with you? Stop being so boisterous. You look like the cat that got the cream.'

Later, as she was dressing, Emma said: 'I don't know how you can be so happy when we've only got another three days left here. I'm just getting more and more miserable. I don't want to leave here. I just want to stay here forever.'

'Well, you must make the most of these three days then. Are you seeing Steve today?'

'Yes,' Emma said sadly, 'couldn't we stay another week?'

'No, we couldn't.'

'Why not?'

'A. Because we haven't been invited to stay another week; B. Because our flights are booked and cannot be changed and, C. Because you have a job to get back to.'

Emma sighed. 'It's just been such magic. It's a different existence – this beautiful, beautiful place and being part of a family and everything. I never knew such happiness existed; I just can't bear the thought of leaving it all behind – Charlie, the Aunts, Bridie and the Limbus.'

'And Steve?'

Revelations

'Yes, Steve as well, but he's only part of it.'

'And Frances?'

'No, Mummy! I think we can both live without Frances. It's just that the last month has seemed like normality and our life in London so grey and somehow artificial.'

'You didn't think so at the time.'

'I didn't know anything better, did I? Since Daddy died, there's never been anyone else apart from the two of us. Weren't you lonely, Mummy?'

'Yes, I suppose I was.'

'It really was very brave of you to come out here; for all we knew they might all have given us the cold shoulder, like Frances.'

'I'm very glad they didn't.'

'Now, you've got them eating out of your hand, they all adore you, especially Charlie. He's going to miss you, you know.'

'I think he'll miss us both.'

'It's terrible when you think of all the years we have wasted, when we could have been a family. And all it took was for us to meet each other and spend a little time together.'

'The first move had to come from them.'

'Yes, I see that. Do you think that, now the ice has been broken, and we all get on so well, we'll be able to keep properly in touch with them, and come out here regularly?'

'I think they would be disappointed if we didn't.'

'And Uncle Charlie, do you think he'll visit us in London occasionally?'

'I expect so.'

'I hope so; things just won't be the same without him, will they? He's such tremendous fun.'

'He's more than that. He's one of the most decent, most honourable, most wonderful men you're ever likely to meet.'

'Mummy!' Emma said in astonishment then, in a tone which implied a conflict between suspicion and understanding: 'Do I detect something rather more than sisterly affection?' Sylvia just smiled.

'Mummy! Tell me! What's going on?'

'Nothing is going on.'

'Tell me! Tell me!'

'Well,' Sylvia hesitated, 'well yes, you do detect something more than sisterly affection.'

'Tell me! Tell me! Come on, out with it!' she sat down in front of her mother and took both her hands.

'Well, I'm in love with him, I suppose.'

'Oh, Mummy.' Emma was speechless for a moment, then: 'And what about him?'

'What about him?'

'How does he feel about you?'

'Well, I think he's fond of me.'

'He's more than that. You can see it in his eyes every time he looks at you; and the way he follows you around like a little puppy dog.'

'Do you think so?'

'I know so. Hasn't he said *anything*?'

'You know Charlie, he's so reserved.'

'Hasn't he said *anything*?'

'Well, sort of. He said he loved the magical ripple of my laugh.' which was the only phrase from last night which she could immediately call to mind.

'Good grief!' Emma tossed her head and cast her eyes to heaven, 'Is that all, Mummy?'

'No. There were other things, but neither of us has actually spoken the three magic words.'

'Well, it's high time you did.'

'This conversation is the wrong way around. Mothers are supposed to advise their daughters on their love life.'

'Mummy! This is simply the most fantastic, the most unbelievable, most mega-wonderful thing that has ever happened.' She hugged her mother impetuously, her mind flooding with the possibilities that this amazing news

Revelations

presented and feeling, even in the heat of the moment, just a little ashamed that she was also thinking of the effect it might have on her. 'But let me give you some daughterly advice: Don't let this all slip through your fingers because both of you are too gauche to tell the other how you feel. If you love him, tell him. Think of all the years we've already wasted through poor communications. Don't let's waste any more.'

'Thank you, darling; thank you very much; so you approve?'

'*Approve*? I'm absolutely over *the moon*; I'm so *thrilled*, so *delighted* for you; I can't tell you how happy you have made me. Just don't blow it now, I implore you.'

'I'll try not to, darling.'

Later, seeing Charlie emerging from the dining room, Emma rushed at him, flung her arms round his neck and hugged him with all the strength her slender form could muster. He thought that she would never let him go and, when at last she released him, he saw there were tears running down her cheeks.

'What's all this about?' he asked gently, but she did not answer and, with a final huge, wet kiss on his cheek, she was gone.

* * *

Rupert Saint John Powell had finished his examination of the paintings in time for a glass of champagne with the family. He had been in the attics with the Aunts and Mr. Pontefract for nearly two and a half hours and came onto the veranda with Kate who was looking slightly dazed. A violent sniffing from behind indicated that Herbert was following.

'I believe you have met Charlie, my nephew?' Aunt Kate said.

'Yes, yes, we were in Osnabrück together. How are you Colonel?' Charlie remembered that their two regiments had overlapped for a time and that he had not liked this bumptious man any more than he did now.

'Very well, thank you. A glass of champagne?'

'Never been known to refuse, ha, ha, ha.'

Introductions were effected and Saint John Powell continued: 'Yes, I think Jimmy Riddel was garrison commander at the time. Do you see anything of old Jimmy?' he asked, implying a familiarity which Charlie, who knew Brigadier Riddel well, knew to be highly improbable.

'No, I haven't seen him for some time.'

'Well now, the paintings.' Rupert turned to Kate with a look which enquired whether it was in order to speak in front of Charlie.

'Yes,' Kate said, 'my nephew knows all our affairs.'

'We will, of course, be sending you a detailed inventory and valuation, but, to give you some idea in advance, I would say, at auction today, assuming all the paintings were placed on the market at the same time, we are talking of somewhere in the region of fourteen to sixteen million.'

'About what you thought, Aunt Kate.' Charlie said casually, determined not to give Saint John Powell the satisfaction of a reaction like a surprised participant in *'The Antiques Roadshow.'*

'If, however, you decided to release them over a period of time, they could make considerably more. Had the same situation with Margaret Pelham last year – you know, Lady Margaret Pelham of the Norfolk Pelhams.'

'That is something which my aunt will have to decide in due course.'

'Yes, of course, and, in the meantime, I would strongly advise you to review your insurance cover. For insurance purposes, the normal rule of thumb is auction value plus twenty-five percent.'

Frances came onto the veranda and Charlie introduced the two men to her.

'And I would also advise you to consider installing a more sophisticated security system then the one you have.' he indicated one of the small radar scanners in the corner.

'We have one already,' Charlie said, 'you saw him as you came into the grounds.'

Saint John Powell looked puzzled for a moment and then guffawed: 'Oh, you mean the little Indian chappie?'

Revelations

'The little Indian chappie, as you call him, is an ex-Gurkha rifleman with twenty-four years service, a Military Medal, a Distinguished Conduct Medal and a very sharp kukri. Security systems do not come more sophisticated than that.'

'Oh quite, I take your point, ha, ha, ha.'

Charlie was relieved when Frances, who was very much into fine art and antiques, led Rupert away and engaged him in arty talk in a far corner of the veranda from where his braying laugh and persistent name dropping were slightly less offensive.

Aunt Kate and Charlie talked to Herbert Pontefract who impressed them greatly with his knowledge of furniture in the course of a sniffing eulogy on some ladder-back Regency chairs he had spotted in the dining room.

When it was time for the Christebys men to go, Frances, flushed and smiling said: 'Rupert and I have had such an interesting talk. He's going to come over and look at my Fletcher watercolours when we all get back.'

Kate said that she hoped that Mr. Saint John Powell would join them for dinner the following evening when they were having a little dinner party before the family all returned to the UK.

'How very kind, Miss Morton-Stewart, I'd love to.'

'Oh lovely,' said Frances with almost too much animation, 'we can continue our discussion then, Rupert.'

'And, of course, you too Mr. Pontefract, and Mrs. Pontefract.' Kate added.

Herbert, taken unawares, accepted with as much grace as he could muster and Rupert Saint John Powell looked decidedly put out at the diminishment of the invitation by its extension to the awful Pontefracts.

* * *

Henri, he garden boy, still preferring the frivolous levity of French patisserie to the wholesome solidity of good Irish baking, was not overjoyed by the extra slice of fruit cake which Bridie slid maternally on to his plate, but did not miss the approbation which the gesture bespoke.

Easter at the Villa Victoria

'There you are now. We'll make a good, strong boy of you yet, chust, a good, strong boy of you yet.'

'Merci, Madame Hogan.'

Bridie and the Limbus had been planning the dinner party for the following night with all the excitement of an end-of-term midnight feast. There would be fourteen for dinner and the house had not seen such a party for nearly two years.

'It would be when the Colonel was down with his army friends and that lady and her son from Edinburgh were in the house,' Bridie said, 'we had fifteen then, chust, we had fifteen then.'

'I think it was sixteen,' Manju said, 'I remember I could only get scallops for fifteen and then one of the ladies said she couldn't have them as she was allergic to them.'

'Oh yes, I think you're right, chust, I think you're right; there were sixteen.'

Dhani had brought in two extra leaves for the dining table, which were stored in the coach house, and had polished them in readiness. Now, in apron and white cotton gloves, he was polishing the table silver. Monsieur Verrechia, he who had been a waiter at the Martinez, had been contacted and would report for duty at six o'clock the following evening.

Dhani, as was his wont on such occasions, would be doing drinks and wine so Henri, the garden boy, was to come back in the evening, clean and wearing a jacket and tie, to do the gates as the guests arrived and departed. This, he looked forward to as a privilege but, as he would, unusually, be going home in the dark, he would have to do something about the lights on his motor bike which had not been working for some time.

'Miss Kate will want the flowers ready for ten tomorrow morning when she comes down to do the table decorations,' Bridie said, 'has she told you what she wants, Dhani?'

'She walk round garden with me first thing tomorrow,' Dhani replied, 'she tell me then.'

'And the wine? Have you seen Colonel Charlie about it?'

Revelations

'Claret up and standing in the pantry. We get whites up tomorrow.'

'Oh!' Bridie said in sudden alarm, 'what will I put Miss Mattie in? She's dirtied every dress she has, chust, she's dirtied every dress she has.' She hurried through the door en route for the laundry room.

'And Bridie,' Manju called after her, 'you won't forget the cheese tomorrow, will you?'

'No, dear,' I've got it on my line, chust, I've got it on my line.'

The kitchen was buzzing with excitement. Nothing must be overlooked or done in less than perfect fashion. The ghost of Lady Florence and all those other Morton-Stewarts who had entertained the cream of Riviera society in this house so many years ago, would be looking down to see if standards had declined. The success, or otherwise, of the evening would reflect on the good name of the house and the professional ability of its staff. They would not be found wanting.

This happy anticipation in the kitchen was tarnished only by the knowledge that, the day after the dinner party, the family would start returning to UK and the bustle and joyousness of the past month would be over.

23. Preparations

At their flat off the promenade des Anglais, Maud Pontefract was less pleased with the dinner invitation than Herbert had expected. 'It's such short notice. What am I going to wear?'

'What about that nice dress you wore at our anniversary lunch last week?'

'Quite unsuitable. It will have to be something black. Everyone is bound to be very smart, those sort of people always are. I'll have to go out and buy something now before the shops close.'

'Whatever you think, dear.'

'Won't we feel awfully out of place, Herbert? Especially with that dreadful Powell man who's always trying to put you down?'

'You'll see some of the finest furniture and silver on the Coast; the house is a model of elegance and good taste.' Herbert said with a little anticipatory sniff.

'And the people too, I shouldn't wonder. They'll all be looking down their noses at us.'

'People like the Morton-Stewarts don't look down their noses at anyone, dear. They are far too well bred. It's only jumped up little upstarts like Rupert who do that.'

***

At her villa on the Avenue des Sables, Lady Wroughton instructed her housekeeper: 'Now, we've got Madame Lauvert for tea this afternoon; she'll be on her own, her daughter has returned to Paris.'

'Yes, your ladyship.'

'Then, there's nobody coming tonight so I'll just have a light supper at my usual time. What is it?'

'Lamb, I believe, your ladyship.'

Preparations

'Well please ask cook to do it well. I cannot abide this modern fad for undercooked lamb. Then, tomorrow, I'm dining with the Morton-Stewarts so tell Jacques I'll need the car for 7.20.'

'Yes, your ladyship.'

'And Helene, would you ask the gardener to do something about that loose step at the end of the pergola. It's crumbling and quite unsafe. If I trip over and break my neck, you'll all be out of jobs, won't you?'

'Yes, your ladyship.'

Lady Wroughton was looking forward to the dinner party. She had known the Morton-Stewarts all her life – they were one of the few remaining 'good' families on the Riviera. What fun they had all had in the old days when she, and Mattie and Kate were gels – the parties, the dances, the picnics. Then she had married Hugh and spent the next forty years of her life travelling with him as a camp follower. But when she returned to the South of France, the Morton-Stewarts were still there, living much the same sort of life, although the world had changed around them.

Like all families, they'd had their black sheep. Poor old James! It had broken his heart when his eldest son had married a barmaid; and he'd been in trouble all his life before that; a thoroughly bad lot by all accounts. Thank heavens they'd had Charlie to hold things together, he was always steady like his father, and thank heavens old James had the sense to cut that rotter out of his Will; he'd have spent the lot in no time flat if he'd had the chance.

And yet, the 'barmaid' was not at all what she had expected when Kate and Mattie brought her over to tea the other day; not in the least loud and blowsy; quite the reverse really. She had been surprised at how pleasant and how dignified she was; very pretty, too; a lovely figure, clear skin and beautiful hair. She looked so young, must have been a child when that scoundrel James had married her. And her daughter, (Emma was she called?) – a quite enchanting child; too much makeup, of course, and a very strange haircut, but the young get up to some very peculiar things nowadays.

There was a niece, too, poor Florence's grand-daughter; married to a parson's son who was in some sort of trade; she'd met her some years ago, when they were on their honeymoon; couldn't remember her name but she hadn't struck her as being particularly agreeable.

* * *

In their luxurious modern flat above his consulting rooms in the Boulevard Dugommier, Doctor Marcel Chouard greeted his wife in the manner she had long since abandoned hope of discouraging.

'What Ho! Elise.'

'What Ho! Marcel.'

'You will not forget we are dining with the Misses Morton-Stewart tomorrow, will you?'

'Of course not.'

Elise Chouard was a very glamorous Côte d'Azur blonde from Vence who had oiled her husband's progress to the heights of his profession, in a fashionable and lucrative private practice, with assertive and elegant social support and a fine judgement on with which of his superiors it would be productive to flirt.

They had dined on several occasions at the Villa Victoria where Elise's delight in the excellence of the cuisine was marred only by her husband's anglophilia, which tended to become increasingly bizarre as the evening progressed.

'Cherie,' she said, 'please promise me you won't drink too much tomorrow. You never know, you might have a call.'

'Doctor Pouillard is covering for me tomorrow.'

'Even so, it is best not to drink too much. Remember, the old ladies are your patients.'

'They are also my friends.'

'They are, more importantly, your patients.'

'And Elise, old girl,' she winced, 'you are very chic and very beautiful but it is not mandatory to make every man at the table fall in love with you. Nuff said?'

Preparations

* * *

In the lounge of the Gray d'Albion in Cannes, Steve Fitzgerald waited for his coffee to arrive. He had things to do today but, since he had met Emma, he had found it increasingly difficult to concentrate or apply himself to anything.

There was no future in it, of course, in a couple of days time she would return to London and he to Paris. It was probable that they would never meet again. He could write to her, and she to him, he supposed, but the letters would dry up as the familiarity of her old social group in London reimposed itself on her life and gradually eroded her memory of him. She was so young – far too young to be burdened with a commitment to one man whom she would, necessarily, seldom see.

Were circumstances different, he would woo her – he was intoxicated with her elfin charm, her youth, her vitality and her innocence. He would court her until he won her and could carry her back to Boston to delight his parents and enrich the rest of his life. But *would* she delight his parents? Though his father was a fourth generation American, he was Boston Irish with a deep-seated, hereditary loathing of the English and, more so, of the hated Anglo-Irish aristocracy who, he had been taught from childhood, had exploited his forefathers, and whose blood was in Emma's veins. Perhaps he would never accept her.

Anyway, it was academic. Steve was a career diplomat who must go where his masters sent him. There was no chance of a posting to the London embassy, he had only just recently arrived in Paris; and there was no way he could conduct a long-distance courtship of a girl like Emma, with her passion for life and her endless stream of admirers when, at best, he could only hope to see her for, perhaps, one weekend in four. It really was a hopeless situation.

He was invited to dinner tomorrow at the Villa Victoria and it broke his heart to think that it would probably be the last time he would see his precious, wonderful little Emma.

Easter at the Villa Victoria

* * *

In the foyer of the Hotel Negresco in Nice, Rupert Saint John Powell sat and pondered on why none of his 'friends' on the coast seemed anxious to see him. It was partly due to the difficulty of locating people in the Alpes-Maritime telephone directory, which sub-divided the department into towns so you had to know exactly where someone lived before you could find their number. He had managed to contact two people, both of whom he imagined would have been delighted to hear from him but, in the event, were otherwise engaged, or said they were. How boring people could be.

There was, of course, old Tom Braithwaite who had been in his regiment and had, in fact, always been very decent to him. While many of Rupert's brother officers had tended to look down on him, and shun his company, Tom Braithwaite had always been prepared to give him the time of day. He had retired to the South of France and had a modest flat not far from the Negresco; but the rungs of Rupert's social ladder were not fashioned from elderly, retired officers living on their pensions; Tom Braithwaite had no glamorous or influential friends to whom he might be introduced, and could not afford to wine and dine in the smart places in Nice where Rupert would wish to be seen. Old Tom was simply not worth a visit.

Still, Rupert thought, there was the dinner party at the Villa Victoria tomorrow. That would be a good talking point for when he got home and there were bound to be some other interesting people there, people with rank, and money, who he could add to his circle of 'very good friends'.

* * *

The kitchen at the villa was a powerhouse of activity. To Manju, with her hotel training and experience, a five-course haute-cuisine dinner for fourteen was not the nightmare it might have been to a keen amateur. It needed careful planning, of course, and, in consultation with Miss Kate, she had decided upon a cold terrine, followed by a hot fish course, a hot

Preparations

main course, cheese and then a cold dessert. She was making the terrine now, which would be one thing out of the way. The fish and meat had been ordered and would be collected by Dhani first thing in the morning. She would get as much of the preparatory work done as possible in the morning and then, from tea time onwards, she would be oblivious to the world around her – totally absorbed in the production of a meal which none of the guests would ever forget. Sometimes she missed the frenetic activity of a professional kitchen – the heat, the noise, the bad temper when things went wrong and the elation when they went right. Only on occasions, such as tomorrow's dinner party, did that old feeling of supercharged urgency return to her; and it was nice to experience it again, once in a while.

* * *

'Try not to smoke too much tomorrow evening, dear,' Aunt Kate said to Mattie, 'it's such a disgusting habit and it makes you cough.'

Mattie smiled like a guilty child.

'And you get the ash all over yourself,' she continued, 'Bridie has such a job, forever washing your frocks.'

'They're perfectly all right,' Mattie said, offended, 'a little bit of ash never hurt anyone.'

'And don't encourage Charlie to smoke, either.'

'Keeps the moth out.' Mattie said.

'What keeps the moth out?'

'A bit of ash on a frock.'

'There are no moth here, dear. And don't monopolise the young people tomorrow; 'Frills' will want to talk to them. ('Frills' was their pet name, since childhood, for Lady Wroughton originating, it was thought, from her mother's fondness for dressing her in frilly frocks.)

'Why should I do that, dear?'

'You always do; you shout at them across the table and can't hear a word of what they say in reply.'

'What nonsense, dear.'

'Mattie was quite used to this lecture from Kate before every social gathering. She had been receiving them all her life. Mattie loved parties and meeting people, and simply liked to enter into the spirit of everything and behave naturally. But Kate was so inhibited with ideas about precedence and correct behaviour that she spoiled much of the pleasure.

Certainly, her hearing was not what it used to be, in fact, truth to tell, she heard very little in company. She could still converse on a one-to-one basis when people spoke slowly and distinctly – she could always hear what Charlie said to her – but at a crowded table, with everyone talking at once, she really didn't get much of it at all. But what did it matter? When all was said and done, it was not *wha*t people said but *how* they said it. If they were smiling and laughing, she would smile and laugh back at them and, when someone looked grave, she would look grave too. When someone had asked her a question, which she recognised by raised eyebrows and an interrogative expression, she had developed the technique of pretending to have dropped her napkin, or something, and then launching off on an entirely different subject. So expert had she become in these deceptions, that not many people realised that she was actually as deaf as an adder.

Aunt Kate looked forward to the morrow with her usual concerns. She worried about trivia – would the flowers for the table look all right? Would any of the guests cry off at the last moment leaving a gap at the table? Would anyone get held up in traffic and arrive late, ruining the orchestration of the meal? Would anyone drink too much and embarrass other guests? (Young people drank far too much nowadays.) In her heart, she knew that everything would go well, she had arranged hundreds of dinner parties and they always did. The staff were completely competent and, as always, well prepared; they could cope with any little hiatus that might arise. Charlie and Dhani would have the wine beautifully organised, as they always did. Yes, she knew that everything would be all right but still could not help making herself fractious and edgy by imagining every possible disaster which might occur.

Preparations

* * *

'Charlie.' Sylvia said.

'Yes, darling.'

'If we are going to the Tropique tonight, which I very much hope and assume we are . . .'

'We are.'

'Could we possibly leave about an hour earlier so I can look for a dress in Juan for tomorrow night?'

'I suppose so, if you must.'

'I must, darling. I can't let you down by looking frumpy.'

'You couldn't look frumpy if you tried.' he said and was deeply flattered that she had talked about letting *him* down – an implication of partnership which he found quite thrilling.

Accordingly, they arrived in Juan early and she led him by the arm along the row of smart little boutiques at the eastern end of the Boulevard Charles Guillaumont. 'This will do.' she said decisively outside one of them, 'Come on.' She pulled him towards the door.

'I'm not going in there,' Charlie said with horror, 'I'll wait for you out here.'

'Don't be such a poop, Charlie. Come in with me; nobody is going to eat you.'

He reluctantly followed her inside and the assistant, noticing his discomposure, offered him a chair. 'Perhaps Monsieur would like to wait here for Madame?'

Sylvia rummaged quickly down the row of dresses, plucking one out, holding it up, frowning and putting it back. She eventually selected two.

'I'll try on these two, please.'

'Of course, Madame.' the assistant replied, showing her to a curtained changing cubicle at the back of the shop.

A few minutes later she emerged from the cubicle in one of the dresses. It was a black dress, about three inches above the knee, simple and unadorned yet of obvious quality. It fitted her perfectly and she looked absolutely stunning.

The assistant caught her breath. 'Oh Madame! C'est fantastique!' It was what she said to all her customers but there was something in her look of awe that denoted that, this time, she really meant it. Most of her time was spent in trying to convince women of oddly assorted shapes and sizes that they looked 'fantastique' in the dress which had been hanging on her rails for too many weeks and needed shifting. She knew, from long experience, exactly where, with her hands, to take a tuck, or pull down on a seam, to display the garment to its best advantage as the customer examined herself in the mirror. With this lady, there was no need to touch the dress in any way. Her figure was so perfect she could have made any dress in the shop look 'fantastique'.

Sylvia turned and twisted in front of the mirror looking at herself from different angles. She had left her shoes in the cubicle and the zip at the back of the dress was only half done up where it had snagged on the label which dangled on its string down her back. As she turned from side to side, her soft, shining hair swung from one shoulder to the other and the label, on its string, followed its motion like a pendulum. It was at this moment that Charlie realised that he was hopelessly in love with her and did not want to spend another moment of his life without her.

She made a turn in front of him and said: 'What do you think?'

'Fantastique!' he replied and the assistant smiled indulgently.

'Well,' Sylvia said, 'I don't think there's any need to try on the other dress. If you like this one, let's go firm.' She went to the cubicle to change. Charlie's head was swimming with a strange and violent emotion and, after a few minutes, he followed her to the cubicle and called:

'Are you decent, Sylvia?'

'Wait just a minute.'

He waited for what seemed like an eternity until she parted the curtains and he saw her beautiful face smiling at him through the gap, her eyebrows raised in a question.

Preparations

'I love you, Sylvia.' he said and, taking her head between his hands, he drew her to him through the gap in the curtains and kissed her on the mouth, gently and passionately.

'And I love you, Charlie,' she replied, 'so much that it hurts.'

They looked deeply into each other's eyes for a moment then Sylvia broke away and said: 'And if you want to prove your love, you can get out your credit card and pay for this dress while I finish changing.'

'Certainly, darling.'

'And by the time you've paid, I'll be quite ready for a cool beer at the Tropique.'

'Excellent'.

Much later, family tradition would have it that Charlie actually proposed to Sylvia in the boutique, with his head poking awkwardly through a row of designer dresses. It made for a better story, and good stories are what family tradition is all about. But, in reality, this did not happen until some time later, in the Bar Tropique, in the course of what turned out to be a four-beer evening, at the end of which Charlie arrived late for dinner – for the very first time in his life.

Easter at the Villa Victoria

24. The Dinner Party

The family and their guests had assembled on the veranda at the appointed time, introductions had been made and Kir Royales served and consumed. At eight o'clock Dhani had appeared at the door, in spotless, starched white jacket and black tie and announced to Aunt Kate: 'Dinner is served, Madame.'

The guests moved through to the dining room.

Kate stood by as her guests paused to admire the table before being shown to their places. It looked magnificent. Crystal and polished silver sparkled in the soft light from the two great candelabra; her flower arrangements were the essence of a Côte d'Azur spring and not a knife nor a glass broke rank from their regimented order in front of each diner. Yes, she thought, Mummy would have approved, the table was perfect.

The guests stood by their chairs while Mattie was discreetly dusted off; the Aunts sat down followed by the others. Grace was only said at dinner when there was a clergyman present, which there was not tonight, so napkins were shaken out onto laps while Dhani circulated with water – a choice of still Evian or sparkling Badoit – and the meal began.

Terrine de Poireaux a la Vinaigrette
et Julienne de Truffes

Gewürztraminer Léon Beyer
1991

Manju's terrine was a masterpiece – alternate layers of white and green leeks, garnished with truffles.

The Dinner Party

'Same wonderful cook I see, dear.' Lady Wroughton called across the table to Kate. Then to Rupert on her right: 'Only place on the Coast you can eat like this nowadays, unless you pay a king's ransom at one of these rip-off gourmet places for the film stars.'

'Yes,' Rupert replied, greatly pleased to have been seated next to her. The cost of food in some of these places is quite ridiculous. A friend of mine, Anne MacKrill, you know, Lady Anne MacKrill of the MacKrills of Perthshire – you know her I dare say?'

'No.'

'She had a meal the other day in one of those pseudo-smart places on the Old Brompton Road, and it cost her nearly £300 for two people.'

'What did she have? Smoked MacKrills?'

Rupert laughed dutifully and turned to Frances who was soliciting his attention on his other side.

Charlie, at the veranda end of the table with Lady Wroughton on his right and Maud Pontefract on his left, recognised that the latter was feeling a little out of her depth and set about putting her at her ease. He established that she came from Harrogate.

'Oh, Harrogate; such a beautiful place.'

'You know it, do you?' Maud said with obvious delight.

'Oh yes, it's one of my favourite places. Such lovely gardens and such nice, gentile people live there, don't they?'

'Well, Harrogate folk do have a reputation for being a bit stuck up.'

'Quite understandable. You're bound to get a bit stuck up if you live in a beautiful place like Harrogate.' Maud purred with pleasure.

Elise Chouard, looking very exotic in a Paris couture dress and masses of jewellery, sat between Richard and Herbert Pontefract. She was talking to Herbert, having decided she would leave Richard, who was really quite nice looking, until later. Noting Herbert's hesitant French, she asked: 'You prefer we speak in English?'

'If you don't mind.' he replied.

'I don't mind. My husband loves everything English and we often talk in

English at home. Many of his patients are English, too.'

'He's a doctor?'

'Oui, oui. This terrine is superb, is it not?'

'Yes, delicious.' said Herbert who hated leeks above almost every other food and was having a struggle to get his down.

Steve and Emma, who Kate had reluctantly seated together due to Mattie's pleading, sat rather sad and silent, each aware of the significance of this occasion.

'What time is your flight tomorrow?' he asked.

'About five in the evening. I think I'll just hide up in the attic.'

'That would only delay things. You have to return to London sometime, sad as it is.'

'I just want to stay here forever.' she said plaintively.

Marcel Chouard, sitting between Kate and Maud Pontefract, was far too absorbed in the enjoyment of the terrine to speak to anyone. Where food and wine were concerned, he was a Frenchman through and through and did not believe that it's enjoyment should be interrupted by conversation. Dhani circulating silently behind the diners, topping up glasses, saw the doctor drain his as the bottle approached – a sure sign of a serious epicure – and filled it accordingly.

Charlie laughed, 'You're enjoying that terrine, Marcel.'

'Top hole, old boy.' the doctor replied out of courtesy, then closed his eyes in ecstasy as he savoured the earthy delight of the truffles.

Sylvia, in her simple black dress and with no jewellery, still eclipsed Elise Chouard with all her finery, by virtue of her natural beauty and poise. She sat between Steve and Richard who, being far enough away from Frances to risk a compliment with impunity, said: 'You look quite stunning, Sylvia. How well that dress suits you.'

'Thank you, kind sir.' she replied with a laugh. Then later: 'What time will you have to leave in the morning?'

'I think we must try and be away first thing. I'd like to get the other side of Paris in daylight.'

The Dinner Party

'Yes, it's a long drive and I imagine the twins get very tired on a journey like that?'

'They tend to sleep on the way home from holidays because they're miserable and depressed; but on the way down, when they were all hyped up, they were absolute murder.'

Mattie, sitting in her usual place next to Kate, was wondering how she could annoy her sister for seating her next to this awful little man who was still eating his leeks when everyone else was finished and, moreover, appeared to be in need of a handkerchief.

* * *

Out in the kitchen, Manju, having indulged herself with a discreet peep through the hatch to ensure that the terrine had been well received, had swung into action with the final stages of the fish course. She had placed the turbot, which had been delivered in the morning and was very fresh, in the fridge at lunchtime, covered in milk and ice cubes which would ensure that it remained pure white during cooking. Now it was in the oven, baking in cream and she was checking it every two minutes as it must be cooked absolutely *'à point'*. Meanwhile, she was whisking the quince mousseline and dashing from pot to pot on the top of the range – inspecting, stirring, tasting and seasoning.

Bridie, watching the dining table from the hatch, kept Manju posted on the progress of the first course so she could fine-tune her timings.

'The little sniffing man's not finished yet. He's eating very slow. I don't think he likes leeks, chust, I don't think he likes leeks.'

At last he was finished and Monsieur Verrechia was collecting the plates.

'He's finished,' Bridie called, 'the plates are coming out.'

'Ça marche!' Manju called as she swung the heavy dish of fish from the oven and prepared to arrange it on the row of heated plates behind her.

Easter at the Villa Victoria

*Le Blanc de Turbot
en Mousseline de Coing*

ა⊸

*Puligny-Montrachet Champ-Canet
Etienne Sauzet 1981*

The turbot was placed before them, the pure white flakes of fish fanned out artistically and surrounded by a velvety, light green, cream sauce and garnished with parsley, chervil and tarragon. The next glasses in line were half filled with lush, golden, Côte d'Or Burgundy. Marcel shrugged and sighed and his wife, breaking off her conversation with Richard, frowned at her plate and said, in an exasperated tone: 'How *does* she keep the fish so *white*?'

Maud, seeing herself presented with a second glass of wine, wondered what she should do with the first, which she had not yet finished. She looked out of the corner of her eye at other diners and noted they had all finished their first-course wine. Her anxiety was quickly relieved as Dhani removed the glass, making a mental note not to top this lady up and to dispense her with lesser quantities. The Gewürztraminer, he knew, though good, was not precious but there could be no waste of this Montrachet nor, indeed, of the claret which was to follow. By this stage of the meal he had a good idea of the drinking habits of each guest: the doctor and his wife obviously knew what they were drinking and would need constant attention; so would Lady Wroughton. The Pontefracts were not great drinkers, nor the young American gentleman, and Dhani would service their glasses with discretion to avoid any embarrassment to them and, of even more importance, any waste of precious wines which would displease the Colonel.

Unbeknown to Dhani, there had been no waste so far as Monsieur Verrechia, carrying the used glasses through to the scullery on a tray, had paused at a point in the corridor where he could not be observed from either dining room or kitchen, and had knocked back the remnants of wine in each glass in quick succession.

The Dinner Party

'I love fish,' Lady Wroughton boomed, tucking in heartily, 'but there's no fish like that wot you've caught yourself. D'you fish?' she asked Rupert.

'I try to get a week on the Doune every year. Alasdair Drummond is a friend of mine – you know . . .'

'Yes, I know, *Lord* Drummond of the Drummonds of Banffshire, he's a friend of mine too. Never heard him mention *you* though.' She had clearly got his number and, turning abruptly to Charlie asked: 'D'you get much fishing nowadays, Charlie? Never knew a man tie a salmon fly like your father.'

At the other end of the table, Elise, having finished her turbot was batting her eyelashes at Richard who was trying to finish his and Sylvia, aware of Steve's melancholy, and the reason for it, was trying to cheer him up by asking him questions about his job:

'How long do you think you'll stay in Paris?'

'I should think three years at least, possibly a little longer.'

'And will you come down here for holidays and weekends?'

'Not quite the same incentive after you and Emma have gone home.' he replied pathetically and with a shy smile.

'Ah!' Sylvia and Emma said in unison, each placing a hand over one of Steve's.

Frances regained Rupert's attention and was trying to initiate an arty conversation with him.

'What do you think of this year's winner of the Turnberry Prize?' Rupert asked her; this was a huge, emerald green turd, spiked with cloves and suspended from the ceiling by a rusty bicycle chain.

'Oh *amazing*, so *intimate* and *relevant* . . .'

Lady Wroughton, whose years as an army wife had endowed her with a trooper's vocabulary, interrupted: 'I think it's just what it appears to be, – absolute crap.'

Charlie was still talking to Maud about Harrogate: 'Yes, Valley Gardens, is that what they're called, just below the Crown Hotel?'

'Yes, Valley Gardens and The Crown is a lovely hotel.' even with the reduced quantities of wine she was receiving, Maud had a pleasurable glow and was feeling unusually relaxed in Charlie's attentive and charming company. 'Herbert and I stayed there once when he had to attend an Antiques Fair. You should see the dining room – great high ceiling and magnificent pillars. Reet gradely.'

'Really?' said Charlie, who had stayed at the Crown on a couple of occasions and had found it comfortable, if not reet gradely, 'I must go and stay there next time I'm in Harrogate and have a look at this dining room.'

'You'll not regret it.' Maud assured him.

Herbert, himself, was getting on better with his fish than he had with the leek terrine but his progress was again slowed by Mattie's attempt to converse with him:

'You're in advertising, are you?'

'No, Miss Morton-Stewart, I work for Christebys.'

'Christmas trees?'

'No, Christebys – the auctioneers and fine art house.'

'Doctor Barnardos?'

'No, Miss Morton-Stewart. I deal with furniture and paintings.' and he assisted his explanation by making painting motions with his hand.

'Oh, you're a painter . . . Frills,' Mattie called across the table to Lady Wroughton, 'you wanted your morning room redecorated. This man is a painter.'

'No, no, I'm not.' Herbert said shaking his head emphatically.

Strange little man, doesn't seem to know what he is, Mattie thought and wondered if she could get a quick ciggy in now; or should she wait until after the next course. Better wait, she thought on reflection, don't want Kate getting hysterical.

* * *

Bridie, waiting at the hatch, kept the kitchen posted on progress: 'He's nearly finished now. He's always the last, chust, he's always the last.'

The Dinner Party

Manju drew from the oven a bain-marie dish with rows of courgette timbales, baking in little dariole moulds. She pressed the top of one with a finger; two minutes more, she decided, and they were back in the oven, the door closed. The racks of lamb had rested and were ready for carving.

'Plates!' she called, without panic, and Bridie laid the hot plates before her as she carved the lamb with the speed and finesse which could only have been acquired by years of professional experience. The timbales came out of the oven and Bridie loosened them and turned them out of their moulds – perfect little castles of courgette, olive oil, breadcrumbs, milk, gruyère cheese and eggs. Manju dipped a finger in the glossy sauce which was reducing on the range and tasted: a dash more salt; a vigorous stir and that was it. The timbales were placed beside the carved lamb; one steamed shallot, split in two, was arranged on each plate with three tiny asparagus spears; the sauce was spooned on beside the lamb and a sprig of chervil was placed on top of each timbale.

'Manju, dear,' Bridie said as they stood back and surveyed the rows of plates, 'that's perfect, chust, perfect.'

Les Dos d'Agneau Rôti a l'Os aux Échalotes Marinées
a l'Huile d'Olive Vierge et Vieux Vinaigre de Vin
Flan de Courgettes

ஓஓ

Château Léoville-Barton
2eme Cru Classé Saint Julien 1982

The claret had been decanted that morning and stood in the same Venetian glass decanters, and on the same sideboard, as the family's claret had stood two hundred years before. Dhani, conscious of the liquid gold he was handling, dispensed it with extreme care. Monsieur Verrechia, having cleared the white Burgundy glasses, paused in the corridor to drink the remnants, such as they were, pulled a face of approval, belched, and continued on his way to the scullery. The lamb was placed before each diner, there was a lull in conversation and a sigh of approval went round the table.

Lady Wroughton, having taken a liberal sip of her claret and nodded at Kate in approval, poked Rupert's arm and asked: 'And to what branch of the Saint John Powells do *you* belong?'

Rupert had not yet recovered from her last slight. Lord Drummond had hundreds of friends; why should he have mentioned him to *her* – stupid old woman. She repeated her question in a scornful and challenging tone: 'To what branch of the *Saint John Powells* do *you* belong?'

Rupert sniggered and replied: 'I'm from Surrey, actually.'

'Where in Surrey?'

'Camberley.' he said, thinking it sounded better than Frimley.

'Camberley, eh? I lived in Camberley for a time, just after the war. Don't remember any Saint John Powells though.'

Marcel Chouard withdrew his nose from his glass as Dhani passed to seek confirmation of the vintage, one of the very finest:

'1982?'

'Yes, sir.' Dhani replied and Marcel, knowing of no appropriate Wodehousian expression of appreciation merely mumbled: 'Oh, la, la!' before swirling his glass and returning his nose to the tantalising fragrance.

Charlie, having exhausted his knowledge of Harrogate, had moved on to Hartlepool whence, he learned, Maud's mother came.

'There was a monkey washed ashore from this French ship during the Napoleonic Wars,' she told him with an animation which was increasing with every gulp of wine she took, 'and the folk in Hartlepool thought it was a Frenchman. They'd never seen a Frenchman, you see.'

'Frills!' Mattie called across the table, 'Who was that fellow who put a chamber pot on top of the cathedral?'

'Beau Geste Baynes.'

'Chest pains?'

'No, Beau Geste Baynes. Tell her Kate.' she added impatiently, waving her knife in the Aunts' direction.

The Dinner Party

'Beau Geste Baynes.' Kate shouted in Mattie's ear above the now not inconsiderable hum of conversation. 'They called him Beau Geste because he nearly enlisted in the Foreign Legion one night when he was drunk.'

'Married Lottie Fergus-Ffiennes in the end,' Lady Wroughton added, 'strange couple – spent the first night of their honeymoon tobogganing down the stairs on a silver tray they'd been given as a wedding present.'

'And they hung the monkey,' Maud told Charlie, 'thinking it was a Frenchman, you see.'

'Good heavens! That was a bit draconian, even for a Frenchman.'

'No, it was a monkey.'

'Yes, but they *thought* it was a Frenchman.' Charlie reassured her lest she should doubt his attention to her story. His attention had, in fact, been divided for a moment as he had noticed Monsieur Verrechia at the other end of the room, walking rather unsteadily.

Elise Chouard, who was managing to obtain more than her fair share of the claret, was now turning the full power of her charms onto Richard and was presently delivering a teasing citation on the virility of English men. Richard, knowing that Frances had observed her behaviour, and kept scowling in his direction, decided he would play up to Elise in retribution for Frances's coquettish intimacy with Rupert which was beginning to annoy him.

Herbert Pontefract, determined not to be the last to finish this course, was attacking his lamb with a lack of finesse and appreciation which had not gone unnoticed by the observers at the hatch.

'He's stuffing it down his throat as if it was nothing more than bangers and mash, chust, bangers and mash.'

Emma and Steve were exchanging long, dreamy looks and saying very little despite Sylvia's frequent attempts to start a cheerful conversation going, and Kate was berating Mattie who had announced her intention of slipping out for a little ciggy on the veranda before the next course.

* * *

Easter at the Villa Victoria

The kitchen was enjoying a slight lull. The cheese had been laid out on individual plates and was ready to go through. Each diner would receive a small piece of three, mature, soft-rind cheeses – an unpasteurised Brie, a Langres from the Champagne-Ardennes region and a strong Reblochon de Savoie. They had been bought that morning, in perfect condition, from a specialist fromagerie in the Old Town. A Bougon had been planned but was rejected at the last moment as it was not quite ready. The cheese would be eaten without bread or biscuits, with a knife and fork in the French manner and would be accompanied by a powerful Northern Rhône.

Les Fromages

Hermitage de la Sizeranne
Chapoutier 1978

Monsieur Verrechia, on his way out with the claret glasses, observed that Dhani's careful management of the wine had left him with only a very modest collective draught. However, he noticed that cook had left a scarcely-breached bottle of marsala near the kitchen door and, with a lifetime's experience in such matters, it would not take him long to create the necessary diversion which would enable him to purloin it.

Mattie and Charlie returned from the veranda where they had smoked a hurried, half cigarette and the guests started on their cheese.

Dhani, having circulated with the Rhone and found the take-up rate to have been higher than expected, hurried to the scullery to open two more bottles where he surprised Monsieur Verrechia, who scarcely had time to conceal the bottle of marsala behind his back.

With the abundant hospitality of the house, any previous inhibitions which may have been harboured by any of the guests had long since been abandoned. The room resounded with cheerful laughter and loud, animated conversation.

The Dinner Party

Charlie was back in Hartlepool.

'If you want to *reeeally* upset someone from Hartlepool,' Maud told him, 'you just have to say to them 'Hung any monkeys lately'?'

Charlie laughed encouragingly although he could not envisage any circumstance where he would be likely to wish to upset someone from Hartlepool.

Rupert, who had decided to concentrate his attention on Frances, and keep well clear of Lady Wroughton, felt her prodding finger on his left arm. He turned towards her reluctantly.

'Knew a builder in Camberley called Powell. Fitted a new downstairs lavatory for us.'

'You know where it is, dear.' said Mattie who had picked up one word.

'Any relation of yours?' Lady Wroughton asked Rupert.

'No.' he replied curtly and turned again to Frances wondering, now, if this wretched old woman had heard about his background from someone and was trying, deliberately, to embarrass him.

Frances, however, was not as receptive as she had been earlier and was glaring with unconcealed anger at her husband who was now holding Elise by the wrist and was *shshushing* her in an intimate and flirtatious way.

Aunt Kate had also noted Madame Chouard's behaviour. A very common woman, she thought, but she could hardly invite the doctor without her. Everyone had been drinking rather a lot tonight, the table had become very noisy and undignified. She would hasten on the dessert, she thought, and was about to beckon Monsieur Verrechia to tell him when she noticed he seemed to be staggering a bit. Was he ill, she wondered.

* * *

Manju put the finishing touches to her dessert – little choux pastry horns filled with Chantilly cream and home-made pistachio icecream, surrounded by fans of sliced kiwi fruit, mangoes and pears lying on a rich, highly reduced raspberry coulis; the whole garnished with glazed strawberries, mint sprigs and verbena. Of all the dishes she had prepared tonight, it was this of which she was most proud but she realised, with a little sadness, that judging by the amount of wine which had been drunk, it was the offering which would be least appreciated.

La Corone d'Abondance aux Fruits Glaces

Château la Tour Blanche
1er Cru Classé Sauternes 1966

Manju's fears were not fully realised as, although some of the guests were in no condition to appreciate the full depth of her artistry, others were. Elise Chouard broke off her seduction of Richard for long enough to gasp and shout 'Bravo!' in the general direction of the kitchen and Marcel, having stared at his plate for a full minute, was moved to go over to the hatch and call a compliment through to Manju who accepted it with smiling delight. The sight of Dhani circulating with the ice-cold sauternes, however, sent him scurrying back to his seat.

Lady Wroughton, too, was sufficiently impressed with the dessert to catch the Aunts' eye and shout: 'Fantastic!'

'Elastic, dear?' Mattie replied in puzzlement.

Having picked off and eaten her glazed strawberries and taken a liberal sip of her sauternes, to which she said: 'Mmm! Yum, Yum!' Frills Wroughton returned to her persecution of Rupert and, prodding him again with her finger, said: 'Imprisoned for indecent exposure – several times.'

'I beg your pardon, Lady Wroughton?' Rupert said with as much surprise and mystification in his voice as he could muster.

'Powell the builder,' she boomed, 'they used to call him 'Flasher' – 'Flasher' Powell.'

'Afterwards,' Elise said to Richard, 'we take a little walk in ze garden and you show me ze pretty flowers, huh?'

The Dinner Party

'No, no,' Richard replied in alarm, 'far too cold.'

'The weather? Or you?' she mocked.

Charlie, meanwhile, had moved on from Hartlepool to the Yorkshire Dales and Herbert was delivering a sniff-punctuated dissertation on the problems of woodworm in antique furniture, quite unconcerned by the fact that nobody was listening to him. Marcel had finished his dessert and sat slumped in his chair, swirling and sniffing his wine and mumbling: 'Spiffing, simply spiffing.'

Dhani leaned over to top up Maud's wine and Charlie, fearing an imminent rendering of 'On Ilka Moor baht'ad' if she drunk any more, gave an imperceptible frown which Dhani immediately interpreted and only topped her glass up by the smallest amount.

At this point, there was a dull thud from the end of the room and all heads turned to the doorway where Monsieur Verrechia lay prostrate on the floor. Marcel was instantly in attendance and, after a cursory examination, beckoned Dhani to help carry him out to the staff sitting room. When he returned to the dining room Marcel said: 'Nothing serious, no cause for concern.'

'Poor man.' Aunt Kate said sympathetically. 'I thought he looked ill.'

'Drunk as a fiddler's bitch if you ask me.' Frills grunted.

Marcel leaned over Charlie as he passed behind his chair: 'Pissed as a fart, old boy.' he whispered.

'I thought as much.' Charlie replied.

Kate led the ladies out to the drawing room where Bridie was waiting with coffee and petit fours. Emma pouted and sulked at being separated from Steve. Frances glared at Richard with overt hostility and Lady Wroughton informed Charlie that she would require some cognac with her coffee. Then, as she passed Rupert's chair on her way out, she prodded him in the back and said:

'Flasher Powell, that's what they called him. He used to drop his breeks in front of school girls.'

'So you have told me, Lady Wroughton, on several occasions.' he replied, not without style.

The men shuffled up to Charlie's end of the table and, after some manly talk over the port, and a Ratzputz for Herbert, prescribed by Doctor Chouard to 'settle' him, the gentlemen joined the ladies in the drawing room and, shortly thereafter, it being well past midnight, the party broke up. The guests were loud in their praise for the magnificent meal and in their gratitude to the Aunts for such a wonderful evening. The Chouards called at the kitchen on their way out to thank the chef. Marcel shook her hand and Elise attempted to prise from her the secret for keeping fish so white.

Emma's eyes filled with tears as she said goodbye to Steve and he promised to phone her next day before they left for the airport. Maud told Charlie that she'd never had such a wonderful evening and, in the taxi on the way home, told Herbert that her glamorous vision of the Riviera had now been fulfilled. Rupert managed to avoid another poke from Lady Wroughton's bony finger by keeping well out of her way until she left, and Richard avoided a fate worse than death by hiding in a broom cupboard while Elise Chouard was departing.

When the guests were all gone, the Aunts retired, well satisfied with the success of the evening. Emma kissed everyone and went tearfully to bed and Frances led her husband upstairs with an urgent and malevolent look in her eye.

'Alone at last.' Charlie said to Sylvia.

'Yes, darling. It was a splendid party, I think everyone had a simply marvellous time.'

'Except Emma.' Charlie said.

'Yes, except my poor little Emma, but that will all come right tomorrow, won't it?'

25. Solution

After breakfast while everyone was still seated at the table, Charlie tapped his glass with a spoon, like an after-dinner speaker, and said: 'May I have everyone's attention for a few minutes please. I know you are anxious to be off, Richard, I won't delay you much; this won't take long.'

The family turned to him expectantly.

'You will remember that at our meeting the other day, it was suggested that I might come and live out here and I agreed to give it some thought. Well, I have given it some thought and I've reached a decision.

'Now, quite independently of this, Aunt Kate and Mattie subsequently approached Sylvia and asked her if, in the event of my deciding *not* to move down, whether she would consider coming to live here to look after them and manage the house.

'Well, we have both given it a lot of thought and, to cut a long story short, we have both decided we want the job.'

Both Aunts were beaming with pleasure.

'Now, again quite independently to all of this, Sylvia and I have decided to get married.'

A gasp went round the room.

'That is, if we're allowed to – we are not quite sure if it is legal for a man to marry his brother's widow, but we'll be finding out about this tomorrow.'

'What if it's not?' Frances asked in a surly tone.

'Then we'll just have to live in sin.'

Richard rose to his feet and embraced Sylvia. Then he crossed to Charlie and shook him heartily by the hand. 'This is wonderful news.' He said in quite genuine delight, 'congratulations to you both; it couldn't have happened to two nicer people.'

The Aunts closed in and there was much hugging, kissing, hand shaking and tears of joy, then Emma said plaintively:

'Can I come too?'

'Where else would you go, my little waif?' her mother replied, throwing her arms around her and hugging her.

'When will it all *happen*?' Emma asked, bouncing between Sylvia and Charlie, her excitement intense.

'Well, we have a few things to sort out in the UK first.' Charlie said.

'Including the small matter of a marriage.' Sylvia added.

'But they shouldn't take more than three to four weeks,' Charlie continued, 'so, all things being equal, we should all be out here late May, early June.'

'For good?'

'For good.'

'I must telephone Steve.' She rushed towards the door.

'No, hang on just a minute.' Charlie called her back, 'Aunt Kate has something she wants to say.'

They all turned towards the old lady.

'Yes, dears. Well, Mattie and I wanted you to know how grateful we are to you all for your kindness and consideration to us. It has been a simply wonderful few weeks for us; we have become a family again and it has been an enormously happy change to our dreary old lives. Hasn't it Mattie?'

'Oh yes, dear.'

'Charlie and I will be deciding over the next few months, the best way of dealing with Aunt Sade's money. There will be trust funds, of course, for all the younger members of the family and a little extra capital for the older ones; but Mattie and I thought we would like to make just one small claim on the proceeds; didn't we Mattie?'

'We did, dear.'

'This little reunion' Kate continued, 'has been such a happy time for all of us that we thought how nice it would be if we could do the same every year with as many members of the family as possible coming.'

'We would like it to become a family tradition,' Mattie added, 'Easter at the Villa Victoria.'

Solution

'What a lovely idea.' Richard said.

'And we thought that just a little of Aunt Sade's money should be put aside to cover everyone's travelling expenses so the cost, at least, would never prevent anyone from coming.'

'Brilliant!' said Emma.

'We'll book our tickets for next year as soon as we get back.' Richard said laughing, as the family dispersed to continue with their packing.

* * *

Frances closed the door when the others had left the room leaving herself alone with Charlie. Her expression was grave and accusing.

'I am absolutely shocked and appalled, Uncle Charlie.' she said.

'And why are you absolutely shocked and appalled, Frances dear?' he replied with restraint.

'Because you have flouted the rules and conventions which we were all brought up to believe were important and of which I have always regarded *you* to be the family custodian.'

'What conventions are these, Frances?'

'You know perfectly well what conventions. The maintaining of standards in an increasingly *vulgar* and *common* society. I never dreamed that *you*, of all people, would ever do anything to discredit the family.'

'And you consider that I have?'

'You're about to.'

'You mean my marriage to Sylvia?'

'Of course I do. When Uncle James married her, at least the family stuck together and ostracised them, as they deserved. And let me remind you – *you* were party to that decision, we younger ones took our lead from *you*.'

'To my enduring shame, Frances.'

'Well, you shouldn't be ashamed about *that*. It's your actions *now* which are bringing disgrace to the family. From the very earliest age we were always taught that People Like Us did not marry people from a lower social order to our own. Every friend I ever made at school had to be vetted by my parents to make sure they were 'suitable'. My childhood was a nightmare of repression, forever wondering whether or not I could make friends with him or her; whether or not they were of our *'Jart'*. You wouldn't believe the friends and functions I missed out on because they were not considered PLU. And you, Uncle Charlie, were always held up to us as the model of correct behaviour who would never, *ever*, compromise the good standing of the family.'

Charlie noticed there were tears on anger and frustration in her eyes as the underlying reason for her hostility started to become clear to him. Could it be that a dutiful acceptance of the social disciplines of an earlier generation had inhibited the enjoyment of her youth to the point that her perceived loss could only now be mitigated by her imposition of the same disciplines on others? His initial feeling of anger towards her changed to one of sympathy and understanding.

'I'm truly sorry, Frances,' he said, 'if my decision to marry the woman I love distresses you, as it clearly does, or leads you to believe that I am letting you, and the family, down in any way.'

'You are.'

He ignored the accusation. 'You see, in any established and well-ordered family, each generation accepts *part* of the values of the previous generation and augments them with their own which evolve from the changing circumstances of the age and their own ideas of what is proper within its context. In this way, the best and most important aspects of behaviour are probably retained and the less important parts continually modified. Things *must* change you know, Frances.' He smiled at her gently.

'That is what made our family so special,' she replied, 'things *didn't* change. There was a wonderful, secure feeling of continuity, a recognition of the importance of old fashioned behaviour and principles. Look at the way this household functioned – there were no concessions to modern vulgarity here; until Emma brought that poisonous little Italian oik into the house, that is.' she added contemptuously.

Solution

'Our family *is* special, Frances; and I would imagine that, over the years, we have retained more of the old principles than most. But some things *must* change; it's called progress. Only a couple of days ago you were telling me that my ideas of sporting behaviour were out of date. Remember?'

'That's just typical of you, Uncle Charlie. It's 'bad form' to show triumph when you score a goal but it's OK to marry a barmaid. You just want to retain those aspects of decent behaviour which suit your own comfort and convenience and abandon those which don't.'

'I suspect we are all a bit like that, Frances. Ultimately, each one of us has to decide what we feel is worth preserving and what needs changing.'

'Well, you obviously have decided and in so doing you have, in my opinion, let yourself and the family down badly. I'm sorry, Uncle Charlie, but my upbringing is too strong to permit the slightest degree of understanding or sympathy for your apparent moral emancipation.'

Frances left the room with the last word and, as she closed the door behind her, Charlie realised with horror that, until a few weeks ago, he and she would have had very little about which to argue. But he would not leave things like this. Charlie liked everyone to be happy and he could not bear the thought of poor Frances being so deeply upset and brooding over a situation for which she believed him to be responsible. He would talk to her again; he would visit her in London; he would work on her and try to convince her that certain of her prejudices were out of date and must be discarded before they sapped the joy from the rest of her life. He was confident he could change her so that, at their next reunion in one year's time, Frances could be as happy and relaxed as everyone else.

* * *

That evening, the house had returned to its normal calm and Bridie sat with Manju at the kitchen table preparing haricots verts for the evening meal.

'Miss Kate says they're to have the room that was Lady Florence's. We'll have to get them boxes out and put them away, chust, put them away.'

'And Dhani can give the walls a coat of paint to freshen things up before they get back.'

'There'll be linen for the big bed in the second store room. We'll need to go up and look tomorrow, chust, we must look tomorrow.'

'Colonel Charlie says they could be back in as little as four weeks. There's a lot to be done. We'll have to get cracking tomorrow, Bridie, everything must be perfect for them when they arrive.'

'Ah, sure, everything *will* be perfect for them when they arrive. Everything will be tickety-boo, chust, everything will be tickety-boo.'

* * *

Out in the garden, by Hetty's Leap, Dhani stood motionless in the evening air, his kukri in his hand. Occasionally, he would look upwards to the sky and bend his head to one side as if he was listening for something. Eventually his patience was rewarded by the distant whine of jet engines on full thrust as the British Airways evening flight for London left the runway at Nice and, climbing steeply, headed out to sea. The sun caught on its silver fuselage as the aircraft banked and began its turn. Dhani watched as it cut back across the coast and, climbing all the time, headed north towards the distant Alpine peaks. He watched until the ever-diminishing speck in the sky had disappeared and he could no longer hear the sound of its engines.

They were beyond his care now, but they would return.

With a sudden flash of his kukri, too swift for the eye to follow, he deadheaded a row of cyclamens with surgical precision. He collected the spent and severed blooms and made his way back to the house smiling and chuckling to himself.

Epilogue

The golden globe of the sun dragged itself clear of the horizon and climbed behind the citadel of Fort Carre, stamping the shadow of its ancient battlements on the town of Antibes. The tide of its light rolled steadily inland, surging up the wide boulevards and flooding the white houses on the hillside with its golden warmth. Its progress challenged the dampness of the morning dew and vanquished the hitherto dominant brilliance of the flashing lighthouse on the heights of Notre Dame.

Soon, it raised the veil of darkness from the Villa Victoria, which had stood on its hilltop each morning for over a hundred years awaiting the kiss of the dawn. Its white, stucco walls and green louvred shutters had shielded successive generations of occupants from the fierce heat of the morning sun and had borne witness to the changing fortunes of many lives – their trials and their triumphs, their joys and their sadnesses.

The house had stood firm through the devastation of two world wars and had turned its head from the tide of social change which had followed each. It had withstood all threats to its integrity, and its privileged milieu, and had repelled all attempts to encroach upon its policies or impair its prospect.

Only recently had it witnessed some concession to the change outwith its walls, and some mitigation of the obdurate conventions its establishment had for so long supported. It had seen the challenge and rejection of prejudice, and the birth and growth of a simple and noble-minded love which would shortly be consummated and established within its walls. It had seen the desire to preserve the best parts of tradition and a willingness to review the worst. It had seen the loyalty, love and inter-dependence which a common morality inspires in all people and which no force on earth can weaken or subvert.

Easter at the Villa Victoria

The time would doubtless come when its bastions would fall to the allied forces of social progress and urban demand, and its graceful walls would tremble and collapse beneath the swinging, iron ball of a demolition contractor. A great block of flats would arise from its ashes, enabling many to benefit from the wonderful views and peaceful aspects of the place which had previously only been enjoyed by a few.

And in time, all memories of the old house on the hill would be erased and the occupants of the apartments would not know, nor care, that they stood on the spot where Lady Cargill had entertained the great and the good, in regal style, and old Captain Stewart had belted his kilt in preparation for an audience with his queen.

But that time had not arrived. There would be life and love in the Villa Victoria for some years yet to come.

– The End –